Hail th

By Timothy Ellis

The Hunter Legacy, Book Five

One

"Oh, hell no!" I exclaimed.

I felt disjointed for a brief moment, as if time had just jumped back a few seconds, and I'd heard myself exclaim the same thing twice. Or maybe it was just a mental echo brought about by a shock discovery.

"Get Yorktown moving, NOW!" I yelled.

People around me winced, as team coms amplified my voice in their heads.

"They're about to jump on top of you. Cruisers, Corvettes, and Excalibur pilots, stand your ships on their nose and push Yorktown down! For divine's sake, do it, NOW."

"Jon, what's going on?" asked Vonda.

"The Midgard fleet is about to jump into Miami, right on top of the American ships. And what's worse, they have two giant battering rams going first, presumably to make a path through the debris field that isn't there anymore."

I could hear Yorktown's Captain bellowing orders in the background, overlaid by those of Greer and Miriam, as they exhorted their pilots to do as I'd told them.

Lined up behind the two strange looking ships, were four walls of six Missile Cruisers, with Talon Squadrons in between. Between us and them, was another twenty four Cruisers, deployed in a defensive wall.

"Four walls of six Missile Cruisers about to jump," I said for the American's benefit, who couldn't see what I saw.

"American defensive ships, get an immediate target lock on the jump point."

Barely ten seconds later, the first two dull red dots jumped. On the scanner screen, the dull red dots merged with the green dots.

Two yellow dots appeared for just a second. The scanner feed from the other side vanished.

"What just happened?" I demanded.

"Feed lost at the source," said Jane. "Coms lost as well."

I sat there, stunned, for several seconds.

"Perhaps today *is* a good day to die," I sub-vocalized to myself.

"Shut up, Jon!" said Amanda, sub-vocalizing as well.

"Sorry," I whispered.

"Ka-Plaa," sub-vocalized Eric.

"Success," I translated, still sub-vocalizing. "Indeed."

His pronunciation needed work, but it had been a great response to my all too public musing. Only those on team coms would have heard what we said.

"All ships," I said normally, "advance. Prepare to fire. Jane, mark out positions to stop, for all ships, in range of all guns. Allow the Battleships room to turn enough to bring all guns to bear. Launch the Hives."

"Confirmed."

Time stopped for me. What was it with me and time?

There is no time. Focus.

The battlefield was laid out to my sight below me.

My fleet was arrayed in a wall formation. BigMother was in the middle. Warspite was on my left, Repulse on my right. John Wayne was above, with the Guardians on both sides. A line of Corvettes was above them. A line of Cruisers and Destroyers was below BigMother.

The enemy fleet was divided into two halves.

The closest half was a defensive formation between us and the jump point. A wall of Missile Cruisers was six wide and four high, sideways on to us. Seven hundred and twenty Talon medium fighters were behind them, positioned to fire through the gaps, and around the sides of the wall.

The other half of the enemy fleet was lined up in four rows of six, behind each other, so six Missile Cruisers could jump into the Miami system together. Between each group of Cruisers, were fifteen squadrons of twelve Talon fighters, with the last group of Talons in the tail position.

I looked down on the battlefield, and a fierce cold touched my heart.

Time sped back to normal, as did my vision.

My fleet shot forward, obeying my order to advance, raggedly at first, but coming back into formation quickly.

The first rank of six enemy Missile Cruisers jumped out.

"Fire missiles as soon as they come in range. Fire Hive torpedoes as soon as you can get a target for them."

"Confirmed."

Midgard fired first, as if they'd been waiting for us to arrive. Four thousand, eight hundred capital ship missiles headed towards us. Talons streamed through the jump point, going the other way, to attack the American fleet on the other side.

Fifty Mosquito launchers belched in response.

Our missile launchers fired a second later.

The second rank of Missile Cruisers jumped.

A wall of Talon missiles headed towards us.

The Hives fired off salvos of torpedoes. It looked like they would arrive at much the same time as our missiles.

I sat there watching. There was nothing else I could do now. The Bridge around me was silent, as everyone's attention was glued to the scanner. I zoomed it in so only the space between us and the jump point was visible.

"Get the salvage droid out of there, Jane."

"Confirmed."

It had played its part, sneaking us a look at the enemy position without revealing our presence. There was no point in it, or the comnavsat it carried, being destroyed in the fighting.

Any sort of plan was out the window. Midgard had surprised me this time, and given us no time to adapt. All we could do was slug it out.

Missiles met Mosquitos, and space in front of us lit up.

The third rank of Missile Cruisers jumped.

Our missile launchers fired a second time, this time aimed at the remaining wall of Missile Cruisers, still waiting to jump. A cloud of Talons were in front of them.

Twenty four Missile Cruisers exploded in the space of three seconds.

Point Defenses opened up at the approaching anti-fighter missiles.

Several missiles impacted on BigMother's shields, and I checked to see what was happening fleet wide. The Corvettes were having the hardest time, but most other ships were holding their own.

"Corvettes, duck behind a bigger ship, before you lose too much shielding."

I watched them all fall out of position, and move into protected spaces. Their shields began to improve.

The last six Missile Cruisers jumped out.

"Shit!" I said, as I realized what was about to happen next.

"What?" asked Alison.

"Our last salvos of missiles are going to jump through into Miami."

"Oh."

"No-one ask how bad that is please. I don't know."

"Duh!" said Amanda and Aleesha together.

The last salvos of missiles vanished into the jump point as expected.

The next wall of incoming Talon missiles launched at us. The Mosquito launchers belched again.

"All ships, launch FF's."

The Talon cloud surged towards us, now they weren't trying to protect their capital ships. Seven hundred and twenty fighters. They started winking out almost immediately.

The fleet kept up the missile launches.

The cloud surrounded us. Point Defense turrets sought out missiles, Corvette and Destroyer guns sought out Talons, and they continued to wink out.

"BigMother pilots, launch. Corvettes and fighters, break and attack."

"About bloody time," said a British voice.

The two Gunbus, Camels, Excaliburs, and a Centurion launched, and joined with the other Corvettes in dogfighting Talons.

"Sir?" asked Lacey, who was in the Assault Frigate General Custer.

"Go."

Custer dropped from underneath BigMother, and dived into the middle of the cloud. Normally suicidal for a Frigate, this one could dogfight with the best of them. It was designed for me, and whatever I flew, handled like a fighter. Even BigMother.

Every fiber of my being wanted to dive BigMother in after Custer. I resisted. I found myself checking what guns I could link to my joystick, and discovered BigMother had the same gun and front launcher setup as Gunbus did, so technically I could dogfight her the same way. The mind boggled though, and I resisted even more strongly. BigMother was longer than a Cruiser, but shorter than a Battleship. Dogfighting in the middle of a fleet was out of the question. All the same, my fingers itched.

The number of Talons dropped to below one hundred, and they peeled away from the fleet, trying to escape back towards Midgard.

"Pursue."

Our smaller ships went after them, while the larger ones continued launching missiles.

Fifty Talons. Twenty nine. Thirteen. None.

I breathed a sigh of relief, and drained the remaining water in my bottle. I couldn't recall actually drinking from it, but obviously I had. Jeeves replaced it with another one.

"All ships. Crews can refresh themselves, but remain on high alert. We may have to do this again in Miami as soon as we can jump in. BigMother team, RTB. Fleet coms are now ended for now."

Jane caught my eye, and I nodded to her. Fleet and Team coms shut off.

The whole battle had lasted just under fifteen minutes. The debris field was huge. Talon wrecks were all around us.

"Jane, send out the salvage droids. Haul the salvageable Talons into the Guardian's cargo holds. If they fill, create a parking area. Clear the debris from around us into a mountain well away from us, and then I want the jump corridor cleared as rapidly as possible."

"Confirmed."

"Is it over?" asked Amy.

"Yes, at least until we can jump a comnavsat into Miami, and find out what happened there."

"Admiral," said Vonda. "Can you explain what happened here?"

I sighed.

"We arrived just as Midgard were jumping into Miami. My guess is, they planned to attack from both jump points at the same time, using what they thought were overwhelming numbers, and are probably unaware we took the other jump point. The first ships to jump out looked like huge walls attached to the front of two Cruisers. They'd obviously guessed a few days ago their fleets were not getting through the debris field on the other side, or maybe a Talon survived the jump to jump back and tell them. They devised a way of pushing through it, to clear the down jump lane, for their fleet to follow. The problem was, Yorktown, whatever Pocket Battleships they had, the Gunbus squadron, and the Excalibur wing, were all waiting to jump through to here."

"So what happened?" asked Amanda.

"I don't know. They had maybe thirty seconds warning to move Yorktown out of the way. Immediately after the two battering ram ships jumped, two missiles were fired, and we lost all contact. I don't know why."

"Could have been nukes," said Alana. Everyone looked at her. She was the demolition specialist. "The EMP from an explosion that close would have fried the jump point comsat and the navsat on any ship in the blast range. Might even have taken out ship ID's. Ships not caught in the initial blast should have been okay otherwise."

Good explanation for the troops, but it didn't explain the loss of coms, which had been going AI to AI, through Jane, not the comsat. And I wasn't about to tell them.

"We can only hope," said Annabelle.

"Everyone take some downtime while you can," I said. "I'm going to email Miami, and hope we get a response. It's going to be at least an hour, likely more, before we can safely approach the jump point. I'll be in my Ready Room if anyone needs me."

I jumped up, groaned, stretched, and limped in, sinking into a lounge chair. Angel followed me, and sat on my lap purring. Vonda followed as well. Jane closed the door behind me. I started a vid.

"Marshall, Admirals, Generals. The Midgard side of the Miami jump point is ours. We arrived almost to the moment when Midgard started to jump a forty eight Missile Cruiser force through the jump point. The first two ships through were like battering rams, as if they expected to have to hammer their way through a debris field to make a passage for their Cruisers and fighters. Seconds after the jump, there were two missiles fired, and we immediately lost both nav data and coms with Miami. The first is explainable if the missiles were nukes, but the coms loss is a mystery, since they were going AI to AI. I'm trying not to think the worst."

"We know Yorktown was right at the jump point, and only had less than thirty seconds to move clear. For now, I'm hoping they did, and their offensive force remained intact to deal with the twenty four Missile Cruisers, and sixty squadrons of Talons that followed. The other half of the force engaged us, and was handled without any major issues, and no casualties. Once again, the Mosquito missile system proved to be the decisive factor in handling the barrages."

"Marshall, I don't know how the American fleet faired. If you receive no contact from Admiral's Jedburgh or Hallington in Miami, please send this vid on to whoever is the appropriate authority for urgent action. I would assume there's at least one Rear Admiral still left there on the other Carrier, but I don't have contact details for that person. Have someone contact me with a sitrep. I sincerely hope this won't be necessary."

"In any case, as soon as we can clear a passage to the jump point, I'll send in another comnavsat. The state of the other side of the jump point and who controls it, will determine my subsequent actions. In the meantime, all we can do here is wait and hope. Hunter out."

I sighed, assembled the email, and sent it off.

"Well put," said Vonda.

"Did I miss anything important?"

"No. I'll leave you to planning our next step."

She stood, and left.

I sent a quick text email to Miriam, asking her to confirm she was alright, hoping it would be answered quickly.

It wasn't.

Two

I sat there wondering if I'd killed Miriam.

It had been my idea to mount their new Pocket Battleships, Gunbus squadron, and Excalibur wing, on top of Yorktown, and have her pushed into the jump sideways by a Cruiser.

It was my fault their Fleet Carrier was sitting there sideways on, totally vulnerable to anything jumping in at them. It had never occurred to me that Midgard might attack there again.

True, I couldn't have foreseen what had happened, but the blame was still mine.

I started down the emotional spiral. My Fault. I'm to blame. Guilty of arrogance and stupidity. Risen to the level of incompetence.

Was this my karma coming back at me? I'd killed those two assassins without even thinking about it. And before that, I'd flushed the mercenary team out an airlock. I'd killed when I hadn't needed to. Was this my punishment? And what about sleeping with Alison while I had something going with Miriam? Was this punishment for that too?

In a dream, I'd seen Miriam vanish in purple smoke. Was it trying to tell me she was soon to die?

I looked upwards, seeking guidance.

Tell me you haven't taken my lover's life to pay me back for those I killed.

Tell me I'm not damned to remember her the rest of my life as a curse for losing my spiritual way.

Tell me she hasn't paid my debts.

Silence.

Tears came to my eyes.

A noise caught my attention. BA had her head poked around a barely open door.

"No you don't," she said. "You're not doing this!"

"Which this is that?"

The flippant answer rolled off my tongue without requiring thought.

She came in fully.

"You're beating yourself up about what might have happened over there, because you suggested it. You're rapidly convincing yourself you killed Miriam. Am I right?"

I looked at her miserably.

She pulled me out of my seat, causing Angel to jump onto the chair rapidly from my lap, and hugged me. For a full five minutes she held me, before pushing me away, and turning to Angel.

"I'm going to borrow him for a while, sweetie. Is that alright?"

Mew.

"Thanks. I'll bring him back when he's thinking straighter. Why don't you visit your cat bed for a while?"

Mraa, mraa. Angel jumped off the chair, and ran out.

"Follow," she said to me.

She led me down through the ship, into Custer, and to the Gun Ranges. She programmed a two person assault course. I was about to point out I didn't have my guns, when she took two assault rifles from a gun rack I didn't know was there.

For the next two hours, she bullied me through the course repeatedly.

Eventually, Jane announced the jump corridor would be cleared in about ten minutes, and we headed back up the ship.

I hurt. Really hurt. BA hadn't let up. She'd pushed me to the limit of physical exhaustion, and my bruises hadn't liked it. But I savored the pain. I deserved it.

I limped back onto the Bridge, and sat. BA and I were the last ones to enter.

I emptied the bottle of water waiting for me. Jeeves quietly took the empty and dropped another full bottle in the holder.

"Jane... Ouch!"

I looked around to see BA step back with a medical device in her hand.

"Sorry Jon, I pushed you as hard as I had to, but we need you pain free now."

"Just as well you're a superb combat soldier, because you're a lousy nurse."

There was a titter of laugher around the room.

"Jane, sitrep."

"Almost ready."

"Send the comnavsat as soon as you can."

"Confirmed."

I waited impatiently. I had to suppress the urge to get up and pace.

"Droid away."

It took another minute to jump. The scan data for Miami popped onto the screen again.

There was a mass of grey dots. No green ones at all. Dread seized my heart and squeezed.

"What the hell happened?" asked Eric, down in one of the Camels.

I hadn't realized team coms was back on.

A huge area was marked as a navigation hazard, but oddly, the down jump corridor was clear. And now I looked closely, there appeared to be a line of grey dots ending in an arrow head, pointing into Miami. Some of my dread lifted.

"Let's go find out," I responded.

I opened a channel to Repulse.

"BigMother is jumping into Miami. Admiral Bentley, you have the fleet until I return."

"Aye, sir," she replied.

Unlike me, she was professional enough to not show any emotion. The channel closed.

I nodded to Jane, and she moved us forward, and into the jump at a low speed.

Three

The first seven ships we passed were all Gunbus class. The next fifteen were Excaliburs. They moved to follow us, showing they were still operational.

"Coms?" I asked Jane.

"None."

I tried pinging Miriam with a simple 'please answer this ping' message.

"What took you so long?" came back.

I grinned.

I looked around, and they were all grinning, seeing the dots following us.

"Sitrep," I pinged her.

"The first two ships missed us by inches. Yorktown and Lexington were both damaged by missiles, and can't land fighters. Two Gunbus were lost. Seven Excaliburs lost. Twenty three other fighters lost before we could join the fight. Almost all ships of Corvette size or smaller are damaged. Can you take the worst of us? At least we can ping basic instructions to each other, so I can tell people to land if you can take us."

"Yes. We can take four squadrons for now. Send them in worst first. The Excaliburs should fit in through the rear of the Flight Deck, but some of you will need to spacewalk to an airlock, as there aren't enough bays. Six Gunbus can dock at our external airlocks. If Greer is still with us, you and he report to my Ready Room, please."

I threw her ping to a side screen so everyone could read it.

"Jane, prepare for fighters landing. Get every repair droid we have to the Maintenance Deck, and the Flight Deck. Find out why they have no coms, and repair whatever the problem is on the Corvettes and Excaliburs first."

"Confirmed."

"Both on our way," answered Miriam.

"BigMother Corvettes and fighters, launch please. We need all available docking for incoming damaged ships. Custer as well please. I want a general inspection of all ships in the American fleet. If you get close enough, pings work, so see if you can make contact with each one. Squadron Leader, take Lexington. Wing Commander, take the Yorktown. See if we can set up any form of communication with them. If you can make contact with an Admiral, I want to know immediately. Oh, and Wing Commander, deploy a comnavsat please."

There was a chorus of acknowledgments, and ships began to launch. Slice also acknowledged the additional order.

I asked Abagail to cancel team coms, and opened a vid.

"Marshall, Admiral, and Generals. I'm in Miami, and the American fleet prevailed. However, it was at some cost. Both Carriers are damaged to the level they cannot recover fighters. Nine of their new Corvette and Privateer ships were lost, with twenty three other losses. Most of their smaller ships are damaged, and I'm recovering the worst of them now."

"Something odd has happened here. The entire American fleet is without coms, and their ships display on the scanner as if dead. I have no contact as yet with anyone above the rank of Commander. I'll keep you informed as we learn anything new. Hunter out."

I sent the vid off, having added Admiral Bentley to the recipients, so she would know what had happened.

I turned to Jane.

"Did the work on the Pilot's and Crew Mess's get completed?"

"Confirmed."

"Fully ready for occupation?"

"Duh!"

The twins smiled at hearing Jane copy their favourite saying. I looked around the Bridge.

"Volunteers to meet American pilots, please. Take them to the Pilot's Mess. Overflow to use the Crew Mess instead. You'll need to get directions, as I don't even know where they are."

"Confirmed."

Everyone laughed. As a tension releaser, Jane was doing well. Most of the team left the Bridge.

I moved into my Ready Room, and had no sooner sat in a lounge chair, when a flash of white landed in my lap. I gave her a huge cuddle. A random thought told me Angel was now eleven weeks old.

"You're getting bigger, sweetie pie," I told her. "Soon you'll be able to jump up on things without using a ramp."

Meow!

She looked pleased with that comment. She tried to jump to the top of the chair, landed two thirds the way up, and climbed the rest of the way. She was soon fast asleep on top.

I tried to look at emails to pass the time, but found I couldn't concentrate.

Fifteen minutes passed, and midnight ticked over. I started pacing.

"Jon," said Jane through coms, "there's an email you must view now."

I took my pad out, saw the email highlighted with an urgent flag, and threw the vid to the wall. An American four star General looked out at me.

"Vice Admiral Hunter. I'm General Patton, of the American Joint Chiefs. Your communications about the Miami situation have been received via the British Fleet. We appreciate you ensuring we received your updates, in spite of not having the proper channels available. You are hereby recalled to active duty. Until the status of Admiral Jedburgh is established, you are placed in command of all American ships and personnel, within the Miami and Midgard systems. You will please send all ships requiring shipyard work back to Dallas, as soon as they can either move themselves, or be towed."

"You are ordered to destroy all missile launchers on the surface of Midgard, and to blockade the Midgard planet, in preparation for the arrival of a diplomatic mission. You are further ordered to investigate the system for other inhabited planets, moons, or stations. You will remove Midgard's ability to wage war."

"Orders are being sent to all ship captains and unit commanders. I understand you don't have an aide. You will immediately appoint yourself one, who will communicate with my aide, to receive copies of these orders, for communication through local means."

"Admiral, please keep us up to date with all new information, no matter how trivial it may seem. Patton out."

There were contact details attached to the email.

"Jane, whisper to Alison, and get her in here ASAP, please."

"Confirmed."

I responded with an orders received and understood message, adding we had no new information at this time, but we were trying to make contact with each ship now.

I stood again to start pacing, when a whirlwind crossed the room, grabbed me, and started to hug the life out of me.

I hugged her back for a good two minutes, before disentangling myself.

"Hi," I said. "For a while, I thought you were dead."

Miriam looked at me steadily. Then she laughed.

"I came oh so close, but you don't get rid of me that easy, buster."

This time she kissed me.

"Ahem," came a voice from the doorway.

We broke apart, and I turned to find Alison.

"You wanted me, Jon?" she asked.

I let go of Miriam, and walked to my conference table, waving them both there as well. We sat.

"Are you up to speed on the duties of an Admiral's aide?" I asked Alison.

"Sure. Do you know an Admiral who needs one?"

"Me. In fact, I've been ordered to have one. Would you like the job?"

"Is this a trick?"

I laughed. Miriam didn't seem to understand what was going on.

"No, I need an aide, and I need one now."

"Okay Jon, you have an aide."

"Good. When we finish here, claim an office, and have Jeeves put your name on it." I pinged her the contact details I'd received. "I need you to contact General Patton's aide immediately. Identify yourself as my aide. You'll be sent a series of orders. Identify who those orders are for, and where they're located at the moment. Jane will need the list."

"On it."

She went blank as she began to compose an email. I turned to Miriam.

"Who's the senior American officer of those who came on board with you? Or who is coming on board if not already here?" I asked her.

"Greer. He was promoted a few minutes ahead of me, so he has marginal seniority. He's getting things organized in the Pilot's Mess, but should be here soon."

"Get him up here now, please."

"Okay."

I pinged Vonda for her and Alsop to join us, and pinged Annabelle as well.

"What's happening, Jon?" asked Miriam.

"Patience. I'll explain when the others get here."

We waited. Annabelle was first in. Vonda and Alsop walked in together not far behind, and I waved them to the table. Vonda had no sooner sat down, when she went blank. Presumably she had a ping or email to view.

Greer came in almost at a run, and I waved him to the table as well. He sat, looking very curious. Vonda was back with us now I saw.

"Thanks for coming. You all need to see this."

I threw the General's vid to the wall, and watched the two Americans as it played.

"Orders, sir?" asked Greer, after the screen vanished.

"Commander, I need you to take a shuttle to every ship in the Miami system. You'll take a copy of the vid you just watched, and show it to every ship's captain, or whoever currently has command. Start with the Carriers. I need to know what happened to the Admirals. I want everyone on the list Alison will give you, or whoever has their command now, here for a meeting at nine in the morning, at which time they'll receive orders direct from General Patton."

"The same applies for unit commanders. I would assume that includes all Squadron Leaders, and Marine Colonels, and above. Alison is acting as my aide from now on. I'm sorry you won't be getting much sleep, but with coms down, someone senior has to deliver the orders. That's you. Jane will be flying the shuttle. She is to receive the combat feed from each ship. Keep her up to date with anything you discover. If need be, she can pass the information straight on to me. Suggest to each captain or unit commander they bring with them a report to be transmitted off to ASF Command. As soon as you return, send off any information you find out, so the Joint Chiefs have some sort of update before morning."

"Yes sir. Leave now?"

"Yes. Jane, prep a shuttle, and direct the Commander to it."

"Confirmed."

Greer stood, saluted, and left.

I sighed.

"Someone up there hates me," I mumbled.

"Maybe so, Jon," said Vonda, "because I have to make this worse for you."

She threw another vid to the wall.

"Lieutenant General Wellington," said the officer with four stars on his shoulders. "You are relieved of your current duties, and appointed temporary Military Governor of the Midgard system. You will pass command of the multi-sector fleet to Vice Admiral Hunter. You are to assist him in the pacification of the Midgard system. When safe for diplomats, you will work with the initial diplomatic team the Americans are sending, to establish a peace. If Midgard don't agree to peace, you will command a blockade force around the Midgard planet, until other measures can be considered, and put into place. Hopefully they'll agree to peace, in which case you will restrain all members of the current government, in preparation for war crimes trials, and administer the system until relieved. Admiral Hunter is receiving orders from the Americans. You will assist him in the execution of those orders. Price out."

There was silence around the table.

"What is thy bidding, my master?" asked Jane through the coms. Her voice changed. "What does the head honcho require?"

"Stop," I said. "Let's not go through the whole list. We'll assume the jokes were original, and we all laughed."

"Spoilsport, your big cheesiness."

I looked around the table. They were all trying to keep their grins under control. And failing. I turned to Miriam.

"Commander, you better see to your pilots. When you're ready to sleep, use one of the suites on Deck Two."

She looked about to say something, but thought better of it. She nodded and stood.

"Sirs."

She turned, and left.

"Jane, how are we off for food, water, and consumables?"

"The ship was only provisioned for thirty for a month, plus what we brought over from the station for the marines. All the same, we're running through the provisions rapidly. Jeeves was going to recommend a food order in another day from now."

"Launch the small freighter. Give it a new avatar, so any people it deals with will think it has a captain. Do a speed run to the Dallas Military Orbital. Pick up what's waiting there, and get it all back here, as fast as possible. Also, how many fighters are still flying out there?"

"Confirmed. Three squadrons."

"Commander," I said to Alsop. "Can you communicate with Dallas Military, and organize us food, water, and consumables, for two hundred people, for a week?"

"Yes sir. I'll use what we ordered for your station, before the Avon battle, as a base to work from."

"Also, we'll need parts for the fighters. Jane will give you an idea of what we need, but get them to send us enough parts to repair seven squadrons of all the usual battle damage. Plus what the Excaliburs and Gunbus need."

"Yes, sir."

He went blank.

"Jane, you may need to do two trips. Food and supplies for two days first. Parts second. The rest of the food third. When the parts arrive, start repairing ships, starting with the least damaged."

"Confirmed."

I pinged Miriam to get her pilots to sleep, warned that as soon as their ships were repaired, they would be swapping with someone still out there. She acknowledged.

"Jane, give each pilot a minimum of six hours sleep. As a ship is repaired, and after the six hours are up, get the pilot up and launched, with instructions to tell the next fighter which needs repair, to land. We need to repair as many as possible as fast as possible. I don't want us having to stick around here babysitting fighters for days on end."

"Confirmed."

I sighed again.

"Congratulations, boss," said Annabelle with a grin.

I sighed yet again, and Annabelle, Alison, and Vonda laughed. Alsop was in his own world, and hadn't noticed. I looked at Annabelle.

"Did you find out if the Americans have troops with them?"

"They don't."

"At least that's something. We could have taken fifty or so, but no more. Let's just hope we don't need them."

I pondered for a few moments.

"Jane, how many more fighters can we take aboard?"

"The receiving and maintenance bays are full. The Midway class was only designed for four squadrons."

"What about moving the least damaged ones into the launch bays, with the outer doors sealed?"

"Confirmed. It'll be a tight fit, but we could get in another thirty six fighters that way."

"Prep another shuttle for Miriam please."

"Confirmed."

I pinged Miriam to take a shuttle out, and have the rest of the fighters land. I told her we'd worked out where to store them. They would need to enter through the forward end of the Flight Deck, as the rear had parked ships. She pinged back to say she was on her way.

I sighed again.

"You need sleep, Jon," said Vonda. "Let the weight settle for the rest of the night, and pick it up again in the morning."

"I agree," said Annabelle.

I noticed Alison wasn't there. Neither was Alsop.

"Angel," I said.

Meow?

"Bed time, sweetie."

She stood, stretched, jumped down from the back of the chair, and ran down her ramp. The white flash vanished out the door.

We also stood, and with a series of goodnights, we headed for our suites.

In my bedroom, I managed to switch my suit back to a belt, shuck my briefs in favour of boxers and t-shirt, and climb into bed. Angel settled next to my neck as usual. I stroked her a few times, and to the sound of her purr, I fell asleep.

Four

I woke to find myself draped with naked females.

Miriam was on one side of me, and Alison on the other. Angel was curled into my neck as usual.

I gaped at the women in turn. I'd half expected Miriam, but Alison as well? My mind boggled.

I gently moved the draped anatomy off me, and crawled out, ducking into the shower.

"Time," I said to Jane.

"Seven fifty five," she replied through coms. "I'm waking everyone in five minutes."

"Good."

"Where are you holding the meeting?"

"Conference Room big enough?"

"Just."

"There will do. It won't be for long."

"Where are you, Jon?" asked Miriam loudly.

"Shower," I called back.

Two naked women walked into my bathroom. I looked at them. I closed my eyes, and opened them again, expecting to find myself alone. They were still there.

"Wait," I said. "You're Amanda and Aleesha playing a joke on me, with good suit programming."

"Wrong," they both said together, smiling widely.

Miriam entered the shower first, followed by Alison.

"Umm," I said, not really having any clue as to what to say next.

"He's clueless," said Miriam.

"You're surprised about that?" responded Alison.

They both laughed at my obvious puzzlement.

"Put him out of his misery," went on Alison.

"It's alright, Jon. I know about you and Alison. She contacted me, and asked my permission, before the Avon battle. I'm a pilot. I get the whole tomorrow-we-might-be-dead thing. Lord knows, all three of us have nearly died in the last week. You thought I'd be upset?"

I nodded.

She kissed me, and turned to Alison.

"I get the front, you get the back."

"Why do I get the back?"

"I outrank you."

"Oh."

"GOOD MORNING, MIAMI!"

By the time I was able to exit the shower, I was well and truly washed.

The three of us headed along to the Dining Room for breakfast. For once, I was starving, and ate the full porky. I didn't linger, but headed up to my Ready Room. Alison followed me. We sat at the conference table.

"Sitrep, Jane."

"All requested commanders are on the way. All fighters were recovered. Freighter is due back in approximately two hours. Work is in progress on the coms issue."

"What was the problem?"

"The EMP from the two nukes fried most external circuitry. So while coms were actually fine, every antenna array in the fleet was rendered inoperable. Something like thirty percent of external turrets were also affected, which is why so many of the Corvettes and Privateers died. They just didn't have enough working Point Defense for what was fired at them."

"Hell. It's always the simple things which get you in the end. We have the parts for the antenna arrays?"

"Yes, for the fighters anyway. The capital ships should be able to do their own. If not, they'll need a shipyard. As far as other repairs go, we don't have parts for Sabres and Epees, let alone Excaliburs. Two hours for them to arrive. Repairs will take the best part of a day."

"Gunbus and Excaliburs first. The rest in order of least damage."

"Confirmed."

I turned to Alison.

"Can you go to the Conference Room now please? As each person enters, ask their name, or who they're representing, and ping them their orders. Seating is by rank. I'd suggest you make a plan of the table and allocate, and tell people where to sit, or not, as they enter. Put Yorktown on my left and Lexington on my right. Greer and Young next to them. Then the two Pocket Battleships, and the Missile Cruiser."

"I can do that."

She left with a smile on her face. It wasn't often a Lieutenant was able to boss around higher ranks.

I reached for my pad, and checked for any important emails.

A Lieutenant Colonel Ashdale, General Patton's aide, had emailed asking for more information on the fleet's condition. Jane told me the battle feeds, and a brief summary, had been sent off, when Greer returned from his midnight jaunt. I replied I was meeting with all ship commanders at nine, after which all of them would be submitting reports, if they'd not already done so on arrival on board. I would send an update after the meeting myself.

I continued wading through the daily accumulation.

Precisely at nine, I walked into the Conference Room from the Bridge.

"Admiral on deck," said someone, and the room came to attention.

"As you were," I said.

Those at the table, sat. The rest stood easy.

The room was filled to capacity, with only a corridor of space to let me get to my seat. Everyone in the room looked at me expectantly. A few of them frowned when they saw my age for the first time. I ignored them, and took my seat at the head of the table. To both sides were Commanders. A few of the Captains further down the table looked upset at the placement of junior ranks ahead of them. Greer looked tired for some reason.

"For those who don't know me," I began, "I'm Vice Admiral Hunter. The purpose of this meeting has already been achieved, being the delivery of your orders from General Patton. As per my instructions, I formally take command of all American forces in the Miami system."

I turned to Yorktown.

"Sitrep," I said to her.

"Commander Bowrey, sir. Temporarily in command of Yorktown. Yorktown survived the initial incursion because of your orders sir. We were pushed down far enough for the first two Cruiser, whatever they were, to miss the ships on our hull by inches. The two nukes they fired, resulted in complete coms failure, and a lot of smaller turret failures. Unfortunately, we ended up to the side of, and slightly below, the jump point, and a Missile Cruiser was fast enough to get a barrage off at us, while still in down jump. Combined Point Defense from the ships still on our hull took out half the barrage, but the other half hit us. Yorktown needs a shipyard. We have engines again, as of a short time ago, but won't be making any speed records. The Flight Deck was substantially damaged, and we can't land anything. The Launch tube system was also badly damaged, so we can't launch either."

She looked at me helplessly.

"Senior officers?" I prompted.

"The Bridge was badly hit. All the senior officers are in medical Care Units. I was the senior officer in the CIC, otherwise I'd either be dead, or in medical also."

"Thank you."

I turned to Lexington, and nodded to him.

"Commander Atwell, sir. The first group of Missile Cruisers had time to turn and line us up really well. We took most of a barrage. I'm not sure, but I think Lexington will have to be scrapped. The Bridge was destroyed, the Admiral and Captain killed. I was also in the CIC. We have major casualties. After Commander Greer left, we started receiving damage control teams, and medical help from other ships, so we're holding our own for now. But Lexington will need to be towed back to Dallas, sir."

"Thank you." I looked towards the first of the Captains. "Pocket Battleships and Missile Cruiser sitrep."

The senior of the three Captains said, "Captain Johansson, sir, of Harrison Ford. This is Captain Dunning of the Mark Hamill, and Captain Channing of the Missile Cruiser Backblast. All three ships are in good shape sir, thanks to the Mosquito systems, and Point Defense. We took a few missiles each, but didn't lose shields. We expect to have coms back up by the time we return to our ships."

"Good. As soon as you're back aboard, jump your ships through to Midgard, and report to Commodore O'Neil. You'll join his fleet."

"Daniel O'Neil sir? Last I heard he had the Mercenary Frigate General Custer."

"That's him. He works for me now. He has command of the John Wayne."

There were smiles from quite a few down the table.

"About time that son of a gun lived up to his potential," grinned a white haired Captain, sitting next to Captain Channing. Sounded like there was a story there, but now wasn't the time.

"Anyone else damaged enough to need a shipyard?" I asked.

A dozen hands were raised at the table, and just as many among the standing officers. The former presumably had Cruisers, and the latter most likely Destroyers, Frigates or Corvettes. With their lack of Point Defense, the Talons had big juicy targets to aim their missiles at. Each individual missile wouldn't have done much, but a squadron launch at a single ship, if they all hit, would have done a lot of damage.

"Who is senior Captain among those ships not damaged?"

The white haired Captain raised his hand.

"Captain Pleasance, of the Nicolas Cage".

"Form an escort for the Carriers out of those ships also needing a shipyard. Have Lexington towed by the most appropriate ship for the task. Include a tow vessel for Yorktown in case she needs one as well. Leave behind all salvage droids to continue with the cleanup. When you arrive at Dallas Shipyard, contact General Patton for further orders."

"Aye, sir."

"Who's next in seniority, who won't be going back to Dallas?"

"Me sir." A hand was raised next to Captain Pleasance. "Captain Holloway, of the Tom Cruise."

"The remaining undamaged ships will stay to blockade this jump point. Please supervise the cleanup. All debris is to be cleared into a mountain well away from the jump point. No one is allowed through except for the following. I have a freighter doing supply runs at the moment. And the diplomatic ship Command is sending, with its escort. They should jump into Midgard, and request instructions before proceeding any further. Anyone else with what sounds like a good reason, should be referred to me for a decision. Until we sweep the entire system, fingers will stay on the triggers, so I don't want any accidents with unexpected guests."

"Yes, sir."

"Anyone not able to fix their own coms?"

Greer and Miriam looked at me, and I gave them a small head shake to mean not them.

No one moved.

"Good. No-one leaves this ship without first sending a full report of the battle off to General Patton's aide, including a complete status report of their ship or command. The Joint Chiefs want to know what happened, and how many pieces need picking up. If you need an office, there are some you can use on this level, otherwise there's a Rec Room on the next level down. Let's get on with it. Dismissed."

I stood, and everyone stood as well. I walked out, and returned to my Ready Room.

Five

I'd barely sunk into a lounge chair, when three Commanders turned up at my door.

"Can we have a minute, sir?" asked Miriam.

I waved them in, and into lounge chairs.

"We need to thank you, sir," said Commander Bowrey.

"What for?" I responded.

"You saved everyone on Yorktown, and the ships on her hull, when you told them to push us down. If you hadn't ordered that action, the first ship through would have torn us apart."

Greer and Miriam nodded.

"I'm also the one who put you there in the first place. I think the one negates the other."

"No, sir," said Bowrey emphatically. "We'd been on the ready line since seven in the morning. We were all lined up until your suggestion changed our deployment. Without that change, none of us stood a chance. The first two ships were designed for tearing debris fields apart, and pushing the bits out of the down jump area. They would have torn through most of us before we even knew what was happening. The next wave would have down jumped into what was left, and completed the job. Until your suggestion changed things, we were already dead, and didn't know it yet. You gave us all a chance to survive."

"Thank you," they all said together.

I looked at them with a lack of understanding. I'd almost killed them, and they thanked me for saving them? What sort of logic was that?

"You're welcome," I said. "Please don't make me do it again."

They laughed. I looked at Greer.

"You look like you need some sleep, Commander."

"Ah, yes sir. How long before our ships will be ready to fight again?"

"The parts they need should be here soon. The repairs will begin with the Corvettes, followed by the Excaliburs, and finally the fighters. You have time to get some sleep. Jane will wake you when your ship is ready for you, or team coms will wake you if something happens. In the meantime, I need you rested for the next phase."

"Yes, sir."

The three of them rose, saluted, and left.

I assembled an email for Lieutenant Colonel Ashdale, including a brief summary of what I'd heard, and the recording of the meeting. The reports from all the captains would fill in the blanks.

Not long after sending it off, the freighter landed on the Flight Deck, and was transported down to be unloaded.

Jane and I discussed how to go about finding the other habitable planet or moon, and any other inhabited structures in the Midgard system. Especially given the nav scanners didn't work properly there.

An hour or so later, she informed me the last of the captains had left, as had the freighter on its second run.

I moved back to the Bridge.

"Where are we at?" I asked Jane.

"The three ships you wanted in Midgard have jumped. The remaining Gunbus went with them. Repairs to Greer's Starman have begun. She should be ready to undock, and give her place to the last Gunbus, in an hour or so. We are go for returning to Midgard."

"Starman?"

"They went with using their call signs as ship names."

I smiled at that. Easy solution. Fighters generally weren't named. But Corvettes always were, and so usually were Privateers. Although Gladiator convention was to tag a number on the end. All ships were named with the class and a number to start with, but this was changed when the owner took possession. The two Camels for example, were currently named Camel 01 and Camel 02, since they'd been pressed into war service instead of me taking delivery normally. Among capital ships, the first in the class was named a way the rest of the class would follow. Hence the Actor class, with the names of ships being past actors who were now immortal. Using call signs to name what were larger than usual fighters, was a great idea.

"Jump us out of here, Jane."

"Confirmed.

We jumped back into Midgard, and I called a senior officers meeting for as soon as everyone could arrive. I told Jane to specially make sure Greer wasn't woken up. He needed the sleep, and he wasn't going to be needed for what I had in mind.

I was sitting in the Conference Room as people started to come in. Miriam was first, and she was going to be the most junior present. She sat as far away from me as she could get, knowing her place in the ranks. General Wellington took her place to my left.

The room quickly filled. Admiral Bentley entered last, slightly behind Admiral Dingle, and General Smith, who was talking to O'Neil as they entered. I shook hands with Dingle for the first time, having never actually come face to face with him before. For an officer I'd first considered promoted too high, he'd certainly performed as well as could be expected so far. There were many captains I'd not met before, from the Cruisers and Destroyers of the combined fleet. Alison closed the door behind her, and stood just inside the door, next to Alsop.

I stood.

"As of this morning, the command of the multi-sector fleet has passed to me. General Wellington has been appointed Military Governor of the Midgard system."

There was a general stir around the table.

"We have several objectives now. The first is to pacify the planet Midgard, in preparation for the diplomats. The second is to ensure the entire system is disarmed. The Shipyard was neutralized yesterday. We suspect there's either a second habitable planet in the system, or a moon. Midgard itself ought to have an Orbital station, but it doesn't. So we need to look for it."

"Admiral Bentley will be breaking the fleet up into small groups. Each group will be assigned a patrol area. If you come across a planet or moon with life signs, or any kind of station, you will inform me immediately, and take no further action except observation. Our response will depend on what we find. I want no one biting off more than they can chew because they find something which they think they can handle. If there's another Midgard force in this system, and there could be two of them, we handle them with our full force, not piecemeal. I don't want to be forced to explain the loss of one of our ships, because the captain proved to be overly gung-ho. If you find a fleet, you back off and shadow, until the main force can arrive."

"Let me be clear about something. There will be NO retaliation against civilians. We'll need the planets' station back here for General Wellington to use as a base. There will be no accidents. Understand me?"

I looked everyone in the eyes, one by one. Most of them nodded as I looked at them.

"Wing Commander Slice."

"Sir?"

"You will deploy a comnavsat in orbit of every planet in this system. You will also check for areas where one is not enough. We can't cover the entire system, but we can cover all the real estate. You'll have an escort to watch your back. No unnecessary risks. If you find an opposing force, you will deploy a comnavsat, and get the hell out of there. Even if the comnavsat doesn't last long, we'll get enough to plan an attack."

"Yes, sir."

"The main force will be heading straight to Midgard. That's where I expect any remaining fleet to be. But don't assume it. There's at least one other inhabited location in this system, and it could also have a significant fleet there."

I looked down the table at everyone.

"Let's get this finished today. No last minute casualties please. There have been far too many already. Admiral Bentley will give you your assignments shortly. Dismissed."

I looked at Susan, Vonda, and Annabelle, motioning them to stay. The rest filed out.

"Jane will give you the patrol areas we worked out, Susan," I said. "Divide up the Sci-Fi and British ships. Slice needs a bigger escort, as he's most likely to come across something interesting. Better give him at least one Cruiser, with a sensible Captain who will let him lead. He doesn't have the rank the Cruiser captains have, but for the job I gave him, he is the most experienced person in the fleet. Exploration is his mission." She nodded. "The idea is, we cover the entire system as fast as possible. So if you see something we missed, by all means tweak the plan. Emphasize the no action directive. I want to find out what's here, before we blunder in and do something stupid. There have been enough surprises in the last few days. I don't want any more."

"Agreed," they said together, and we all laughed.

"Annabelle, it's about four hours to Midgard. Prep the troops. I'm hoping we can take out the missile sites from orbit, but if not, you go in, and neutralize them."

"We'll be ready."

"Have I missed anything?" I asked Vonda.

"I don't think so."

"Admiral, form up the main fleet into line abreast formation. Have BigMother's support ships form a second line above the main formation, and get the rest moving. I fancy dinner at Midgard."

"Confirmed," answered Susan, and we all laughed as we stood, and left.

Six

Once the fleet was moving, I sent off a 'We are moving to Midgard' email, and we went down for lunch.

Greer turned up looking a lot better than he had earlier. He took me aside.

"Jane told me my ship has been repaired, and swapped for the last Gunbus. What did you want me to do?"

"Relax for now. Go back to bed if you still need sleep. As the Corvettes and Privateers are repaired, their pilots should launch them, and join the line formation above the main force. Re-dock yours when you can. You and Miriam stay aboard until just before we get there. As soon as the underside airlock is clear, tell Lacey to dock."

"Yes sir."

I waved him towards the table, and we took seats.

After lunch, Miriam found me playing with Angel, and joined in, until Angel lost interest, and went to sleep on her kitty castle. I introduced her to 'Who' episodes. She didn't really follow what I tried to tell her about the backstory, but she enjoyed the actual story itself.

BA dropped past to ask a question, although I never found out what it was, because she became engrossed with what we were watching.

I looked around at one point to find Alison in the next chair. Sometime later, the twins were lounging on the floor.

As one episode finished, Abigail asked what this was, so I went through the backstory again. To my surprise, she understood the basics, and started explaining it a different way to the others. Even Annabelle seemed to understand time travel was involved, by the time she finished.

Jane kept me updated with the repair work through my PC, as the afternoon wore on. By the time the next episode finished, all the Gunbus ships were on station in the line above us, with the exception of Greer's. Several of the Excaliburs were as well. Miriam's was ready for her. All I had to do was get her away from the entertainment.

"Time to go back to work people," I announced.

"We have to do this again," said Aline. "I never knew the old stuff could be so interesting."

"Me either," said Alana.

The whole team seemed to have wondered in without me noticing. I shooed them out. They needed to prep for possible ground combat. I needed to get to the Bridge.

Angel beat me up there, even though I'd started well ahead of her. She took her place on her console mat.

Miriam and Greer undocked, and the three junior 266 pilots landed, so they could pilot the drop ships if needed.

Alison, Vonda, and Alsop, joined me on the Bridge. Jane was there, as usual. Amy ran in a few moments later, and took a seat at the back.

As the time clicked over past four in the afternoon, the planet Midgard was large in the view screen.

"Jane," I said, "deploy a comnavsat, please."

"Confirmed."

The comnavsat exited through a droid airlock on the Cargo Deck, and took up an orbit around Midgard.

"Hey," said Jane, with a laugh in her voice. "They put their beans in upside down!"

We laughed, although Alsop looked like he really didn't get the joke.

"What have we got?"

"One hundred and twenty missile launchers, all grouped in a series of compounds, well away from any population center."

"Any ships?"

"Negative."

"Ready for the meet and greet?"

"Confirmed."

"Meet and greet?" asked Vonda.

"Jane has a greeting in their own language prepared to send."

I opened a channel to the planet. Immediately we received their answering service.

"Die Heathen, thou who would bring Ragnarok upon us. Those who worship technology will bring the end of all, if we do not stop you. Die Heathen..."

I muted the channel, and nodded to Jane. She nodded back, and threw the just sent message translation onto a side screen.

Government of Midgard, you have committed acts of war against the Sci-Fi and American sectors. You will surrender to us now, or face the consequences.

"Missile launch," announced Jane.

"Surprise, surprise," I said. "Mosquitos please."

Two hundred Mosquito missiles met one hundred and twenty capital ship missiles in the upper atmosphere.

"I wonder how they'll explain that to their people?" asked Alison.

"Or this," I added.

One hundred and twenty missiles launched from Guardians, and headed down to the planet. After a short pause, there was a noticeable plume on the surface, where each of the compounds had been.

"All sites destroyed," said Jane.

"Send the message again."

"Confirmed."

A side screen popped up with several people showing, next to the screen with the translation from before. One of them spoke in what we assumed was Old Norse. The translation went up on the other screen.

Who are you to defile our planet?

"Vice Admiral Hunter, of the multi-sector fleet. You have waged war against us, and you lost. You will now surrender."

I nodded to Jane, and she translated it.

The effect was instant and completely unexpected. One of the men turned to the other, and struck him across the face. The man reeled back, and fell.

The Hunter! You told us the wrath of the hunter was of no consequence. We took you at your word. The hunter was of our own people you said, and his wrath was meaningless. You fool. We are now doomed!

"Jane, ask him what he's talking about."

The man still standing, bowed.

The prophecy of Ragnarok has a little known codicil. This warns of a special doom if we leave our planet before the dawn of Ragnarok itself. The wrath of the hunter would descend on us, all who left our system would die, and we would suffer as no others will. Our Seers told us the hunter was one of us, and as a simple woodsman, could not do anything to hurt our people. Tell me truthfully, what of those we sent out on Crusade?

"All dead. Many of them took their own lives rather than be captured."

We have been deceived by those who interpreted prophecy. You are the Hunter. Are you to be our doom ahead of the rest?

"What is the prophecy of Ragnarok?"

Forbidden. Those who must know, will know. Those who follow, must follow on faith alone.

"I need to know."

He looked at me, as if really seeing me for the first time.

You are the Hunter. You will know. But it's not my place to be the instrument of enlightenment.

"Fine." I was getting tired of this. "Do you surrender?"

Midgard is at your mercy. But I cannot surrender to you. I am but the humble caretaker of this planet. Those who rule, removed the abomination from the sky. To where, I do not know. They make their will known through Seers.

I could see Vonda's sudden smile, and the shake of her head. Her understanding hit me as well, and I couldn't stop myself from snorting. It sounded like a classic political scam. The Seers were the real rulers themselves, with people they could manipulate doing the talking for them. They send people off on a grand crusade, thus ridding themselves of all the troublemakers.

I indicated Vonda.

"This is General Wellington. She is the new Military Governor of Midgard, until the Sci-Fi sector government decides otherwise."

I waved Vonda forward. The Midgard official bowed to her.

"You will place all Seers in immediate detention," she said, "and surrender them to me, when ordered to do so. Diplomats will be arriving soon. You will prepare a place where we can meet to discuss peace, and the future of Midgard."

We await your diplomats. I ask only one thing.

"Which is?"

Return to us those who have been sent to the embarkation point, that they should avoid the Hunter's wrath.

"Agreed. Where is this place you speak of?"

The first man savagely kicked the second man, who was still on the floor.

Tell them.

The fourth moon, of the fifth planet.

"Thank you," said Vonda. "Lock up all the seers. I'll be in touch with you again soon."

Your will be done. Will you send the Hunter away before he destroys us?

The man was terrified of me!

"I cannot send him anywhere. However, he will be leaving soon."

I await your next command.

He bowed low, and the channel closed.

Seven

I opened a channel to Custer.

"You can stand down, General. There's no need for a ground action. We are however, going to visit a station, so we may need you then."

"Understood."

The channel closed.

"What just happened?" asked Amy.

"Which part?" asked Alison. "Someone being terrified of Jon? Or the war being based on a lie?"

"Both."

I put my face in my hands, and just sat there.

"Classic power play in my opinion," said Vonda. "Exploit something the people worry deeply about, gain power for yourselves, create an enemy, and get rid of those people who might threaten you by sending them to fight. It never occurred to them the prophecy might contain a real person, who would stop them."

"Doesn't explain why he was terrified of Jon though," said Amy.

"I don't know," said Vonda. "Wrath is a pretty powerful word to bandy about."

"Who are you really, Jon?" asked Alison. "Or what are you?"

I let my hands fall away from my face, and looked at her. She had her serious face on, but the twinkle in her eye, and the twitch of her lips, told me she wasn't being serious.

Vonda laughed at Alsop's expression. He had that swallowed-a-frog look on his face again.

"Email from Slice, Jon," said Jane.

I dug out my pad, and threw the vid to a side screen.

"Admiral, first planet done, moving to the second. Have you checked the tactical display for this system? If not, I think you'll find it interesting."

"What's he talking about, Jane?" I asked her.

"This."

Another screen popped up showing the positions of the planets around the star.

"Hooley, dooley," I exclaimed.

"What are we looking at?" asked Amy.

"This," I said with a flourish, "is how the system looks from above at the moment. All the planets are almost lined up in one neat line, nearly ninety degrees around from the jump points. There's less than a five percent deviation."

"Is this good?" asked Alison.

"It's very rare," said Jane. "In some systems, it only occurs once in tens of thousands of years."

"And it's happening here now?" asked Vonda. "Is that significant?"

"Could be," I said. "For Seers, it's too obvious an omen to pass up on using to justify whatever you want people to do for you. Wars have been fought before based on much less of an omen than this one."

"Makes Slice's job easier too," said Jane. "Took him the same time as us to get to the first planet. Now he can do all of them in the same amount of time, instead of having to cover the entire width and length. Also means the Orbital station is not all that far from us. Half an hour or so, depending on exactly where it is."

"What do you want to do now, General?" I asked her. "The main fleet needs to find this missing station, but you probably should remain here."

"I could move to Custer."

"No, better make it Warspite. They need to see something significant in orbit for a while. When the rest of the Sci-Fi fleet finishes their patrols, they can form a blockade around the planet. I'll leave the Americans here for now, in case any ships try to escape. We didn't detect any, but it doesn't mean they don't have some hangered somewhere."

"Fine with me. Who tells who what?"

It took me a moment to shift mental gears.

"Your bailiwick, your announcement."

She nodded, and opened a vid.

"Generals and Marshall. While Midgard hasn't actually surrendered, their ability to threaten anyone has been ended. They've agreed to accept a diplomatic mission, and I'm hopeful, this war is now over. There remains at least one loose end, which Admiral Hunter will now pursue. Governor Wellington out."

She nodded to Alsop, and he went blank while he assembled the email, and sent it off.

"Captain's Gig for the Governor, please Jane."

"Confirmed."

As soon as Alsop finished, the two of them left.

I opened a channel to Greer and Miriam.

"Commanders, we've been given the location of the Orbital station. General Wellington is remaining here, on Warspite. I'm assigning the smaller American ships as a temporary blockade force around Midgard. Commander Greer, deploy so no ship from the surface can escape. Capture is better than destroying, but no ship leaves this planet. Commander Young, dock with BigMother please, you'll assume command of the pilots still aboard."

"Yes, sir," they said together.

I closed the channel, and opened another to BigMother's ships.

"Dock please people. As soon as you're all aboard, we're moving out again."

They acknowledged, and I closed the channel.

A half hour later, we were on our way to the fifth planet. The main wait was the Gig doing a round trip. George and the 266 pilots appeared on the Bridge, and took seats. Annette followed them in a minute later.

There wasn't any point in leaving the Bridge, so pad still being in hand, I started checking emails. A number of invoices were waiting for my attention, so I paid them. Seems Jeeves had ordered a few things, given the opportunity the freighter runs provided. One of the invoices was two complete sets of Angel's stuff. It made sense. There was no point in continually shifting her stuff around, especially the kitty castle, wall, and ramps. Might as well have a set in Gunbus and Custer, for future use. Seemed Cat World considered me a safe customer, as the pallets had been delivered to the freighter, before the invoice was paid.

"Heads up," said Jane.

We were about half way to the fifth planet, Midgard having been the fourth in the system. Ahead of us, and somewhat below our course line, was an asteroid belt.

A black dot was now showing on the scanner. There were no ships showing, but this didn't mean there weren't any docked at whatever station this was. We watched as the station came into visual range, and progressively grew bigger.

As we reached a point where the fleet was about to pass it by, I called a halt. Jane took us down, relatively speaking, and BigMother approached the station. It was located on the edge of the asteroid belt itself, just far enough away to avoid any possibility of a collision with a rock.

"Mining station," said George. "Looks like we found the Shipyard's feeding ground."

"Looks like it," I said, with a grin. "Jane, send the following. Midgard has surrendered, please do the same, or you will be destroyed."

"Confirmed." There was a minute's pause. "The station has surrendered."

"What ships are docked?"

"One super-freighter, and a mixture of large and medium freighters. Nine in all."

"Can you take control of them?"

"Yes, but for basic functions only."

"Anyone on them?"

"Not many."

"Tell them to leave the ships immediately. Once they're empty, undock them."

"Confirmed."

"What are you up to, Jon?" asked Alison.

I gave her the Maniac grin.

"Oh, shit," said George. He knew that look all too well.

"Jane, take us back to the fleet please. Have the freighters follow along behind us."

"Confirmed."

I opened a channel to the Mark Hamill.

"Captain Dunning, do you have towing capability?"

"Yes sir. You want the station to be moved?"

"Yes, please. Take it back to Midgard, and put it in synchronous orbit over the capital city. Inform General Wellington she now has a base, with my compliments."

"Aye, sir. After?"

"Form up with Warspite, and wait for us to return."

"Yes, sir."

The channel closed. Mark Hamill peeled out of formation, and headed down towards the station. When she was clear, I ordered the fleet to continue.

Five minutes later, another black dot appeared on the scanner. We made a slight course change to bring us straight to it. I was surprised we hadn't seen it already on the front view, as the HUD details showed it to be huge. At least as big as the Sydney jump point station, which being a combined military and civilian station, was bigger than most. All the same, it wasn't visible until we passed a small moon, and found it in orbit of another moon. The planet the moons orbited was a large gas giant.

The fleet stopped at a healthy distance, within weapons range.

"Same message, Jane."

"Confirmed."

There was a very long pause.

"They don't believe the planet surrendered."

"Figures. Can you clone yourself to their computer?"

"Done. The clone's name is Janice. Should it get a little stuffy over there?"

"You couldn't do that with the shipyard."

"No, but here we can. The life support system here is a lot different."

"Do so. Put a life support failure message on every screen."

"Confirmed."

"What ships have they got?"

"The six Cruisers which evacuated the Shipyard, and three medium freighters."

"Are they enough to evacuate everyone?"

"No. Looks like they have three full fleets worth of people here, in addition to a crew. It will need most of the freighters we took from the other station to carry them."

"Dock them please. Suggest they have only ten minutes to evacuate, before they lose air completely, and let them know we're sending them more ships."

"Confirmed. Freighters will be here in about five minutes."

"What are you up to, sir?" asked Lacey.

"Just relocating Midgard citizens back to their planet."

"Bollocks," one of the pilots mumbled.

I grinned at them.

"That's bollocks, sir," I responded, still grinning.

We watched as the freighters docked. The first of the Cruisers pulled back from the station.

"Jane, tell the Cruisers to hold their positions. When all ships are loaded, they'll be escorted safely back to Midgard. Any attempt to escape will result in the destruction of the ships."

"Confirmed."

"Isn't that a bit harsh?" asked George.

"Sure. I wouldn't do it though. They only need to hear it. If need be, we can tow the lot of them back."

There were a few relieved faces.

"There are some life signs on the station which appear to be ignoring the life support failure," said Jane.

"George, take Custer over to the station, and have the team do a sweep through it. I want every civilian off that station. If need be, stun them, and haul them to a ship."

"You've got it."

He stood, and ran out.

I opened a channel to Custer, and repeated the orders to Annabelle.

In record time, indicating George must have run the whole way he couldn't trolley, Custer undocked, and moved across to the station. I threw suit cams onto the view screen, and we watched as the team were guided by Janice to where people gathered. All of them were wearing the same sort of breathing gear we'd encountered when my station had been boarded a week ago.

The biggest group was in administration. Janice told them to surrender peacefully. They refused. We watched the team taking ineffective fire from them, as one by one they were all stunned. Cargo droids from Custer hauled the bodies off to the nearest ship.

It took an hour to subdue and remove the remaining people. The freighters sealed their airlocks, and undocked. The one's Jane controlled, moved out to form a line behind the fleet. The others were directed to join them. At first they refused. I had Jane threaten to destroy them. It took all the turrets on the fleet pointed at them, to change their minds. The ships moved into a rough formation with the other freighters. I had four of the Guardians take positions behind them.

Custer undocked as well, and re-docked with BigMother.

I stood, changed my suit to 'slinky red', and sat again.

"You're not," said Alison, with her mouth left open.

"I'm claiming this abandoned station. Jane, have one of the Guardian's take the station under tow please. Two others for escort. Take it to where the Shipyard is. Get Janine to build more station tugs, sufficient for moving both stations."

"Confirmed."

"Isn't this piracy?" asked Lacey.

"No, Privateer Law. I captured the station, in a time of war, using my AI, and my own troops, who were fired upon after calling for surrender. No-one else is here to dispute the claim. It's the same principal as claiming a ship after a battle, except war claims need no adjudication when abandoned."

"I guess so."

I grinned at him.

"And since you're all crew on the BigMother at the time of capture, under the terms of our contract, you're all listed as crew members of the station, and entitled to a share of the income it produces."

There was a mixture of smiles and shakes of the head. I beamed at them until they were all smiling back.

It took another half hour to attach the tow, and for station and escort to move off. The fleet started back to Midgard. I switched my suit back to fatigues.

We all went down for a late dinner, where we found the rest of the team, just arriving from Custer.

Eight

Dinner was a boisterous affair, now the war seemed to be over.

We were still lingering over desserts (me), and coffee (everyone else), when we arrived back at Midgard. The return trip had taken more than twice as long as the outbound trip, because we were escorting slow freighters.

The Cruisers were instructed to dock at the station, and offload everyone. All the freighters followed them. The station was going to be crowded for a while, until everyone was ferried down to the surface.

Jane sent her security droids in for crowd control, using my shuttles, but not the Gig, which I didn't want to get trashed. Each shuttle also carried five combat droids. The security droids, who appeared to be human, and thus wouldn't alarm anyone, started loading operations.

I instructed every ship with its own shuttle, to provide a military escort for the pilot, and begin taking people down. As well as the shuttle dock, we configured some of the main docks to take shuttles.

The drop off point was a large field outside the capital city. Those who were still out from stunning, went first, and were literally dropped in a heap out of the way.

Once the Cruisers and freighters were empty, I had Jane send over repair droids with fighter computers, so Jane could use the ships fully. They also gave the ships Hunter ID overlays. As each one was completed, it docked with a Pocket Battleship, loaded up with the salvaged hulls it was carrying, and Jane sent it to the jump point, to dock with the station. The super-freighter loaded all the remaining hulls, and was the last to leave.

My small freighter landed on the Flight Deck, was taken down, and unloaded. It didn't need to do another trip, so it joined the shuttles in moving people. The last lot of parts would hopefully see the rest of the fighters' combat ready by the morning. The ships might be ready, but I doubted the pilots would be. Miriam had gone down to check on them, and found a party in progress. By the sound of things, there would be hangovers in the morning.

Vonda came back aboard, and we conferred in my Ready Room. She sent off a vid announcing that two stations had been neutralized, and subject to the patrols not finding anything else, the war would be declared over the following morning.

We joined in the celebrations downstairs, which had moved into the Rec Room. I was surprised to find Angel in there. She was getting plenty of attention, and lapping it up.

Around eleven, I decided to called it a night. I picked up Angel, received a mwow of protest, and a lot of wiggling, and put her down again. She went off to seek someone else to pat her. I quietly left.

I was in boxers and t-shirt when I heard my door open and close. Miriam walked in with a grin on her face, pushed me down onto the bed, and did a strip tease.

All thoughts of sleep, vanished. It was some time later before we did.

"GOOD MORNING, MIDGARD!"

I jerked awake, as did Miriam beside me.

"Jane, did you do that to the whole ship?"

"I certainly did," she said with a laugh.

"Sadist."

"That's one of the milder comments."

The laugh echoed around the room.

"I bet," said Miriam.

"You have orders, Jon."

Miriam pecked me on the lips, moved her breasts against my chest, and ....

"YOU HAVE ORDERS, JON!"

I rocketed up, Miriam pushed aside, and fell out of bed, on my left side.

Miriam looked over the side at me.

"You okay?"

"No."

"Jon, don't make me send in a combat droid," said Jane.

"Yes, mum."

Miriam giggled.

I dragged myself up, and headed for the shower. Miriam followed. Jane at least gave us time for a leisurely wash and dry. Back in fatigues, Miriam headed for breakfast, and I to my Ready Room.

"Sitrep," I said, when comfortably seated.

"Most of the pilots and marines are hung over."

"No surprise there. Tell me something I don't know."

"All ships are back from their patrols. Nothing addition-al found. General Wellington formally announced the war to be over a half hour ago. The comnavsats are all placed. We now have an unbroken coverage of ship movements all the way to Nexus."

"Show me."

The scanner map went up on the main screen. It did indeed show all ship movements between here and the Nexus 618 system. Nexus was the central hub of the Australian sector. I was interested to see a lot of traffic heading in and out of Midnight, past my station, Hunter's Redoubt. As I watched, a blue dot detached from the station, and headed towards an Australian destination.

I dragged my attention away from it.

"You mentioned orders?"

"Check your emails."

Indeed there were.

The first was from General Patton.

"Vice Admiral, congratulations on a job well done. As soon as General Wellington can release you, you are to proceed to Dallas Orbital. Bring the Corvettes and Privateers with you. They'll go into the shipyard to complete their repairs. Once you arrive, have the Sabres and Epees transfer to the Military Orbital, or Shipyard, depending on their condition. Advise my aide when you jump into Dallas."

"On a personal note, I must say when your promotions came up each time, I strenuously argued against them, based on your age, and short experience. I admit I was wrong. You have conducted the war better than most of the Generals and Admirals I know could have."

"There will be further orders for you once you reach Dallas Orbital. I'm sure the civilians will want a formal celebration, so be prepared for one. Patton out."

I sat back for a moment, absorbing what I'd heard. A four star General apologizing? When I'd been responsible for getting so many Americans killed? He was right in the first place, for Gaia's sake. It didn't make sense.

I moved on to the next one, being General Harriman.

"Congratulations, Jon. You did the impossible. And while I know you're sitting there wondering what all the fuss is about, take it from me, Australian sector is very grateful to you. The Americans caught a series of bad breaks, and we feel for them. But all the same, Midgard never entered American space, so their sacrifice was not in vain. Don't beat yourself up about the losses. It's part of command."

"Your station is becoming a hub of activity here, as traffic between the sectors gets back to normal. It'll be a shame to move it now. Are you sure you want to do that? Let me know. I'm sure I can convince Sci-Fi sector to allow it to remain here."

"Enjoy the celebrations. That's an order!"

He grinned at me briefly, and the vid ended. I started one to send back.

"Walter, thanks for your email. Order accepted." I gave him a grin. "The station can stay where it is. However, make sure it's well away from the jump point, and not in the line towards Bad Wolf. I've taken possession of another station, one the size of Sydney station. It will be heading your direction as soon as I can organize it. It'll go to the center of the Nexus system, just off the traffic routes between the jump points. You can advise the merchants of the new station, and where it'll be. I'll let them have first choice of moving to the new station if they wish, or establishing themselves on both stations. Let David know, so he can make preparations for moving there, and duplicating the administration section.

It'll need some work first, so there'll be no hurry to do anything."

"I'm ordered to Dallas, and assume there'll be a delay in leaving there. At this point, I have no idea when you can expect me back. But I'll send the stations on soon, regardless of when I can leave. I'll advise you further when I know anything. Hunter out."

The next email was from General Price.

"Congratulations, Vice Admiral. Job well done. I have to admit I had my doubts about you at first, but your conduct has been exemplary. Proceed to Dallas, and offload the Americans. Leave the Avon troops with General Wellington. I'll have further orders for you when you get there. Price out."

Marshall Bigglesworth had the last word.

"Vice Admiral. Congratulations on a job well done. I've heard nothing but good things from Admiral Bentley. I look forward to meeting you soon, as do a few others here on London. Bigglesworth out."

I wondered what he meant by that. London wasn't in the general direction I intended going. Even if I was ordered back to Avon, London wasn't on the way.

I sighed. It would be good to get back into my own uniform. It would be even better to get back into civvies for a while.

I called a meeting of senior officers for nine.

Nine

I looked around the room.

Seated at the conference table were General's Wellington and Smith, Admiral's Bentley and Dingle, Commodore O'Neal, Captain's Johansson, Dunning, and Channing, and Commanders Greer and Young. Alsop and Alison sat at the other end.

"End of this road," I said with a smile. "I have orders to take the American pilots to Dallas."

"I also have orders for Dallas," said Susan Bentley.

"Admiral," I said to Dingle, "You'll command the Sci-Fi ships, under General Wellington. Give her all the support she needs as Governor of the system. You report to General Price, through Commander Alsop. I've had no word about the status of this system, but for now, assume it's quarantined. You'll need to put ships at the Azgard jump point to stop people jumping in. I have assets there at the moment doing the job, but they'll be gone within two days. So work up a deployment plan that blockades this planet and system. You won't need to worry about the Miami jump point yet. The Americans have a sizable fleet still there. If that changes, someone will let you know. Although at some point, Sci-Fi sector will need to take responsibility for that jump point as well."

"Yes, sir."

"Captain Johansson. Harrison Ford, Mark Hamill, and Backblast, will form the primary escort for the Diplomatic Mission which is on its way. You'll wait at the Miami jump point for their arrival. In all other respects, which don't inter-fere with the Diplomatic Mission, you'll report to Admiral Dingle, until a more senior American officer arrives, or you're recalled."

"Yes, sir."

"General Smith, the Avon troops will be remaining here. Debark them to the station, with enough supplies for three days. The Senior Colonel has the command, reporting di-rectly to General Wellington. Move them to Custer, and have George dock her at the station for the transfer. They can clean the station to keep them busy. Identify a place to con-vert into an armoury."

"Yes, sir."

"Commanders, your squadrons will be returning to Dal-las for repairs. Arrow formation ahead of the fleet please. No point in having a normal CAP while we're on the move."

Why did that sound like famous last words?

"Sir," said Greer, and Miriam nodded.

I turned to Alsop.

"Commander, have you done provisioning orders for the station yet?"

"No, sir. I was going to inventory before ordering."

"I think you can order without doing that. The station will need a full complement of building, repair, butler, maid, and cleaning droids. Add salvage, and search and rescue to the list, as well as the normal amount of trolleys, shuttles, and maintenance scooters. It needs a new station computer as fast as one can be delivered. Assume the accommodations will need rebuilding, or at the least, refurbishing, and order new beds, and bed linens. Also everything else for kitchens, bathrooms, and Rec Areas. Order enough food for five hundred people, for three months. Add whatever a normal station administration requires, and anything Governor Wellington wants for her comfort and wellbeing. Think of everything a station normally has, which a tech hating people would destroy or remove. Get the order off as soon as you can. I assume Avon will order from Dallas, and it'll all be here tomorrow."

"Yes sir."

"Then you inventory. It's faster to assume there's nothing on the station but empty space, and change orders after, if need be. In the meantime, unless you find the miners lived high on the hog, the Governor had better stay on Warspite until renovations are complete. Talking of which, VIP quarters are first priority, followed by Diplomatic meeting rooms, and administration. The Diplomats are going to be here for a long time I suspect, and they won't be wanting to sleep in tents on the surface, or in some miner's barracks."

"Understood sir. I'll get right on it."

"Governor?"

"It's been a long road for all of us. Most of the fleet has had its brushes with death. Pass on to your people, it's been a job well done." There were smiles and nods all round. "Good luck to all of you who are moving on. It's been a pleasure working with you."

The meeting degenerated into a general expression of pleasure session, and broke up. Vonda remained behind after everyone else had left.

"Jon," she said, "I never did figure out if you were a homicidal madman, or not." We both laughed. "But in spite of your age, you're a natural leader. You joining the Australian Militia was the best thing you could have done, and three sectors are damned lucky you did."

"I was drafted."

"Drafted? You're not serious?"

"Yes, I am. Australian sector lost most of its pilots to pirates before I left Outback, and was down to only a single patrol. I made ace on my first flight in a fighter, and General Harriman drafted me when I arrived back at the station. I've never been happy about it, but events proved it was probably for the best. It kept me on the straight and narrow, and gave me some legitimacy. Without it, I might have become some sort of pirate myself. I've skirted close a few times. Lacey was concerned yesterday that I was turning pirate. I had to explain Privateer Law to him."

"Oh? What did you privateer this time?"

"Midgard's original Orbital station."

She burst out laughing.

"You're not content with a station dressed up like a Battleship, and a huge shipyard, you want another station? What else do you want?"

She couldn't say that with a straight face, and continued laughing.

"Actually, there's something you can do for me in that regard. General Harriman is going to be asking Sci-Fi sector for permission for Hunter's Redoubt to remain in Midnight as a control point for ships entering Australian space. It could go in Nexus, but Midnight makes a lot more sense, as it gives the sector a buffer zone if anything undesirable gets past. The Orbital station is considerably larger, and is better suited to the center of Nexus, which I have permission for already. If you could put in a word on my behalf for permission to have a station in Midnight permanently, I'd appreciate it."

The laugh died. She gave me a long speculative look.

"Done. And it's my pleasure. It's been an experience working with you, Admiral. I hope we cross paths again some time."

"Likewise. If you're ever in my neck of the woods, you'll be most welcome."

"On that note, I'd better get moving. Take care of yourself, Jon."

"You too, Vonda."

We shook hands, and Vonda hugged me.

Ten

I spent the rest of the morning on the Bridge, monitoring the preparations to leave.

It was just as well we didn't need a CAP, as most of the American pilots were in no condition to fly. Only the ones on their Corvettes and Privateers were still fully functional. In a way, they were a sort of CAP, but an unconventional one.

Jane and I discussed the new station. She displayed a schematic, and we looked it over, with a view to what work needed to be done to bring it up to a suitable standard. She and Janice communed, and Janice sent us a more up to date version, and a summary of the condition of each area.

It was almost identical to Sydney Station, except it was much older. The design went back to old Earth days, and this one had been among the last built there. So it wasn't surprising it was showing its age. It didn't help having never been upgraded at all. Before it could be used, it needed a complete makeover.

I looked up Sydney's station, and it turned out theirs had been built in place from the now normal kits. I'd never paid much attention. It was a station in space, was about as much thought I'd given it when I was living there. Now, I paid attention to its design.

Imagine you built a modern city of skyscrapers on a round metal plate. Only because this is space, where there's no up or down, you built a second city on the other side of the plate. That's roughly what the station looked like.

The plate itself provides a huge circumference for a hundred docking ports, fighter dock, shuttle dock, and a central strata of decks. In itself a major city, but each space-scraper is almost its own smaller city. A bit like a city on a planet, the disk was the city center, and the space-scrapers were suburbs.

Jane and I started dividing up the space. The central space-scraper on one side was designated administration. This would include traffic and docking control. The largest one on the other side was to be solely for the Hunter family and corporation. We assigned a whole section of both sides for Military use, half being for Hunter ships, and the other half for the Australian Militia. Each area contained a space-scraper, and a set of docks. Control points were designed so each was self-contained, and access could be limited to authorized people only.

They would get Flag, Officer, and Barracks accommodation along the same lines as Custer, but be able to house more than five hundred people at a time. Accommodation also including office space and the equivalent of a CCC for each. A General or Admiral would want a control center and meeting rooms, as well as offices. Both needed armories. I set Jane to design plans for them, taking into account any possible military scenario the space could handle. The Hunter space would definitely include gun ranges.

One of the smaller space-scrapers was designated for Australian sector Customs.

Within the central plate section, the center was set aside for a giant park, including a fresh water lake, and multi-level high waterfalls. The levels above the Dock Level were designated for retail, and was to be extensively windowed, so there was a complete view of space from everywhere around the deck, with the internal side overlooking the park and lake. Business spaces around the park were allocated to food, drinking and entertainment, with many general eating areas.

Below the Dock Level, was to be a modern freight handling facility, with several of the lower space-scrapers dedicated to storage.

The remaining space-scrapers were ear-marked for residential living spaces, offices, and more retail. The residential included a number of large hotels, and ultra-luxurious apartments, especially on the tips of the space-scrapers, where an all-around view could be made.

Given the size of the station, we made provision for both full sized hospitals, and smaller medical clinics.

By the time we were finally interrupted, it was almost midday, and I found Angel asleep in my lap.

It was getting to be a concern how things were happening around me, which I didn't notice. I made a reminder to actually follow medical advice, and get a checkup when we arrived in Dallas.

It was George who interrupted us, walking onto the Bridge and announcing the troops were all moved, and Custer was ready to go. I suggested he should park the second Excalibur in Custer. My Excalibur was on the Flight Deck, but I asked him to move it to the closest bay to the access shafts, so I'd have as short a way to go to get to it as possible.

George looked at me for a moment, as if to argue over whose ship it was. I stared him down, and he left without a word. I smiled at his retreating back, knowing exactly what he'd been thinking. He'd spent so much time in my Excalibur in the last few weeks, he'd started thinking of it as his.

I went down to the Deck Two Dining Room for lunch. Most of the team were there before me. George joined us while we were still eating.

Once I finished, I stood and looked down the table. People noticed, and talk subsided.

"It's a fourteen hour trip to Dallas Orbital. We're all on stand down until we get there. Take it easy for the rest of the day. We can expect tomorrow to have something official planned, so make sure you're bright eyed and bushy tailed in the morning." There were a number of smiles. "Commander," I said to Greer, "Pass the message on to all your pilots."

"Yes, sir," he responded. "Do you want us in our ships?" He indicated Miriam.

"No need. Give your seconds a chance to lead for once."

"Fine, sir. When are we leaving?"

"As soon as the fleet forms up."

He nodded.

"Jon," said Aline. "Can we watch some more of that flat screen?"

"Do you want to continue on from where we left off? Or actually start at the beginning of that remake?"

"Start again please. Might make more sense."

"Okay, but the main character is different, as I was a long way further along when you were watching. It's the same person, but a different persona." She looked puzzled. "Get Abigail to explain it to you. You want them now?"

"Yes, please."

I went into the Rec Room and threw the first season, from way back in 2004, to the main wall. I started the first, and paused it, let Aline know they were on pause waiting for her, and left them to it.

Angel followed me up to the Bridge, and sat on her console mat, looking forward. She turned her head to look at me.

"Yes sweetie pie, we're moving shortly."

She purred, and looked ahead.

Jane reconfigured fleet coms to only the ships leaving with us. We formed up into an arrow formation, with the Corvettes and Privateers forming the head. BigMother was followed by the British Destroyers and Corvettes, with Repulse bringing up the rear.

Four hours to the jump point, seven hours across Miami, and another three hours to Dallas Orbital. With luck, no-one would want me, and I could get a decent night's sleep for a change.

With nothing else to do, I left Angel to her space gazing, and joined the 'Who' watchers in the Rec Room.

I was back on the Bridge for the jump into Miami. The scanner map showed the jump point was clear on the other side, so the arrow head sped up a little, folded back to a double line, and we all jumped through, resuming the formation once we were clear of the debris field and the blockade ships. The debris field had been much reduced in size.

The whole team was there when I returned. I hadn't missed anything, as I'd seen these so many times over the years. But all the same, I settled down in a lounge chair, and resumed enjoyment. It was good not to have anything to worry about for a while. Angel trotted in at one point, demanded a pat from me, and did the rounds of the room.

At dinner time, Aline switched the entertainment system to play in both rooms, and we continued watching as we ate.

I'd always thought there was nothing like a good 'Who' marathon to pass the time. Apparently my new converts agreed with me.

Around ten thirty, I was back on the Bridge for the jump into Dallas. I sent off an email to General Patton's aide to say we were now in the Dallas system. I gave Jane instructions to let me sleep, unless something really urgent came in, in which case she should let me sleep anyway. If a more senior officer wanted my attention before seven in the morning, they better have a damned good reason for it. If the universe ended during the night, I didn't want to know until the hollo-documentary came out.

I found Angel asleep on her kitty castle, and Miriam draped seductively across my bed.

So much for getting a full night's sleep.

Eleven

"GOOD MORNING, DALLAS!"

I bolted upright in bed. A half remembered dream of gold ribbon and purple smoke, fell away, and vanished.

"Stop doing that, Jane," I yelled.

Meow!

Angel jumped up, waggled her left rear paw in my direction, rushed to the side of the bed, and launched herself off. She landed lightly on the floor, and shot out the door.

I sat there gaping after her. I'd never seen her jump so far before. She was growing up rapidly.

"Jon?" said Miriam sleepily from beside me. "What are you yelling about?"

"You didn't hear Jane just now?"

"No. Should I have?"

I suddenly realized Jane had bellowed at me only, through my PC, for once.

"Sadist," I muttered.

"Who is?"

"Jane."

"You rang?" said Jane through the room coms. "Jon, I let you sleep as long as I could. You have a seven thirty meeting on the Military Orbital, and it's already five past. Put your skates on. The Gig is ready for you. Miriam, you have orders as well. Sorry Jon, but get it in gear, Mon Capitan."

"Is Jane getting even more eccentric now?" asked Miriam.

"MOVE IT, JON. You have a four star waiting for you."

I leapt out of bed, and jumped for the shower. Miriam followed, but I didn't let her slow me down. I was out, and drying off, while she was still soapy.

Angel was eating her breakfast when I found her in the kitchen.

"I'll be out for a lot of today, sweetie. Can't be helped, I'm afraid. And later on, we'll all be out, so you'll need to entertain yourself."

She stopped eating, and looked at me.

Mew.

She went back to eating.

I headed down to the Cargo Deck, where I touched down in the access shaft, with only a slight twinge from my left knee. A trolley took me to the down shaft, where the Gig was waiting on the Launch Deck. Jane had moved the Gig as close to the access shaft as it could get. I boarded, and settled into the co-pilot's seat. Jane was sitting in the pilot's. The Gig moved to the lift, and we started rising.

"Sitrep."

"The fleet arrived at one thirty this morning. The crewed ships are all docked with the Civilian Orbital station, which apparently booted a lot of civvies out to accommodate us all. The exception is John Wayne, which docked at the Military Orbital instead. O'Neal and his crew moved to BigMother as soon as they completed docking."

The Gig rose from the Flight Deck, and headed out the rear entrance. I noticed Unthinkable was missing.

"Unthinkable?"

"All damaged ships were moved to the Shipyard before we docked. ETA on the repairs is sometime this evening. My avatar took Camel over personally, and I updated all the ship ID's as you requested."

"Good."

A thought struck me.

"What uniform am I supposed to be wearing?"

I was in Sci-Fi fatigues.

"I'll ask." She was silent for a moment. "American fatigues."

I shifted uniforms, and checked I'd updated the rank insignia correctly.

"Who did you ask?"

"Admiral Jedburgh's aide. And no, I don't know who you're meeting with."

"What about the American ships?"

"All moved to the Shipyard. The pilots were not impressed with the two o'clock wake up call. They gathered their gear, and were gone by two thirty. Neither Carrier is out of Repair Dock yet, so the pilots are now on the Military Orbital."

Speaking of which, we were now on approach to it. Jane swept us in the shuttle dock entrance at a faster than normal speed, and within minutes we were docked to an airlock. The airlock door opened, and Jane followed me through. An Ensign was waiting on the other side, and he headed off into the bustling maze of corridors.

Precisely at seven thirty, I was shown into a large office.

Admiral Darius Jedburgh didn't look well. He waved me to a chair.

"Good to see you again, Vice Admiral. Forgive me not greeting you properly, but I feel like you look."

He was referring to my head bruise, which was still a mottled yellow colour.

"I was only released from hospital a few hours ago, and I had to bully my way out. Too much to do to pander to doctors."

I knew the feeling. He partly rose, and offered his hand across the desk. We shook.

"Thank you. Without your quick response at the Miami jump point, I'd be dead, and most of my fleet with me."

"Sir? It was my recommendation that put you in that situ..."

"No, Jon," he interrupted me. "You're not going there. I was told you felt badly about the whole situation, but nothing was your fault. There isn't an officer in the entire fleet who had any inkling Midgard would attempt another incursion into Miami. And I did ask. We had a senior officer's think tank after your suggestion came in. No one even thought of it, let alone voiced the possibility."

"But..."

"No buts. Had the situation been what we expected, your recommendation was precisely what we needed to bring our ships into the fight, quickly and decisively. What happened was entirely due to the fog of war, and my stupidity in not acquiring the specs for your comnavsat. Had I sent one in that morning, we would have known what was going down, and prepared for it. As it was, your warning, and the very quick orders you gave, saved Yorktown, four Cruiser sized ships, and the Corvettes and Privateers, from a very unexpected death."

"Actually..."

"No again. You were about to say some of the pilots would have been fast enough to save themselves. Perhaps so. But Yorktown would've been dead. Carriers are like a small city. The loss of life was bad, but being destroyed would have been much worse. And before you interrupt me again, our being hit was none of your fault either."

I closed my mouth, and he went straight on.

"What happened to Yorktown was just plain bad luck. One enemy captain out of twenty four, was good enough to recognize an opportunity, and take it. Without the nukes, we might have taken out most of the missiles before they hit, but it's doubtful given how close we were at the time. It's what happens in war. No plan survives contact with the enemy, and even when you win, you can still get your butt kicked solidly."

He paused and looked at me.

"We'll be going to an awards ceremony at nine. I understand you have a suit definition for Sci-Fi Dress?" I nodded. "Close enough. Wear those, although if you can match ours, all the better. Ribbons are fine."

"I'll need a scan of yours. If any of your officers are already in Dress uniform, I can scan those."

"Admiral Hallington is in the outer office, you can use his to scan."

"Thank you, sir."

"This afternoon at four, there'll be a civilian reception on the Orbital station. Everyone from your ships is invited. It'll be followed by a state dinner. Dress uniforms. You can expect a late night. Have you checked your emails this morning?"

The change in topic caught me by surprise.

"Ah, no. I took the opportunity for a good night's sleep. I didn't get that far on the ride over."

"Check them now. You should have one from Marshall Bigglesworth. Throw it to the wall."

I pulled my pad from its hip pouch. Sure enough, there was such an email. I threw it to the wall as requested.

"Vice Admiral Hunter. You and your people are invited to London for a reception at the Palace. We're inviting all the major players in the Midgard war to attend, save those on blockade duty in Midgard itself. Please reply with your acceptance of this invitation, and a probable ETA. Bigglesworth out."

"Sir..."

"Call me Darius, Jon. You're wanting to know when you can leave?" I nodded. "We'll all be leaving at oh seven hundred tomorrow. In fact, I wanted to ask you a favour. We don't have a fast enough Command ship. Can I hitch a ride with you? I have a Battlecruiser which can follow after to bring me, Admiral Hallington, and my staff, home."

I grinned at him.

"No problem. I've flag accommodation onboard you can both use. Your staff can stay on the Battlecruiser. I had a modification done to my Carrier, so we can actually dock your ship underneath. As long as that doesn't offend her captain."

He laughed.

"You never cease to amaze me, Jon. Done and done. You better send off a reply now, as you won't get much chance from now on."

I did the math on how long the trip to London would take from here. The direct route was Kansas, Washington, London, so not a long trip. Roughly twenty one hours in total. So we should get there about four, the morning after leaving. I did a quick vid accepting the invitation, and giving the ETA for us, and the American contingent.

"Now," Darius said when I was done, "if you'll excuse me, I need to dress. Admiral Hallington is outside, he'll show you to the ceremony."

He rose, offered his hand again, and we shook.

I walked out into the outer office. Admiral Hallington was waiting with his arm outstretched. We shook. He didn't look a lot better than Darius did.

"Nice to see you again sir, and thank you for your actions the other day."

I chuckled to myself over the role reversal which suddenly occurred to me.

"Call me, Jon."

"Chet. I understand you want to scan my Dress uniform?"

"Yes, please."

He stood still while I scanned an image. Once I had it, I motioned him to a seat, and sat myself, while I made up the suit definition, removed his insignia and medals, and added my own. I stood again, and shifted into American Dress.

"It's amazing how you do that."

I chuckled, and he joined in.

"You should be using these too."

"It's been proposed already. Neither Admiral Jedburgh nor I would have suffered as badly as we did, had we been wearing them. Both Greer and Young have been pressing for them, but the wheels grind slowly at times. Having lost one Admiral, and almost lost two more, in a single engagement, and it being preventable, is making a powerful argument. Had the entire crew of the Yorktown been wearing them, the casualty list would have been a lot shorter. Anyway, what's done is done, and we'll be moving heaven and Dallas to get them now. Let's be moving. It won't hurt to be early, and will save our aides fussing over getting us there on time."

"When should the ceremony be finished by, Chet?"

"Ten thirty at the latest."

"Good."

He chuckled, and set me off again.

I pinged Annabelle to assemble everyone in the Rec Room at eleven.

Chet rose, and we both limped out, Jane following.

Twelve

Alison was waiting with several Commanders, in a room off the meeting room the ceremony was to be held in.

She was wearing Hunter Dress. We settled into extremely comfortable chairs to wait. There was already the sounds of people moving in the next room.

"Sir," she said to me, "we need to fix your salute."

"What's wrong with my salute?"

"What's right with it, you mean."

She had a point. I'd never been taught. She spent the next five minutes teaching me, and bullied me for the next ten in practicing. Chet and one of the Commanders found the whole thing funny. The other Commander obviously couldn't figure out why an Admiral wouldn't know how to do something as basic as saluting. Fortunately, it was using my right arm, as the left one still wouldn't function too well above shoulder height. Another reason for getting a checkup while I was here.

"Now," said Alison, when she thought I had it, "you'll stand to the left of Admiral Jedburgh, and as he recites the citation, Commander Wantanbe will pass you the medal."

"He'll what?" I interrupted.

"He'll pass you the medal."

"Why?"

She sighed.

"Get a grip Jon, will you. You're presenting the medals as the commander of the campaign."

There was an immediate frown from the one Commander, and wider grins from Chet and the other.

"It's so hard to get respectful help these days," I said to Chet.

The two of them laughed, and the other frowned even more.

"Focus," said Alison. "Commander Wantanbe will hand you the medal. When the recipient is at attention in front of you, you'll hand them the medal, shake hands with your right hand, and then answer their salute. There will be no hugs."

Chet lost it.

A lieutenant poked his head around a door and announced, "They're almost ready for you, sirs," before vanishing again.

Chet made an effort to bring his face under control.

At precisely nine, we walked into the ceremony room. As soon as we were in place at the front, Admiral Jedburgh entered, and took his place at the speaker's podium. Alison jogged me with an elbow from the side that hid her from the officers facing us, and I stepped forward to stand on Jedburgh's left. The frown Commander took his place next and slightly behind me, with a table of small boxes next to him. Alison was behind me, the only person in the room not in American Dress.

"We are gathered here," said Jedburgh, "to honour those whose actions in the past few weeks have brought honour to themselves, and the American Space Force. As the commander of our forces in the Midgard system, and for the last few days of the war, Admiral Hunter will be making the awards."

He read out a long list of names, all of whom had been awarded medals posthumously.

Then he started in on the living. Time and faces blurred, as I handed out medals, shook hands, and saluted. Some were promoted at the same time. Greer came before me, followed by Miriam. I could see she was making as much effort to keep her face neutral as I was, while she took several medals from me, shook my hand, and we saluted. The blur continued with higher ranks.

Finally, the flow of officers stopped. Four boxes remained.

"Vice Admiral Hunter," said Admiral Jedburgh. "Front and center please."

Oh hell. Not again. This isn't right. I moved to stand in front of him, and braced to attention. He talked past me.

"This admittedly young man, came to us as a pilot, and quickly showed our pilots how it's done. We let him go, before we realized we had a relentless foe on our doorstep who refused to communicate. He went on to be the strategic and tactical mind behind a multi-sector battle fleet. And at the last, his quick thinking saved many of us from a sudden and unexpected death."

He could see me looking extremely uncomfortable with this, but he was the only person who could.

"This man can't see what his actions meant for us in the final battle. He gave an incredible sounding order, which was followed immediately by Commanders who trusted his judgement, influencing Captains who didn't know him, and so successful was his order, that Yorktown and the ships with her all survived certain destruction."

"He couldn't see what we could, when his final missile salvo jumped to our side, and destroyed the last six Missile Cruisers, seconds before they fired towards an already badly damaged Lexington. He ordered the impossible, and it was done. He did the impossible, and the day was saved. Yet he's so humble, he can't see past putting Yorktown and her fleet in harm's way, through his suggestion of tactics we adopted. Was it his fault we were in harm's way?"

"HELL NO SIR!" said the entire room, as if they were on a parade ground.

"Where do we live?"

"IN HARMS WAY!"

"Was he responsible for victory that day?"

"SIR YES SIR!"

It took a huge effort at that point, for me to not cry where I stood, and I was dangerously close to collapsing, hyper aware of my bruises. All I could do was lock my suit so I couldn't move. A room full of officers were behaving like troops on a parade ground, and I just couldn't wrap my head around it. My left temple began to throb. I upped my pain medication.

Finally, Admiral Jedburgh looked directly at me.

"Vice Admiral Hunter. You are awarded a silver star for the final battle of the Miami jump point, a Distinguished Service Cross for the missiles which destroyed the final six Missile Cruisers, and the Medal of Honour for leadership, tactical and strategic brilliance on the battlefield, while at risk of your own life. Normally a Medal of Honour is awarded by the President of the American Sector, but it was considered in this case to be more important the award be made now, in the aftermath of a war just won, while the recipient is still a member of the American Space Force. Congratulations, Admiral Hunter."

Commander Wantanbe passed him the medal boxes, I unlocked my suit arms, he passed them to me, we shook hands, and saluted each other. The room went crazy behind us.

"Attention to orders," bellowed Commander Wantanbe.

The room reluctantly quieted.

"There are two last items of business today. Vice Admiral Hunter, you are hereby promoted to the rank of Admiral, effective immediately, and retired from service with the American Space Force, effective at oh seven hundred tomorrow. Congratulations, Admiral."

I just about passed out on the spot. Only my locked suit held me up.

Commander Wantanbe passed him the last box, he gave it to me, and we shook and saluted once more.

"This ceremony is at an end. Dismissed. See you all at the celebration this afternoon."

The mass of officers began to file out. I released the suit lock, and made an effort to stay on my feet.

Darius led me back into the room we'd come out of, and sat me down in a chair. He wore a huge grin on his face, as did Chet and Alison.

"You're out of uniform, Admiral," he said, when we were all comfortable.

I shook my head, still having a hard time believing what had just happened. I opened each box, and removed the medals and insignia. I scanned the insignia, and added them to my American uniforms. Next I scanned each medal ribbon and added them to all my uniforms, reordering them from high to low merit. I added Hunter four star insignia to my Hunter epaulettes. Finally, I changed my American Dress to show the new additions.

"Congratulations, sir," said Chet, and we shook.

Alison pulled me out of my chair and hugged me. The Admirals smiled. She finally released me, and I sank back into the chair. A lieutenant offered me a ginger ale, and then offered drinks to the Admirals and Alison after me. He even offered a drink to Jane, standing quietly out of the way. I drank without really tasting anything. Except for my bruises, I was numb.

"Jon," said Darius, "you're officially off duty now until the celebration at four. We'll see you there."

They left me sitting there with Alison. I told her what I wanted to do next, and pinged George to be ready.

Thirteen

Precisely at eleven, Alison, Jane, and I, me now in Hunter Dress uniform, strode into the Rec Room on Deck Two of BigMother.

The room went crazy, and I was hugged by all the women, and hand shaken by all the men.

When things started to calm down, I looked at Alison.

"You pinged Annabelle during the ceremony, didn't you?"

"Of course," she laughed.

I shook my head in wonder, and moved to stand against the main wall. Alison moved to my side. I nodded to George, and he also moved to my side.

"Attention to orders," bellowed Alison.

At least she tried to bellow, but she didn't really have a parade ground voice.

The room came to attention.

"Dress uniforms, please," I said.

The room shifted as suits changed.

"As your name is called," said Alison, "come front and center please."

A mutter went around the room, and was quickly silenced.

"George is going to pulse you new uniforms," I said. "Please update both your normal wear and Dress, and display your new Dress uniform. Hunter Security is instituting new ranks and insignia. Epaulettes will now indicate which service branch you belong to, by colour. Green is ground based ranks. Grey is fleet. Blue is fighter. Insignia are now standardized, although rank names will vary between branches. Some of these ranks vary from other services, and several are unique to Hunter. George will pulse you the full list after this ceremony. Regardless of the insignia you wear, you will please display your rank at all times on your PC profiles. At times, some of them will cause confusion outside of Hunter, but if you're displaying them publically, this can hopefully be minimized."

I watched as they all received their pulse, and changed to the new uniform.

I nodded to Alison.

"Specialist's Aline Takai, Agatha Merritt, and Alana Henquist."

Aline, Agatha, and Alana came forward, now wearing the insignia of a Corporal.

"There's no rank of Specialist within Hunter Security," I said, "hence the rank of Corporal, those who were a Specialist are now wearing. Corporal's Takai, Merritt, and Henquist, you are promoted to the rank of Sergeant. Congratulation's."

They tried to shake hands formally, but couldn't stop themselves hugging me as well. George sent them new uniforms, and they shifted into them. The room applauded as they went back to their places.

"Sergeant Abigail Weaver," said Alison.

She braced to attention in front of me.

"Sergeant Weaver, you are promoted to the rank of Senior Sergeant. Congratulations."

We shook and hugged, and she returned to her place.

"Flight Officers Jones, Taylor, and Williams."

The three of them looked very surprised as they came forward, and braced to attention.

"Flight Officers, you are promoted to Flight Lieutenant. Congratulations. In addition, you are each assigned to fly brand new Excalibur Privateers, which should be delivered this evening. The ship names and AI's, match your call signs."

They looked elated as they shook my hand, changed their uniforms, and moved back. I could understand why. Once they left British Fleet to be mercenaries, they'd lost any expectation of promotion. It's not that promotion didn't happen in mercenary units, but small units didn't have much need for rank. And they all wanted to fly Excaliburs.

Alison opened her mouth to say the next name, but I beat her to it.

"Lieutenant Alison Vogane," I said.

Looking surprised, she braced in front of me, wearing green epaulettes.

"There's no rank of Captain within Hunter Security. A captain is considered a title, and not a rank. Therefore Lieutenant, you are promoted to the rank of Major. Congratulations."

George pulsed her the new uniforms as we shook, and then hugged. There was a stir around the room when she activated them.

"You will notice Alison and I both have red epaulettes. Red is my command colour, and will be worn only by myself, and my staff. Alison took on the role of my aide the other day, and is now confirmed in that role." I looked at

Annabelle. "This won't preclude her team duties when required."

She smiled and nodded. Alison had been the team's administrator and medic, before joining me.

I nodded to Alison, and she stepped back to her place beside me.

"Lieutenant's Peck," she announced.

Amanda and Aleesha braced before me.

"Lieutenants, you are also promoted to Major. Congratulations."

They both hugged me at the same time. They stepped back beaming.

"Flight Lieutenant Brown."

He braced in front of me, and gave me a quivering salute.

"Flight Lieutenant, you are promoted to the rank of Squadron Leader. Congratulations. You are also assigned to a new Excalibur."

He shook my hand, gave me another quivering salute, which I returned this time without the quiver, and returned to stand with his squadron mates.

"Eric Neilson."

Eric was shocked to be called forward. He'd been standing towards the back with John Slice, quietly enjoying the show.

He came forward, and braced.

"Eric. You dropped unexpectedly into a warzone, and were almost killed after you bailed out. Most civilians, even military trained ones, would be expected to seek a safe place for the duration, after such an experience. Not only did you not hide, you were there when you were needed, putting your life on the line with everyone else. No-one asked you, you didn't volunteer, you weren't drafted, or conscripted, but you were simply there. Such duty to friends and sector demand recognition. Eric Neilson, you are offered a commission in Hunter Security with the rank of Flight Lieutenant. Do you accept?"

He was stunned, and looked around to see his boss's reaction. John Slice smiled, and nodded.

"I accept," he said.

"Flight Lieutenant," I began. I'd looked up his record and found it had been his rank when he'd left military service. "You are promoted to Lieutenant Commander, and assigned to command the Camel class Corvette Nascaspider, on indefinite assignment to the Apricot Mapping Service. Congratulations."

He hugged me.

I knew he wanted a Camel desperately, and I was effectively giving him one of the two he'd been flying since Midnight. He'd become a good friend in a short time. And I wanted to make sure he could handle anything exploration threw at him in the future. Sure, Slice was going to build him one eventually anyway, but what use was credits if you couldn't give a good friend a gift now and then.

He released me, saluted, and went back to stand by his boss, now proudly wearing his Hunter uniform. I pinged him to see Alison afterwards. He nodded to me from the back of the room.

"Squadron Leader Lacey."

He literally marched into position, and braced to attention, also with a quivering salute.

"Squadron Leader, your performance at the Midnight Blockade was given a glowing testimonial by General Harriman. Since then, you've flown Camel, and General Custer. You have a choice to make. Would you like to remain with fighters, or move to fleet?"

"Fighters," he said with no hesitation.

"Squadron Leader, you are promoted to Wing Commander, and assigned to command Camel. Congratulations."

We shook hands, saluted, and he returned to his squadron mates.

"Lieutenant Commander Murdock," said Alison.

George looked surprised, which was understandable, because he'd been promoted only recently, and so had no expectation of another one. However, I had something else in mind. He braced before me.

"Lieutenant Commander, you are assigned to command the Excalibur class Privateer Gorilla."

There was general laughter at the name, although everyone knew it was his call sign as well. He grinned as he realized he was getting what he most wanted.

"Further, when I'm not present, you will captain the Assault Frigate General Custer. When I'm present, you will act as her XO. Gorilla will be hangered in Custer. Congratulations."

George hugged me. I pulsed him his new epaulettes, grey ones instead of the blue he was wearing. While a Lieutenant Commander was a fleet rank, it had been awarded first by the Americans, who used the same ranks for both fleet and fighters. He'd been flying fighters since the war started, hence the blue. Now, as Captain of the Custer, he was being moved to fleet officially. If Lacey had asked for Custer, I'd have assigned George to Camel.

As he stepped back, Alison called, "Commodore Daniel O'Neil."

He braced before me, looking proud to be here.

"Commodore, you are promoted to the rank of Fleet Admiral, which is the equivalent of what other services call a Rear Admiral, Lower Half. You will take command of the station Hunters Redoubt, which will stay permanently in the Midnight system. You remain Captain of the John Wayne, and shall command the fleet stationed at the station. Congratulations."

He hugged me too.

He'd never expected to make Cruiser captain, let alone Admiral.

When he released me, I went on, "See me after lunch. I have orders for you and Lieutenant Commander Bronson."

I saw her nod at the mention of her name. Also recently promoted, she wasn't expecting anything, as she already had what she wanted most. Her epaulettes had changed to grey as well, since she also commanded a Corvette.

"Are all your crew out of hospital yet?" I asked O'Neil.

"No sir, the last come out tomorrow. But I'd like you to meet someone who came out today."

He beckoned to a lady his own age, I'd not seen before. She walked over slowly.

"Sir," he said, "may I present my wife Leonic, my XO on Custer."

"I'm delighted to meet you," I said. "Will you join him on John Wayne?"

"I will," she said.

"Admiral, you'll need to get your last crew out of hospital this afternoon. If need be, move them to the Medical Bay here. Also have each one report to Alison, so they can be formally employed. As I told you, they'll be back dated so they began the day you did."

"Thank you, sir."

He led his wife back to where they'd been. She patted his right star as if she couldn't believe it was there.

"Jane, please."

That surprised everyone.

Her avatar came to attention before me.

"Jane, you are given the rank of Fleet Captain. This avatar will wear the red epaulette with the full bird, as the Americans say." Her suit changed immediately. "Your avatar's running the Liner and freighters, will wear the four thick rings of a civilian senior Captain, on the dull red epaulette."

"Confirmed. And thank you."

"I don't know about everyone else, but you're more than just an AI, or the ship's avatar. And I'm not just thinking about how much more than a normal AI you've had to take on, and master, to keep us alive. You're my friend, and you're part of the team. You deserve an appropriate rank for what you do for us."

"Damned right!" said BA.

Everyone laughed. Jane returned to the corner she'd been observing from, a grin plastered on her face.

"There's one last thing before we have lunch. John Slice please."

He walked over and stood before me, but didn't brace. I held out my hand, and he took it.

"John, we haven't known each other very long, but it's felt like years. In my people's terms, meeting you was like two old souls meeting up once again in a new lifetime. I consider you a friend, and Hunter Security considers the Apricot Mapping Service a friend. If you ever need anything, we'll be there."

"Thank you, Jon," he said with a grin, as we continued to shake.

We broke the grip, and he went back to where Eric was standing.

"That's all for this ceremony. There's a celebration on the Orbital station starting at four, with dinner after. Assemble at the main airlock at three thirty please. We'll move there in formation. Dress uniforms. We head to the London system at seven tomorrow morning. Pilots, I suggest you use the early afternoon to get your Trader and Bounty Hunter Guild memberships. Fleet Admiral, you too please. One of the pilots will explain it to you."

There was a series of nods.

"Now, let's eat!"

BA came up to me before I could move, with her hand raised.

We high fived.

Fourteen

Back in my Ready Room after lunch, I shifted my suit to 'slinky red'.

I'd been pondering general protection levels over lunch, as something had reminded me of my dream that morning, and what it could be trying to tell me. I'd decided a test was in order. Jane came in when I called, and I had her change her suit back to a belt and remove it. I chuckled when the thought popped in about her now standing there naked. Of course, it was just a security droid now.

I changed my own suit to a belt. Taking hers, I put it around my waist as well. As I'd hoped, a pop-up asked me if I wanted to merge both belts. I answered yes, and the two belts became one slightly larger belt. I shifted back to 'slinky red' and checked on the integrity level. It showed a value two hundred and fifty percent higher than before.

I changed back to a belt again, accessed the suit menu in my PC, and separated the two belts, giving Jane hers back. She shifted back into her avatar again, and left. I shifted back to 'slinky red', and sat at my desk.

A memory tickled my mind, and I asked Jane if Alison had ever received boosters for the replacement suit belt she'd received just before the second Avon battle. She told me she hadn't.

I sent off an order to the local Mercenary Outfitters, for delivery as soon as possible. The local 'tool man' responded immediately with an assurance it would be delivered as fast as it could get to me.

I'd no sooner finished the order, when O'Neil and Annette entered. They sat in front of the desk.

"You wanted to see us, sir?" asked O'Neil.

"Have your crew been officially employed yet?"

"Yes sir. I'm stopping by the hospital to bail the last of them out as soon as I finish with the Guilds. Um, why am I getting Guild memberships?"

"Is this for the new HUD?" asked Annette.

"Yes. Jane updated all my ships with my own private HUD overlay. It shows a lot more detail about ships on the scanner and HUD. But a lot of the information comes from all three Guilds. So you need to be members of all three, and subscribe to their data feeds. Once you receive them, the HUD overlay uses the information. You'll see when you're back in space."

"It's brilliant sir," said Annette. "Take my word for it. As soon as I saw what the boss was using, I asked him for a copy."

"Understood," he said. "Bounty Hunter I understand, but how do I gain Trader membership?"

"You don't have to be a trader to gain membership, just be the owner or captain of a ship which can trade. John Wayne has more cargo capacity than a large freighter, so you don't have a problem. Being a senior military officer is enough to demonstrate big ship skills for them, and since you're driving a Pocket Battleship, I don't think they're going to query your skill set. As it happens, you can demonstrate being a trader anyway."

"Sir?"

"Your orders are as follows. After the celebration is over, you are both to head back to the Azgard jump point in

Midgard. By the time you arrive, there should be enough Station Tugs built to move both stations at a reasonable speed. You'll escort them both to the Nexus 618 system. Jane will supply JW with the co-ordinates they're to be taken to. All the ships there will go with you. John Wayne and the three Guardians will be the escort. Annette, you'll take point, and jump first at each jump point. Ensure the other side is completely clear before the stations jump through. If by any chance you find hostiles, you get help if need be to clean them away before the stations jump through. Questions?"

"No, sir," they said together.

"Once they're in position in Nexus Annette, you and one Guardian stay with the stations as a guard. Each of you dock to one station. It's unlikely anything hostile will threaten you, but you're there just in case. There needs to be a presence there anyway, to ensure someone doesn't claim they're derelict."

"Before you enter Midnight, be very sure the station there is well out of your line of advance. Once past, stop and confer with General Harriman. Take a security droid with suit belt from the station there, and have Janet use it for an avatar to put on the Guardian remaining in Nexus. It should fool anyone who tries to communicate with it."

They both nodded.

"Daniel, when the stations are in place, return to Hunters Redoubt, and take command from General Harriman. He'll instruct you on Australian Militia procedures, and the sort of things you can do as an adjunct to the Militia. You should get a Militia feed as well, since part of your role will be a sort of sector police."

"Yes, sir."

"If anyone there asks about moving to Nexus, take their details, but tell them the station there will be undergoing some significant upgrading, and won't be habitable for an unknown length of time. I'm going to offer anyone in Midnight the opportunity to move to Nexus, or operate their businesses from both stations. I'll make a proper announcement when I get back there. And by then, I should have a better understanding of how long the restorations will take."

"Understood sir. Anything else?"

"Yes. While you're at the Traders Guild, mention to them you have a good sized cargo hold, and are heading for the Australian sector. Make sure they understand it'll be a slow trip, but it's very likely they'll have cargo for you to take. They did last time I was here. Tell them you're leaving as soon as possible tomorrow, and to load anything they want shipped overnight. If they do have cargo, see if they can load on the Military Orbital. If not, have JW move John Wayne over here so they can. When you get to Nexus, JW can contact Jane's freighter avatars for pick-up and delivery. Jane will credit John Wayne with the delivery fees, and JW will set you straight on the account keeping for Hunter Security and your crew's share of the profits."

"Phew, learning curve," he said, and I smiled at him.

"Yes. Oh, and on the way, clean up the debris fields we left behind. You can store it all on the station for now. Some of it might be useful. Get Jane to transfer the station's salvage droids I borrowed to John Wayne to speed up the clearing process. That's all I think. If there's anything more, I'll let you know."

"We'll be off to the Guilds then, sir."

They rose and left.

I waded into emails. I threw a vid from Vonda to the wall.

"ADMIRAL, congratulations." She beamed at me. "I'm not surprised the Americans promoted you again. You'll be relieved they retired you at the same time though, I guess. I know you don't like the responsibility we all keep heaping on you, as good as you are at handling it. I expect SFSF will do the same thing shortly, most likely when you get to London. General Price will be attending whatever they have planned there. It's all quiet here, waiting for the arrival of the diplomatic mission. I understand there's a celebration there tonight. Enjoy yourself. There and when you get to London. You've earned it. Again, congratulations. Wellington out."

I sent her back a brief vid thanking her, and expressing my absolute intention to enjoy myself from now on.

Jeeves came in with a package. Opening it up, popped up an invoice, which I paid. I unpacked six new suit belts, with three boosters for each. I added the boosters to each belt.

Again I changed my suit back to a belt, and added a second belt around my waist. The pop-up asked if I wanted to merge, and I answered yes. The belts merged. I checked the protection level, and it was as the test had shown. I also checked if the non-standard nature of my original suit remained active. It had, and in fact, the merged belt had adopted the characteristics of the original completely.

Now for the real test. I looped a third belt around my waist. Another pop-up, and another successful merge. The fourth one refused to merge, so it was the same as a fourth booster refusing to merge.

I set the belt back to 'slinky red'.

I checked the protection level, and was surprised to see it rated the same as a combat suit now.

Feeling adequately protected, I had Jeeves take two of the remaining suits down to my suite, and pinged Alison to come see me.

She limped in about five minutes later.

"Take your belt off, please," I told her.

"Jon? Are you getting frisky?"

She grinned at me.

"No," I answered her. Her face fell. "I've a new one for you. You never received any boosters for that one, so I ordered you a new one. It just arrived."

I handed it over to her. She shifted hers to a belt, removed it, tossed it on my desk, and put the new one on. I watched as she went blank, obviously getting a PC upgrade for it. When complete, she shifted the belt to 'slinky red'.

"Good," I said. "I feel better now you're properly protected. I'm off to the hospital for a checkup. You should come with me for one as well."

She frowned, as if considering refusing, but nodded. She followed me out.

Amanda and Aleesha met us inside the Cargo Deck airlock, and took up flanking positions. I assumed Alison had pinged them I was heading out. Given what had happened the last time I'd gone out onto a civilian station, it made sense.

I stepped to the top of the ramp and took a step down.

My suit snapped into full protection mode with my foot still in the air.

Four golden threads came at me, slamming into my suit at the same place over my heart. Instead of being pulses, the shots continued to hit me in a continuous stream.

The suit reacted as I'd been told it would. The momentum of the hits was transferred down the suit, and into the deck below, lifting me clean off the deck, and propelling me into the air.

As I rose, the golden streams travelled down my body.

My Long Gun was in my hand seconds after the hits began. Targeting went primary. Four targets were identified. From right to left I tracked the gun to each target, squeezing off one shot at each. Four figures in the distance went down one by one. Each golden stream shut off as each target went down, the last one already past my knee and still going down when it ended.

Two meters off the ground, my rise halted, and I came down as fast as I'd gone up.

My feet hit the deck, and agony like I'd never felt before, shot up my left side.

I passed out.

When I came to, I was sitting in my Ready Room, at my conference table.

I was in no pain at all.

There were three of us sitting there. Me at one end, both of them at the other. I couldn't see them very well.

The woman smiled at me.

"Welcome, Jon. You're dead."

Fifteen

"Dead?" I said. "What are you talking about?"

She waved her hand, and a screen opened on the wall.

Three people were kneeling over a fallen figure, while a line of combat droids raced past into the station.

Alison had my head in her lap, and was crying hysterically.

"What?"

"You're dead, Jon. Accept it. Your suit worked as designed, but the trauma underneath it was so great, the pain of touching down stopped your heart. You were dead before your body hit the deck."

I stared at her, then back to the screen. A trolley was approaching at an insane speed.

I looked back to them.

"Where am I? And who are you?"

"You're in your Ready Room, of course. We thought we'd borrow it to provide you with familiar surroundings."

"But who are you?"

"Don't you recognize us?" said the man.

The trolley had stopped, and I watched Jane scoop up my body, dump me on the flatbed, force the girls on to hold me steady, and jump back into the driver's seat. The trolley took off down the ramp as fast as it could go.

I looked back at them. My vision started to clear.

The first thing I noticed was they both had four arms. And what was wrong with the man's face?

I squinted at them, but it didn't help.

The man waved a hand, and I suddenly saw them clearly. My breath would have caught in my throat, only I realized I wasn't breathing.

The man had an elephant's trunk for a nose.

The woman was dressed in antique robes that vaguely reminded me of hollo's of the ancient Indian deities.

My eyes opened wide as I made the connection.

"Kali?"

She nodded.

"Ganesha?"

He nodded. I looked at her.

"Shit! You're the one who's been talking to me all these years."

"Now you're getting it," Kali said, with a laugh.

The Norse and the Egyptians had their gods. The Indian's had their Deities. I was face to face with two of them.

People were diving out of the way of the trolley moving at an insane speed through the station, which only an AI was capable of doing safely. It pulled up outside a hospital. Jane jumped off, picked me up, and raced me inside. The girls followed.

"They won't be able to do anything," said Ganesha.

"You code locked your suit," said Kali. "They won't be able to get it off you."

A medical team took my body, and started to work frantically on reviving me. The suit hindered them. Alison was distraught, and the twins had to pull her away. One of the doctors gave my chest a solid thump.

I looked back at the two Deities.

"So," I said. "What's the deal? Why am I here?"

"There's no deal, Jon," said Kali. "You're here because it's the only way we could get your attention fully. Up until now, you've not really been paying attention to us."

"I always follow what you say to me."

"Jon, you only hear me when I shout at you. You never hear anything we say normally."

"Why don't I?"

"Your head is still too cluttered," said Ganesha.

"You do your releases," she said, "but you never take them to the next level and work on what else your mind is full of. Didn't you listen the day they taught you all this? Or was your mind in your computer game at the time?"

I looked sheepish. It sounded about right for me.

"You needed a clear head, Jon," he said. "Only then would you be able to hear those of us trying to help you. You muddle by as humans do, but you were capable of so much more."

"Capable?"

"You were special, Jon," she said. "You carry my Sceptre."

"Your what?"

"Sceptre."

"I know something of Kali, and she's never been depicted with a sceptre."

"Very true. Do you want to know why?"

"Yes."

"Because the only time I carry my Sceptre is when I bring destruction at a cosmic level. For humans, this would be terminal. The species would end in a blink of my eye."

I looked at her in awe.

"So that's why you're called Kali the Destroyer?"

"He's getting it," said Ganesha, with a grin.

"What do you mean I carry your sceptre?"

"A human is gifted with the Sceptre for one lifetime," said Kali. "Whoever accepts this burden is granted wisdom and power beyond their wildest imaginings. But it's only given to those of pure heart."

"Many die young," said Ganesha. "The burden is too great for them."

"So I failed," I said. "Crashed and burned."

"Technically," he said, "you burned and crashed."

The comment seemed to give him great amusement.

The medical team had given up. I was lying there with wide open eyes, the girls draped over me crying hysterically.

"So that's it? The darkness wins because I couldn't carry the burden properly?"

"What is the darkness to you, Jonathon Hunter," said Kali.

"You tell me. I could never get a straight answer from the Keepers. All I know is the little they told me, and the nightmares. But I've known since the first nightmare, I was here to do something connected to the darkness. I accepted it very early in life."

"Ah yes," said Ganesha, "you worked that clue out quite nicely."

"Clue?"

"When those we speak to do not listen," said Kali, "all we can do is send clues. Sometimes dreams are the only way we can reach you."

"But what was the point if it ends here?"

"We needed to speak at last. You needed to understand."

"Understand? What for? Do I have some choice to make?"

"You already made the choice," said Ganesha. "You're here to understand why you made it."

"What choice are we talking about?"

"Carrying the Sceptre of course," said Kali. "The burden comes with responsibility as well."

"Responsibility for what?"

"To wield it properly," said Ganesha.

"To wield it wisely," said Kali.

"And I haven't been, have I? I killed when I didn't need to."

"You did as we bade," she said. "The question was not would you accept the task, but would you carry it through regardless of the personal cost."

"And I failed?"

"No, Jon. You passed."

Kali looked extremely happy with me. Her tongue extended to its full length. She gazed at me for a moment, and suddenly all four hands thumped down on the table so hard, it bent under her blows.

There was a heavy weight on top of me.

"Fuck that hurts," I said. "For divine's sake, get off me!"

Sixteen

The three girls shot away from me as if they'd been yanked off.

All three of them looked at me speechless. Their tears stopped, but faces remained wet.

A doctor shot in the door as if propelled from an antique cannon. Before he reached me, I changed my suit back to a belt.

He gaped at me without comprehension. But medical instincts kicked in, and he started to work on me. I had a major pain shot as fast as a nurse could bring one, and the agony in my body subsided to a major ache.

From my heart to below my left knee, was a solid blue bruise.

Miriam rushed in at that point, and had to be restrained by Amanda. She was crying, and suddenly confused by the fact the doctors were still there. Amanda told her I was alive, and she collapsed into a chair. Alison sank down next to her, and the twins stayed standing. They were all staring at me.

I was scanned, and checked for broken bones. And given another shot.

I woke to an empty room.

"Jane?" I whispered. "Where are you?"

"Outside your door."

"How long was I out?"

"Ten hours."

"Where is everyone?"

"The celebration is still in progress. The flag officers stepped in, and made sure everyone went."

"What did the doctors say?"

"You have major bruising. They don't think you'll be able to bend your left knee for at least a week, and they plan to keep you under for the whole time."

I did some basic math.

"Time for a midnight flit."

"Jon? You can't possibly by thinking of leaving here."

"Nope, not even thinking about it. Can you get hold of a pain shot?"

"Already have one."

"I need it."

She came straight in, and gave it to me. Major ache became minor ache.

"What's that you're wearing?"

"Security uniform."

"Good thinking. Go out and buy me the best grav chair you can find quickly. One that allows a leg to remain straight."

"You said you weren't thinking about leaving."

"It doesn't require thinking. I'm not losing another week of my life. Go."

She went. I'd already lost a week two months ago, when I'd first been injured. The doctors had kept me out because of a head injury. My head was fine. It was just the rest of me that wasn't.

A nurse came in, and I pretended to be still asleep.

After what seemed like an eternity, broken only by an invoice to pay, and actually being less than half an hour, Jane returned with a grav chair. The left leg support was already in place. Jane was dressed now in an orderly's uniform.

She plucked me off the bed gently, and placed me on the chair. The meds stopped any pain spikes.

I shifted my belt into chameleon mode. Except for a faint outline, my body vanished.

"Home, James," I said to her.

She pushed me out of the room, and towards the hospital exit. Heads turned as an apparently empty chair went past them, but no-one seemed to notice anything out of the ordinary. It was just an orderly going somewhere with a chair. Once outside, with no-one in view, she shifted into the security uniform again.

Neither of us spoke again until we were inside the ship. At the top of the ramp waited a trolley. Jane moved the chair onto the trolley, took the driver's seat, and the trolley started for the other end of the ship. Once a reasonable way from the airlock, I shifted back to 'slinky red'.

"What more did the doctors say?"

"They couldn't understand how you were alive in the first place. You were dead for fifteen minutes, Jon. Total goner. The next thing they couldn't understand was why your heart showed up as being normal for your age. Your heart stopped, and wouldn't start again. There should've been damage preventing the restart. There wasn't. They hadn't a grip on that, when someone pointed out your brain should have been fried by lack of oxygen. After five minutes, brain damage is normal. Your brain was fine. They went through the motions of scans, but except for major bruising, you were perfectly healthy."

"How will they explain it?"

"Not even trying to at the moment. You do realize your midnight flit will cause a lot of trouble when they find you're gone?"

"Not my problem. Can you hack my hospital record?"

"Sure."

"Do so, and mark it 'Patient discharged himself'."

"Confirmed."

We arrived at the access shaft. Jane moved the chair down off the trolley, into the access shaft, and gave a modest push-off.

"Where to?"

"My suite."

She deftly moved the chair out of the shaft on Deck Two, and moved me into my suite. Angel woke as we arrived, looked at me with an alarmed expression, and stood up.

"Hi sweetie. I got hurt badly. Come into the bedroom, and keep me company."

I told Jane to take me to the shower. She stood me up, held me upright, and carried me into the shower. I changed my suit back to a belt, Jane removed my briefs and socks, and washed hospital off me. After drying me, she pulled new briefs and socks back on, and laid me on the bed.

She tossed the sheet completely over me.

I pulled it back from my head with my right hand.

"I'm NOT dead, Jane!"

"Could've fooled me. The only reason they didn't do that in the hospital is the girls wouldn't let them."

I sighed. Even that hurt.

Angel came running up. She sniffed at my bruises, and her claws extended, as if to fight off whoever gave them to me. She looked at me, I smiled at her, and she relaxed, moving to my neck on my right side, and curling up as she usually did.

Seventeen

I woke at six to find four naked women on my bed.

They were lined up next to me. Miriam, Alison, Amanda, and Aleesha. I looked across eight breasts in a row. It was a sight to gladden any young man's ... well let's not go there. It would hurt too much anyway. Just as well it was a king sized bed.

"Jeeves," I said softly. "Pain."

He came in within seconds, and gave me a shot. Jane came in after him, helped me out of bed, and into the bathroom, where she held me up while I used the facilities. My bruised side was in full Technicolor now. The bruises on my head and shoulder were a dull yellow. I couldn't bend my left knee at all. It wasn't that it hurt too much to try, it wouldn't bend. I pondered if the knee itself was damaged.

I shifted into 'slinky red', and she helped me into the grav chair. Angel was eating her breakfast when we went past the kitchen.

She took me to the Medical Bay, and one of the docdroids gave me the once over. I asked it to co-ordinate with Jeeves as to when I could have pain shots. Going into a care unit wasn't on my list of things to do. Its response on my knee was the muscles were too traumatized to be able to move. All of them were down the hit area, not just the knee. But it was the knee, and thigh muscles I noticed couldn't move. It would heal, I was told. Give it time. I had plenty.

I was soon on the Bridge. I bypassed breakfast, even though I hadn't eaten since lunch time yesterday. I wasn't in the least bit hungry.

Jane settled me in my command chair, and used the grav chair to prop up my left leg. Jeeves came in with a pillow and gently padded the top of the chair underneath my ankle.

Angel shot in, and took her usual place on her console pad.

I opened a vid, and recorded a brief message to the effect that contrary to first reports, I was alive, if not kicking, and functional enough that the trip to London was on schedule. I sent it to everyone who mattered, and a few who didn't, but would be wanting to know anyway.

I pinged Admiral Jedburgh's aide to say BigMother was leaving on schedule, asking when the Admiral's party would be coming on board. It took ten minutes to get a reply for thirty minutes later, putting him minutes ahead of official departure time.

I sat there checking emails, answering the few that needed responses, and deleting junk. I lost interest quickly. As a distraction, it wasn't working.

"Jane, who were they?"

"Assassins. Apparently four, who usually work alone, banded together to make sure you were taken out this time."

"Paymaster?"

"Unknown. They haven't said, even under intense interrogation. Dallas military took them off station security's hands before they even woke from your stuns."

I looked up my Bounty Hunter record. I didn't have any new bounties on me.

"Professional hit then," I mused. "I wonder who would go to all the trouble."

"Unknown. Abagail has all the information that could be found. The contact emails were untraceable."

"Emails again. It always comes back to dodgy emails. Have her and Amy come up here after they finish breakfast, and after the brass are finished with me."

"Confirmed."

I thought it a pretty good assumption that Admiral Jedburgh would be on the Bridge to see me as soon as he was on board.

"Jane, you better go down and welcome the Admirals."

"Confirmed."

She left.

I thought I better check what was docked where. Custer was in her underside position. Camel and Gunbus were docked to her, making her look like she had reversed nacelles. Apricot One was attached to the left rear airlock, and Nascaspider to the rear right. Excalibur was on the Flight Deck, and Gorilla was inside Custer, as were the three Dropships. Jane had done some rearranging as the Corvettes had come back from the Shipyard, but the configuration looked good to me. There were four more Excaliburs and five Centurions in docking bays along the inside of the Flight Deck.

A channel opened.

"Starman to BigMother, permission to dock, and where please?"

It was Greer. I checked the scanner. Starman was stopped not far away, and Stiletto was just entering the Flight Deck from the rear.

"Starman, use the mid left cargo airlock. Dock nose on, so the airlocks are the same size."

"Is that really you, sir?"

"No, this is my avatar pretending to be me. Of course it's me. Sheesh!"

"Roger that, sir. Docking now."

Station traffic control were probably having heart attacks about now, as a Corvette sized ship moved too close to the station for comfort. But Greer's AI would be doing the actual docking, so there was no risk.

Stiletto touched down inside a Flight Deck Bay. Since I'd seen Miriam on board already, her AI must have done the transfer.

Apparently they were both invited to London as well.

With the thought of her, she bounded onto the Bridge, with Alison, Amanda, and Aleesha behind her. They stopped abruptly when they saw my leg perched on the grav chair.

"What," I said. "You've never seen someone in a captain's chair before?"

"That's not funny," they all said at once.

I shook my head slightly. My women were now speaking to me in quadrophonic. 'My women'? Now how did that happen? That taunt of 'Hunter's Harem' popped back into my mind. Just as well the man who said it was dead. If BA had ever heard of it, she'd have killed him.

Amanda took out her gun, and wacked me on the right foot with it.

She was angry again. Now what had I done?

"What?"

"Why didn't you tell us you were leaving the hospital?" demanded Amanda.

"Why didn't you wake us up when you woke?" demanded Miriam.

"What are you doing on the Bridge?" demanded Alison.

"What's wrong with your leg?" demanded Aleesha.

I sighed.

Amanda took that the wrong way, and whacked my foot again.

"I didn't announce it, you all looked like you needed the sleep, this is where I'm supposed to be when the ship gets underway, and it doesn't work."

Silence. They glared at me.

"Oh for divine's sake. Why can't you all be happy I'm alive and sitting here?"

Miriam kissed me.

Alison gave her a full minute, hauled her away from me, and kissed me. Amanda gave her thirty seconds and did the same. Aleesha let her sister take as long as she wanted, and then as soon as our lips parted, did the same.

"Go get some breakfast," I said, "before you embarrass me in front of the Admirals coming on board. We'll talk later."

"Yes, we will."

Deadpan quadrophonic. I winced. Then winced because wincing hurt.

"Admiral's Gig is landing on the Flight Deck now," announced Jane.

"Oh hell," said Miriam. "I need to get down there."

Two levels in her chain of command were arriving. She raced out. The others followed her more slowly.

I watched the shuttle arriving on a side screen.

"Is there any reason we can't leave yet, Jane?"

"All present and accounted for. The Battlecruiser will RV with us half an hour out."

"Button us up, and prepare to undock. Advise Dallas Control we're leaving, and have them pulse me the docking fees."

"Confirmed."

The invoice pulse came in a minute later, and I paid it.

Precisely on seven, Jane backed us away from the station. When there was enough distance to not upset the traffic controllers, Jane spun us around, and set course for the Battlecruiser Guam, which I could see in the distance.

I was now retired from the ASF, which was a big relief. I had no responsibilities with either the SFSF or the AM. A weight left my shoulders. For now, I was free to simply be the owner of a mercenary fleet. I had four stars on my shoulders, and no-one was going to be able to promote me ever again.

I could hear laughter in my head for a brief moment, but couldn't tell where it came from. Could have been Kali, but I wasn't sure.

The last promotion actually solved a problem. I'd never have to worry about an employee being a higher rank than me again. As soon as I could shuck the SFSF and AM as well, the happier I'd be.

I'd missed the celebration, which was something of a relief as well. I'd imagined it to be something similar to the one on Avon the night before we left, and I didn't really need another one like it. Getting shot the way I had, wasn't the best way of avoiding people, but it had done the trick.

Ten minutes out, the remaining four Guardians formed up in diamond formation around us, top, bottom, left and right. Repulse took station behind us, with her fleet around her.

Twenty minutes later, Jane slowed us to a stop. The Guardians moved some distance away, as did Repulse and her fleet.

Guam was about the same length as Big Mother, midway between a Battleship and a Cruiser. But she was taller than she was wide. BigMother out massed her by a long shot.

Jane threw her specs on a screen, and we looked for the best way of linking her up.

A large group of people came onto the Bridge behind me. I turned my head, saw the Admirals at the front of the group, and waved them to the VIP chairs. They looked shocked to see me there, but didn't say anything. I guess they expected me to be in my bed for the next week.

Jane and I went on with our discussion. It took us another five minutes to decide the best way to connect her was the left middle underside dock point, grav'ed to the forward highest gun turret. I opened a channel.

"BigMother to Guam. Captain to Captain please."

I was an Admiral in rank, but still captain of the ship. Rank and title, not the same thing. And my rank was no longer active, so I was the captain of a friendly ship, not a superior.

"Captain Patterson speaking. Admiral Hunter?"

"Indeed. Captain, can you release control to my AI please? We'll grav dock you at the front highest turret, to the underside of BigMother. My AI will ensure there's no possibility of accidental collision."

"Aye, sir. Control released."

I nodded to Jane. A screen popped up, and we watched two very large ships come together. Guam moved into position beneath the grav point, and slowly closed the distance until she was merely centimeters away. The grav plate came on, and the ships kissed. Jane tweaked the attitude so she was perfectly aligned with the underside of BigMother, and finally increased the grav to hold her in exactly that position.

"Docking complete," she announced.

The screen vanished and the channel closed. Applause came from around the Bridge.

Jane accelerated us towards the Kansas jump point. BigMother took longer to get up to speed, but our top speed wasn't affected.

Repulse took up the rear position, but slightly above. I assumed Susan wasn't game to be behind in case the dock failed. The Guardians took up formation around us as before.

Another screen popped up with a cam image of how we looked from one of the Guardians.

"Now I've officially seen everything," said Jedburgh. "Including the dead coming back to life."

Jane rose, moved to my chair, and swiveled me around to face the rear, ensuring my leg didn't move, by moving the grav chair with me.

"I'm happy to oblige, sir," I said.

We were the same rank now, but he had the seniority, and we were in public. Everyone was there I noticed. And the two Commanders from the medal ceremony were sitting off to one side.

It was Annabelle who broke the minutes silence following my response.

"How are you alive, Jon? Abagail looked it up. No-one, and I mean absolutely no-one, ever, has come back after fifteen minutes dead, where it didn't involve hypothermia."

"Just lucky I guess," I joked. It went over flat, not even gaining a smile. "How should I know?"

"What did you see, Jon?" asked Miriam. "Did you see the light?"

"Light?" I blinked rapidly. "No light. Actually I spent the entire time in my Ready Room."

"That's not funny," said Alison.

"I'm not joking. I guess you'd call it an out-of-body experience. I was in my Ready Room, watching the girls take me to the hospital on the wall."

"That's really weird," said Aline. "Even for you."

"You're telling me! I was there, and I don't know if I believe it or not."

Check.

"Jane, is there anything different in the Ready Room?"

"Affirmative."

"What?"

"The table is damaged. And there are two largish figurines on the damaged end."

"What are they of?"

"Identical to the ones on the console, only bigger."

My head swiveled around to see the figure of Kali sitting on the console out of the way. I smiled.

"What really happened?" asked Amanda.

"I told you. I was in the Ready Room. There were two indistinct figures there with me, and while I watched the wall, we had a conversation."

"Who were they?"

"You wouldn't believe me if I told you."

"I don't believe a word of this anyway," said grumpy Commander.

Jedburgh gave him a sharp glance, and he looked down at the floor.

"Was there anything strange about my body while I was, err, away?"

"Actually there was," said Alison. "We couldn't close your eyes. That shouldn't have been so. Until rigor sets in, the eyes are closeable."

"I wonder," I started.

"Wonder what?" said Miriam.

"I wonder if I wasn't actually dead."

"You were dead, Jon," said Miriam. "It wasn't an illusion."

The obvious emotion in her voice caused both her bosses to look at her sharply. I guess they didn't know we were an item.

"I'm not saying it was an illusion, I'm saying I wasn't actually there."

"That makes no sense at all," said Annabelle.

"It could," said Eric. "But only if you consider science fiction type answers."

"Here we go," said grumpy Commander, and realized I'd forgotten his name.

He received another sharp glance from his boss.

"Commander, you're dismissed!" said Jedburgh.

He rose, saluted, and quickly left.

"You were saying, ah?" he went on.

"Eric Neilson, sir. Jon was brought up spiritual. His ways and thinking are different from all of us. From what I heard, he may be the first recorded case of actual time travel, as hard as that might be to accept." People looked at him strangely, so he went on quickly. "The point is, strange things happen around him, and to him. Being alive isn't the only mystifying thing. He should've been vaporized. I did a lot of research on the suits when I first heard about them. One Meson blast will render a normal suit useless. Jon wears three boosters. So in theory, after four Meson blasts, his suit would be useless. I asked about what hit him. They were modified Meson Blasters, designed to stream laser instead of pulse. He was hit with the equivalent of twenty four pulses."

That got people's attention. He went on.

"The combined power directed at him, should've vaporized him. But it didn't. Jon, what's your suit integrity?"

I checked and told him. While I'd slept, the suit had regenerated.

"That's impossible," said Alana.

I looked sheepish.

"What did you do?" asked Alison.

"I had a dream about golden streamers, and purple smoke."

The twins startled and looked at each other, indicating they'd shared that dream with me.

"What did you do?" demanded Alison.

"I'm wearing three fully boosted suits," I said quietly.

Eric grinned, while everyone else looked poleaxed.

"Makes sense," he said. "The combination would be about the same integrity as combat suits offer. That explains no vaporizing. But something else had to have been going on."

I could see it in his eyes. He knew there were holes in that explanation as much as I did, but neither of us wanted to point them out. As much protection as I'd had, it still wasn't enough for what hit me.

"Science fiction?" asked Miriam.

"I can offer two theories, but no-one here is going to buy them."

"I will," I said, and I really wanted to hear them too.

The room was still, and dead quiet.

"Well, the first is, at the moment of your death, you were removed from the time stream. Whoever did it, allowed time to go forward before putting you back. At the moment you were back, your medical monitor revived you."

"Doesn't explain the dead body," said Jedburgh.

"True," agreed Eric. "However that can also be explained several ways. The best of which is a droid with a suit was used to replace him. Explains not being able to close his eyes. If it was a suit, the replication was fixed."

I could see he knew there were big holes in that theory as well, but again didn't want to explain them.

"But I think something else happened. He could have been removed from time altogether. His body was dead, but HE was somewhere else. Fifteen minutes later, whoever took him, put him back, and as I said, then his medical monitor revived him."

I nodded to him, indicating they sounded like good theories to me.

"I did experience what many call an out-of-body experience," I said. "Doesn't explain a lot of things, and we'll probably never know exactly what happened. Whatever did happen, I'm just glad to still be here."

Alison and the twins came over, and gently hugged me.

Eighteen

Explanations over, I shooed everyone except Lacey, Abagail, and Amy, off the Bridge.

Everyone else was free to do whatever they liked for the rest of the day. I promised the Admirals a private lunch in my Dining Room.

I looked at Lacey.

"Fancy taking point, Wing Commander?" I asked him.

"Sir?"

"We need someone to go through the jumps ahead of us, and make sure the jump points are completely clear before we go through."

"Yes sir, I can do that. Do you want me out front the whole way?"

"Whatever suits you. You need to be there for ten this morning, five this afternoon, and midnight. You can dock for the rest of the time if you want. I guess it depends on if you prefer solitude, or a crowd."

"I'm easy with both, sir."

"You can delegate if you want to, but I thought a higher rank on the other side of each point would be a good idea in case someone doesn't want to give way."

"I can see that. Undock a half hour before, you think sir?"

"That should do it. We'll have to slow before going through, so you'll have time to jump first. Have your AI communicate direct with Jane as to the timing of jumps."

"Will do, sir."

He saluted, and left.

"What can we do for you sir?" asked Abagail.

I turned to Amy first.

"Amy, can I hire you to do a task for me? Complete and total secrecy?" She stared at me. "I'm serious. You and Abagail have different skills needed to solve a problem I have, and which Australian Security don't seem to be able to crack."

"What can I do to help you?" she asked.

"Research, and following leads. I need an experienced investigator, and you're the closest I know."

"Those skills are why I'm such a good journalist."

"I know, I looked you up."

I hadn't. I'd guessed.

"What's the task?"

"Commitment first. I can hire you as a contractor, or outright employ you. Actually come to think of it, having a journalist on staff could be very useful. You could run a PR department for me."

I don't think she would have been more surprised if I'd levitated to the ceiling. Actually, with the grav chair I could do that now. I chuckled to myself silently.

"Okay," I went on, "how about a contract until we arrive back in Nexus, after which time we can discuss something more permanent. I'll pay whatever your hourly rate is for time you spend on this task."

"Without knowing how long it'll take? You're crazy!"

"Maybe so. Are you in or out?"

"In."

"What's the problem, boss?" asked Abagail.

I gave them the whole story about how everywhere I went, there was an email setting up a hit on me, in several cases when I'd only known hours before I was going to be there. I told them about the emails which never arrived. The one from George that arrived two weeks after being sent. And the one from Annabelle she didn't send.

"A lot of the emails were undoubtedly from the Santiago family, and their history now, so that's a dead end. But someone still wants me dead, and I'm fresh out of options. It's possible this last hit was just revenge from beyond the grave in case Santiago Senior failed, or a group who never received the message the bounties would never be paid. However, the only trail we have is the emails. And I want them followed to wherever they lead."

I looked them both in the eyes.

"General Harriman told me there were other irregularities that had never been adequately explained, but so far, his people have found nothing. That tells me whoever is behind this, is well connected. So there are two ground rules. First, nothing is stored about this matter, or emailed anywhere, which hasn't been encrypted by Jane. She does an encryption which only her clones can access. Second, do whatever it takes."

I looked straight at Abagail.

"Whatever it takes!" I restated for her.

She nodded deliberately. We understood each other.

"Amy, find an office you like, and get a butler to put your name on the door. Abigail, you can use the computer room office, or one up here. Whichever suits you. If you need anything from me, just ask."

They both nodded.

"Where do we start?" asked Amy.

"Get all the data we have from Jane. I know Abigail has some of it, but Jane has all of what we've had shared with us so far. I'll email General Harriman for the rest of the data about the emails he knows about. Discuss this with no one, and that includes everyone on this ship. Complete secrecy. Make sure you're not overheard if you're discussing anything to do with this."

"Understood," they said together.

"Time frame?" asked Abagail.

"As long as it takes. Fit the work in around whatever else is going on. And don't disappear for long enough that people wonder what you're doing. If anyone asks, Amy, you're doing research for your next article, and you better do that for cover anyway," she nodded, "and Abagail, you're doing a computing task for me, which is too complicated for anyone to understand, even if you tried to tell them."

She laughed.

"I won't even need to fake it. I can double bluff anyone, except perhaps you, with computer stuff."

"I'll leave you to it then."

Abagail hesitated as Amy left.

"By the way boss, I don't know if you noticed, but after you were shot on Avon, I took down your vid from the Guilds. I figured with no bounty out on your head now, there was no message to send anymore. Was that okay?"

"Good idea. I should've thought of it myself."

She smiled, and left.

I did a vid for Walter, asking him for all the email data he had. I was going to investigate it myself, as yet another email was behind the assassination attempt on me the day before. I gave him Abagail's contact details. I requested total secrecy, and for him to use Janet to encrypt all emails from him, from now on. Jane encrypted the email, and I sent it off.

I sat there for a few minutes, feeling trapped in my chair, and doomed to being carried around for the next week or two. The thought of being confined was upsetting.

I pulled up a hollo screen, and went looking for medical aids for the immobilized. I surfed my way through a lot of rubbish sites, until I found one for 'Mobility World'. My grin let loose when I saw their range of products. Where were they? Dallas and Kansas Orbitals were both listed.

"Jane, bring up the small freighter please, you're going shopping. Or at least, send another avatar."

"It has one already. What am I buying?"

I told her.

"Bring the ship up, but don't launch for the moment."

"Confirmed."

I pinged Annabelle.

"How many combat suits did you get?"

"Just replacements for the team's," she pinged back. "That was their entire stock of top of the range. As Jane's and yours are in the best condition, I opted to replace the team's first."

"No problem. Did you order any more?"

"No, I wasn't sure I should."

"Okay, I'll put in an order now. Do the team know you bought them?"

"No. They're still in crates on the Cargo Deck somewhere. You should have an invoice to pay somewhere in your emails."

"Don't you think the team should open their presents now?"

The ping back contained a laugh.

I found the invoice email, and paid it.

I thought about ground assaults. I had a professional team, and four hundred and forty eight combat droids. But the droids were lightweights. If we ever came up against a larger team all in combat suits, we were going to be in trouble, droids or not.

"Jane, take the freighter to Kansas Orbital. Buy all the top of the line combat suits available on the station. Up to fifty if they have them. If they'll make the changes for your suit specs, make up another eleven. Do those first, make up the fifty with normal suits after. Get two Pulse Rifles for each suit, and if yours get made up, two Meson Blasters for each. What you can't get on Kansas, have them order for collection on London Orbital. And see if you can get that combat suit backpack for BA, which'll allow her to fire Meson Blasters. If it can be done, get her two Mesons as well. Make sure all suits have arm stunners."

"Confirmed."

BA was bad-arse at the best of times, but with Mesons in each suit hand, she'd be seriously bad-arse. I wondered for a moment if that was what BA actually stood for. I'd always thought it meant bad attitude. But bad-arse fitted her better.

I pinged Amanda and asked.

"Duh!" came back.

I dragged my mind back to shopping.

"Do we have enough charge slots for that number of combat suits?"

"Not on BigMother. But we do between the armoury on Custer and the Marine Barracks armoury."

"Buy the charge slots as well, or what's needed to build them. I think we'll convert a storage bay on the Cargo Deck, nearest one of the side airlocks, into a one hundred charge bay armoury. So buy all the gun charge racks as well. We may as well have a decent central armoury near to where ships can dock and move suits around easily. The one thing which wasn't practical about how Custer is docked, was moving combat suits around. But she can dock nose in to a side air-lock, and the suits then move on the same level. Buy every-thing we need, and when the freighter returns, get the builder droids onto it. Better make it ultra-secure, since Car-go Deck is open when we dock."

"Confirmed."

A screen popped up showing the freighter launching out the left side Flight Deck. It turned to match the way we were heading, and streaked ahead of us.

"Have you been tweaking that freighter again?"

"Indeed," she said with a chuckle.

"Start thinking about how to do a fast courier ship. Avatar and pilot versions. There's a need to move small things around very fast, and it might be nice if our new ship-yard had something to make which people might want. I want one on hand anyway. It would be very useful to have something Gig sized, which could break all the speed records. It wouldn't need guns if it could outrun missiles, but the usual fixed arrangement on front would be nice as well. And it better have Point Defense anyway, in case something happens when speed isn't an option. There's Talon hulls in storage you can play with. Design me a new Courier ship. There's a challenge for you."

"Confirmed."

Squeals of delight came wafting up from below.

Nineteen

Just before we reached the jump point, we slowed.

Camel and Starman launched, ran ahead of us, and jumped. I guess Greer had been ordered to be point man as well. Made sense though, we were in American space, so American military could order people around better than my people could.

"Feed coming through from Starman," said Jane.

A screen popped up showing a split screen of Greer and some civilian pilot. The civilian was arguing he didn't believe there was a fleet coming through. Kansas hadn't seen a fleet in his lifetime, so why would there be one now? In any case, he was here first, he had right of way.

I checked the scanner. We were almost right on top of the jump point.

"Tell Greer to let him jump," I said. "Hold the channel. I want to see this bozo's face after he jumps. Let Greer and Lacey see it too."

"Confirmed."

A medium freighter jumped in ahead of us. I thought he had less than thirty seconds to change course before he crashed into my shields.

His face when he realized his mistake was priceless. A combination of stark terror, and total disbelief. It took him twenty seconds to do anything except gape, and five seconds more to violently change course.

His ship bounced off BigMother's left front shield. His shields failed, and there was a spray of metal for a few sec-

onds, as my shields eroded his hull. As far as I could determine, he didn't have a hull breach, but he'd come damned
close.

I opened a voice only channel.

"Admiral Hunter to unknown ship. The next time you're
told to give way to a military convoy, don't be so bloody stupid! You got lucky. You could have died right there and then,
and it wouldn't have damaged my ship in the slightest. Now,
do you need assistance?"

The voice that came back was suitably awed.

"Sorry, Admiral. No, I won't need assistance. The only
permanent damage was to my underwear. Sorry to have in-
convenienced you."

I closed the channel, and had a good laugh.

A few minutes later, Greer sent through the all clear, and
BigMother jumped. I opened a channel to both ships.

"Commanders, perhaps you better move ahead of us for
the rest of the trip. It might be better to warn civilians further ahead of time, so any more stupid idiots can do the
wrong thing without coming to grief."

They both acknowledged, and the channel closed. The
two Corvettes moved off at top speed. I could see from the
scanner there was traffic up ahead, heading our way, so warning them to stay clear of us was probably a good idea.

I needed to think about this anyway. If I was going to
tootle around the galaxy in a ship this size, I'd need to make
sure unwary civvies didn't crash and burn on us every time
we jumped.

One of the interesting things about jumping was no-one
ever collided during the jump process. But on either side of

the jump point was another matter. The larger you were, the more likely something might jump into you. Collisions were rare, but they did happen. It kept salvage operators in business.

Like as not, I was going to need some pilots for point duties all the time now. The Camel however, was an ideal ship for the job. Big enough to scare off the average stupid, but small enough they weren't at risk of collision themselves. Well, not more than the average freighter was.

The fleet jumped through behind us, and we formed up again.

The next jump point was seven hours away now. There was no point in me staying on the Bridge.

"Jane, can you take me down to my living room, please."

"Sure."

"Angel, want a ride?"

She leapt up from her pad, raced down her ramp and waited at the bottom.

Jane gently lifted me, and set me down in the grav chair. Angel shinned up my right leg, and sat in my lap, purring away. I started patting her.

I was pushed to the access shaft, and we gently wafted down a level, where Jane swung the chair onto Deck Two.

Inside my suite, she lowered me into a lounge chair, Angel riding me down, and propped my leg up on a foot pouffe.

Jeeves had a ginger ale on the table next to me before I was in any way comfortable.

I was still getting comfortable as the room began to fill up. Aline switched on the entertainment unit, and the next episode of 'Who' began to play.

Two hours later, I called Jeeves for a pain shot. I'd done well not moving until then, but Angel jumped back onto my lap after doing the rounds of the room, and hit a bruised area. My flinch made her jump straight off, and reminded me I was overdue for a shot.

Jeeves came over and gave it to me, and then stood there looking at me.

"Will you be lunching here, my Lord?"

Darius choked on his drink. I hadn't even noticed he and Chet had come in. The floor of the room was draped in people, and the two Admirals had been given chairs. There seemed to be more chairs than I normally had as well.

"The Admirals and I will be dining in my Dining Room, the rest will be moving downstairs."

Aline hit the pause with a loud sigh, and everyone except the Admirals, rose and trooped out.

Jane helped me into my grav chair, making me look a bit more mobile than I really was. She pushed me into the Dining Room, and removed a chair to give mine room at the table. The Admirals joined me.

Jeeves had us eating in nothing flat. I wasn't hungry still, and only picked at my food, eating very little of it.

"My Lord?" asked Darius, with a smile on his face.

"The butlers are set to a British setting. They all call me that. My station AI does as well, and she won't stop no matter what I say."

They both laughed.

Chet started the ball rolling.

"Just how are you out of the hospital, Jon? I honestly don't understand why they let you leave."

"What makes you think they did?" I responded, with a grin.

Grins weren't hurting me anymore. I still had a yellow temple area, but it wasn't reacting to facial movements now.

"How then?"

Darius looked like he wanted an answer as well.

"They gave me a shot which put me to sleep for ten hours. When I woke, Jane told me they planned to keep me under for a week. Having already lost a week several months ago, I wasn't keen to do it again. I had her buy this chair for me, and she pushed me out. Basically, I did a midnight flit."

"Why didn't they stop you?" asked Darius.

I switched my suit to chameleon mode, and vanished.

Both of them looked shocked for an instant, before getting hold of themselves, and I switched back into 'slinky red'.

"How did you do that?" asked Darius, with a touch of incredulity in his voice.

"Suit programming. One of my people was dabbling with it when I first met him, and when I asked him if the suit could do a chameleon mode, we found it did. In the hospital, all they saw was an orderly pushing an empty chair around. Once outside, Jane shifted into a security uniform. I stayed hidden until we were back on the ship."

The two of them exchanged glances.

"Yes," I said, "the applications of that are many and varied. We use the suits for far more than clothes and basic protection, but this was the first time I used it to hide. I may do it a lot more in the future. In fact, it gives me a few ideas I should've thought of a long time ago."

"Wouldn't you be better off in hospital?" asked Chet.

"Probably, but I have a state of the art medical bay, which should be able to keep me functional. And I sent Jane off shopping for a few things which should make life easier."

"You amaze me, Jon," said Darius, "you really do. I've heard the stories, but perhaps you would be so kind as to tell us your background. Where did all this strategic and tactical brilliance come from?"

I sighed, and launched into a little of the family history.

"Those Hunters?" said Chet suddenly. "No wonder. I've heard of military dynasties which breed the occasional military genius, but your family has a history which few others match. Not so much military, as space smarts, you could call it. Looks like you inherited the best your family has ever offered down the centuries."

Darius nodded, as if something suddenly made sense for him.

I went on with my early background, building my own computers and simulators, playing every space based computer game I could. They nodded more and more often as I went on.

"So what did happen to you yesterday, Jon?" asked Darius. "The real story this time. I emailed with my daughter who is science fiction mad, and she not only confirmed what your Eric said as possible, she wanted to know who the shadowy figures were, and if you saw them clearly enough to identify them?"

I looked at them both.

"It was pretty much as I said. I passed out from the pain, and found myself in my Ready Room. I was shown the events unfolding with what I assumed was my body, and had a conversation with two entities, one of whom I know has been communicating with me for years now."

"What sort of entities? Are we talking Egyptian god's type entities? Or do you mean Jesus or Elvis?"

I laughed. Six hundred years after his death, the conspiracy theorists still hadn't concluded if Elvis was really dead or not. Or even if he'd been human.

"Not Egyptian gods, but along those lines."

"Is this something to do with your spiritual upbringing?" asked Chet.

"Everything actually. One of the entities talks to me like you do, inside my head, and makes me think about things I'd otherwise miss. I learned never to ignore that voice."

"What's with the claim of time travel?" asked Darius.

"That one I have no clue about. But did you play games at some time in your lives?" They both nodded. "Well it felt like when you die in the game, and have to reload a previous save in order to start again. It's like it took three goes to get something right. How it happened is anyone's guess. Returning the second time threw me against a wall so hard, I still can't use my left arm fully. And it wasn't just me, there were three of us involved."

"No rational explanation at all?"

"None. Maybe the closest is a ghost tipped us out of our chairs."

I grinned at them, and they laughed.

"The thing is though, it wasn't just three people, but also three Dropships. After the first time, I checked them out, and they had logged programming done on them an hour and half after we checked. I can't explain that either."

"As someone put it," said Chet, "you're just a weird mag-net, Jon."

The laughs continued. Lunch went back to generalities after that, for which I was relieved.

The Admirals went off to do some work in one of the of-fices, and I settled where I was, continuing on with emails.

Alison pinged me to ask about spa time, and I told her after dinner. For now, I'd have a hard time getting in and out, even with Jane doing it for me.

Both Bob and Walter had sent 'glad to hear you're still with us' emails. I let them know some of the details, but told them I had no real idea of what happened, just that it had. I asked Bob if he still had a clone of Jane around, and if so, to use it to encrypt his emails from now on. If he didn't, he was to email my station, and ask for a ship to return to sup-ply him a copy of Jane.

Maybe I was late to the paranoia party, but as they say, better late than never. I should've done this a long time ago. If someone was reading Walter's emails, they would have known my movements for all the time before the Door into the Australian sector was closed, and after it opened again. It was somewhere to start anyway, in hunting down the mys-tery assailant, assuming it wasn't Santiago spitting at me from beyond the grave. It was the most likely explanation, but my new state of paranoia demanded we check it out as completely as possible.

Several invoices came in from Jane's shopping expedi-tion, and I paid them without looking at them.

I sent an email to the Avon 'tool man', asking him to send me an encryption key. It came back a few minutes later, so I sent him the details of what had happened, how I'd merged three fully boosted suits, and how the suit had pushed me two meters into the air. I asked him how he was coming with dealing with the hits themselves, given how badly bruised I was now. I suggested he look at how the suit composed itself when it went into protection mode, and if he could change it so it was more like a combat suit in terms of solid protection. It seemed to me the biggest flaw was its skin hugging nature, when things hit it. If it was more like armour, the hit wouldn't get to the skin until the armour was worn away. If there was an energy reflecting surface on it as well, the energy could be reflected before it hit solidly enough to affect the person underneath. In theory.

One word came back. Brilliant!

By this time, I was having difficulty concentrating, and put my head down on my arms for a moment.

I woke up on the bed. It had only been a couple of hours, but Jane had obviously moved me, so I must have fallen asleep at the table.

Jane roused from the corner where she'd been standing.

"Freighter is almost back."

"What did you get?"

"Half the combat suits, and about a third of the requirements to build an armoury. My new suits and the rest are on order for delivery in London."

"What about my new toys?"

"Wait and see!" she laughed at me, lying there almost helpless. I sighed.

A screen popped up, showing the freighter approaching the right side cargo airlock.

"That freighter needs a name," I said. "Let's call it 'Zippy', since it's so fast. Can you do an overlay for its ID?"

"Confirmed."

I watched it dock, and the view switched to an internal cam, showing butler and cargo droids waiting for the lock to cycle open.

As soon as it did, a line of combat suits clanked their way out, and proceeded to move to whichever bay Jane had specified for them to wait in. The butler's moved into the ship after the last one came out. They emerged with a series of boxes and quickly passed out of the cam's view.

A short wait later, Jeeves entered with the first box. He placed it on the floor and proceeded to open it. What emerged reminded me of a time when a friend of mine at school had broken his leg. He'd been given a two wheeled upright scooter to zip around on. His leg was immobilized with a support that wouldn't allow him to put any weight on it, and he zipped around on this scooter for weeks. The technology was old even then, but it was perfect for what he needed to get around.

What came out of the box for me, was something much more advanced. It had no wheels for a start. There wasn't a lot to it. The base unit was a small grav sled just big enough to stand on, but a lot thicker than a usual pad was. From it, a frame rose up into twin hand grips with forearm support.

"Behold," said Jane. "Freedom for the immobile. They call it a medical grav scooter."

I smiled. I knew anyway, since I'd found something similar in the catalogue. But this one seemed different.

"What's different about this unit?"

"Top of the range of course. It has grav's both sides. And it's fully PC controllable."

I opened a channel to the scooter, and its system requested to download to my PC. I lay there and let it.

I explored the new menu it created. When I turned it on, it rose a few centimeters off the floor. I created a set of holographic controls and put it through its paces, moving it in all directions, as if I was on it.

When I thought I had it pegged, I maneuvered it so it was lying directly above me. I eased it down until it was almost touching me, the base unit now underneath my feet. I grasped the hand controls, and switched off the hollo ones. I adjusted the top grav so there was a gentle, only just noticeable, push against my feet. I then began to tilt it, so the top part raised off the bed, pulling me with it. When I was upright, I set it to hover mode, and moved it off the bed. It sank down to about ten centimeters off the floor. There was no pressure on my legs at all, just a feeling of weightlessness.

I moved myself into the living room.

Angel was sitting on top of her kitty castle. She jumped up when she saw me, and arched her back as if preparing to fight.

"It's only me, sweetie. Nothing to worry about. I have a new way to move around."

I moved over to the kitty castle, maneuvered around so she could walk onto my right shoulder. She sat up there, and purred into my ear. I went across to my lounge chair, and picked her off and placed her on top. The next step was going to be interesting. I positioned myself before the chair, started to tilt the scooter backwards, and my butt swung out a bit. There was pain from where leg joined torso. I kept up the tilt and moved the scooter, so I gently eased myself into the chair. Using my PC, I moved the scooter away and let my left leg drop gently onto the pouffe. Any movement of my leg was going to hurt, but it was a momentary spike in the general ache, not a prolonged sharp pain.

Way to go, I thought. I could get around now.

Jeeves came in with three more packages. The first was another pouffe, only designed for supporting injured legs. I lifted my leg slightly, wincing for a moment, and he swapped them over.

"How many did you get, Jane?"

"Six. We'll put one wherever you need one. There's one down in the Rec Room waiting for you now, and another in your Ready Room. One will go to Gunbus and another to Custer."

"What's next?"

Next was a glove. Jeeves unpacked it and handed it to me. I put my right hand inside it, and felt my fingers sliding into finger enclosures within it. Another pop-up asked to install a menu in my PC. I let it do so, and checked it out. I grinned when I saw what the options were.

I changed my suit back to a belt, leaving me sitting in briefs and socks. I pointed the glove at my right foot, and it extended all the way there. I grasped the top of the sock, and peeled it back, until it came off. I tried to put it on again, but couldn't do it one handed.

Jeeves handed me a second glove. With both hands operating down at my feet, pulling the sock back on was easy. I switched the suit back to 'slinky red', and handed the gloves to Jeeves. He took them into my bedroom, and left again.

I called the scooter over, and tilted it to fit how I sat, then allowed it to pull me upright. I sat and rose six times more to get the hang of it, and to speed it up a bit.

Jeeves took the next package past me, so I followed him through the bedroom, and into the bathroom. After unpacking, he placed a grav pad in the shower, covering most of the floor area. He turned the shower on, and I watched the water flow away above the surface of the pad, to curve around its outside edges and then to fall to the floor underneath it. He turned the shower off. I eased up next to the pad, and hopped across using my right leg. I wasn't quite successful in not moving my left leg, and it twinged in pain for a moment. I hopped back onto the scooter with better timing this time, and decided I needed to test something else. I looked through the specs of the scooter to see if I could. Apparently so.

I moved to the spa, raised the scooter over the side, and lowered myself into the bubbling water. There was enough room to tilt enough to sit myself down on the ledge within the water. And I could leave my leg outstretched without needing to bend it. There wasn't a lot of extra room, as this spa was only meant for six people. But it worked. I reversed the procedure and left the spa. My suit of course was dry. The scooter dried off almost as fast as the suit.

I headed out into the bedroom again, laid myself on the bed, left the scooter sitting next to it, and went back to sleep.

Pain woke me up an hour and a half later. I called for Jeeves, and he gave me another shot.

I used the scooter to get up, and went into the bathroom to use the facilities.

When I came out, I visited the Bridge, practicing using the scooter in the access shaft to get up, which proved easy. It only needed a brief down thrust to push me up. At Deck One, I up thrust to slow, and side thrust out. Up and down over the cat wall was easy. Thrust wasn't really the right word, since it was gravity manipulation, but it conveys what was happening.

On the Bridge, I checked our status and found we were now in the Washington system. Washington was one of the few systems to have two Earth like worlds in it. Some others had a second through terraforming, but Washington had them both there waiting for us when the first survey team had jumped in. Predictably, the Americans had called the planets Washington DC and New York.

We were going to pass reasonably close to New York, but Washington, in the inner orbit, was on the other side of the sun from us now.

My chair had been altered, I noticed. It now had an attachment on the left side, which would support my leg at the correct angle. Jane confirmed that Gunbus, Custer, and Excalibur, also had them available should I decide to fly them.

Satisfied with where we were, and I would be comfortable on the Bridge for the next week, I headed into my Ready Room.

The table was indeed damaged, as Jane had said. On each corner, was a figure about thirty centimeters high, looking exactly like the smaller ones on the Bridge console. I moved them so they were each in the middle of the table, a third the distance from each end.

Alison's discarded unboosted belt was still on my desk. I picked it up, and pondered it for a moment.

I called for Jane to come in. It took her a minute to enter. I gave her the belt, and asked her to attach it around the scooter base. She did. I linked to it, took full control of it, and activated full protection mode. It shifted to cover the entire scooter. I changed it to chameleon mode, and it vanished. I shifted it back, and started custom building a new suit definition. When I activated it, the base unit looked bigger than it actually was.

I asked Jane to get my three guns down, and to place them within a newly created hiding space, which sealed when they were inside. There was no way I was allowing myself to be disarmed while I remained as helpless as I was.

The next thing I tried was a lot more complicated. When I activated the new definition, the suit around the scooter, flowed my guns up my body on my right side, leaving my Long Gun in its holster on my right thigh, and both stunners in upper arm holsters designed for opposing draw. So my right hand could draw the gun on the left arm, and left drawing from the right. After transferring my guns to my own suit, the scooter suit returned to its original shape. I practiced moving the guns back into storage, and up to my holsters a few times, until I was happy I could arm myself rapidly. There was no possibility of a quick draw, but I could now move around armed, without seeming to be so. Lastly, I had Jane scan for the guns using standard scanning techniques used by security forces. They weren't detected.

Being almost dinner time, I headed down to the Rec Room.

Twenty

There was no-one in the Rec Room, so I continued on to the Dining Room.

Everyone was already seated, and conversation died as I scooted down the length of the table to the only empty seat, at the head of the table at the far end.

Jason pulled the chair out for me, and I reversed myself into it. Showing more strength than I thought butlers had, he picked up the chair, and pushed me into the table, being very careful not to bang my leg. A pouffe went under my leg before holding it up could get tired. I noticed the next chairs along the table, were far enough away so no-one would knock my leg accidently. It left me a little isolated down the end, but it was better than running the risk.

"Jane told us you were asleep," said Amanda.

"I've had a couple of naps this afternoon, and as you saw, Jane did some shopping for me on Kansas Orbital."

I grinned down the table. Alison opened her mouth to say something.

"Yes," I said to her. There were a few smiles, as well as a few frowns from those not knowing what the byplay meant.

Dinner was strange for me. I felt hungry, and not hungry at the same time. I nibbled at my food without eating much at all. My ache increased the more I ate, so I stopped eating. Instead, I pondered if my bruising went further than skin deep.

Well before anyone else had finished eating, I had Jason pull my chair out, transferred to my scooter, and headed into the communal bathroom. It contained two twenty person spa baths, an area for showering, space toilet cubicles, and several full fresher's. I shifted my suit to a belt, lowered myself into one of the spas, tilted the scooter to allow my butt to settle on the underwater ledge, and moved the scooter to the nearest wall out of the way. All my new bruising was under water. There was no way I could get my underwear off, so I didn't try.

Alison came in about five minutes later. Her suit changed to a belt, her underwear was tossed against the wall near my scooter, and she dropped herself into the spa near me.

"You're feeling better, I take it?" I said.

"How can you tell?"

"You didn't wince getting in."

She laughed.

"I hadn't noticed that. I guess I do."

"So this is what that was about," said Miriam, from the doorway.

She came in and undressed, folding her clothes as she did, putting them in a neat pile on the other side of my scooter from Alison's. She dropped into the spa on the other side of me.

The water hadn't stopped sloshing around from her entry, when Amanda and Aleesha came in, stripped, threw their underwear onto Alison's, and literally jumped in.

BA and Abigail were in next, and the pile of underwear grew again. Aline, Alana, and Agatha followed soon after, and the pile was now a junior mountain. Aline was last in the spa, as she stopped to start a new 'Who' episode first. She climbed in opposite me.

There was silence for a while as we all watched the wall we could see well.

"Jon," said Aline finally. "Show us your bruises."

There was a general mutter of agreement, and nods all round.

I put my hands behind me on the edge of the spa, gathered my good leg under me, and eased myself up so my butt was resting against the top, with my right leg straight and holding me up, and my left lifted slightly, trying not to hurt it. Even so, I winced as my left leg moved at the top of the thigh.

There were a series of shocked gasps, as the girls saw the damage. The bruise was no longer blue, but a bright shade of purple. It ran from slightly above my heart all the way down to below my left knee. My left shoulder was yellow, and I still had other yellow bruises visible.

"Someone's over dressed," said Aline with a sly grin.

The rest of them grinned as well.

Miriam moved in front of me, and without touching my bruises, pulled my briefs down. She moved back to my side, and pointed between my thighs.

"Does that still work?" she said.

"I've no idea," I replied.

"Turn your override off," said Alison.

I looked at her, somewhat shocked.

"Jon," said Amanda, "if you're going to have a problem, its best you know now."

I couldn't fault the logic, but wasn't sure the motivation for offering it was pure.

I hunted the menus for the PC's social setting called 'suppress autonomic sexual reactions'. This was a very useful setting when you were a late teenager who kept getting aroused by the ways some girls dressed. Turning this override on, saved you a lot of bulges in your pants, which led to blushing and other embarrassment when noticed. Not even your belt suit would hide such a bulge fully. I left it on all the time now, except for when a sexual encounter came along. Due to bruising, I'd not had one since before the first Avon battle, when Alison had initiated it.

I turned the override off. Nothing happened.

Aline stood up, and deliberately sat on the edge of the spa, giving me a full view of the entire front side of her body. The rest of the girls did the same, moving so I could see everything all of them had.

"No problems there," announced Miriam, and they all giggled.

My blush suppressor failed again, as I realized they were all looking at the part of me now standing at attention. I went bright red, and turned the override back on, cancelling the error message from the blush suppressor. I really should log an error report about that, as it kept on happening.

"Aww, I wanted to play with that," said Miriam, Alison, and Aline together, as what had been at attention, stood easy instead.

All eyes went to Aline, who blushed a deep red. I looked her in the eyes, and saw interest for the first time. My eyes flowed down her body to her breasts, and then down to her thighs. Both of us went even redder.

She slid off the edge of the spa into the water. I did the same, and suddenly the water was trying to slop out of the spa as the rest did the same together.

I pinged Aline, "I never knew you were interested."

She pinged back, "I always have been. But unlike Alison and the twins, I'm shy."

"What changed?"

"You I guess. You died on me, and you never knew. This was just too good an opportunity to let you know, for me to pass up."

"Oi!" yelled Miriam. "What's going on with you two?" She turned to Aline. "He's mine!" She paused. "Well for the next few days anyway. After I head back to Dallas, you can have your turn."

I looked at her surprised. Miriam grinned at me.

"Jon, I get it. We all live on the edge. None of us is capable of having a decent relationship while we might die tomorrow. None of us will begrudge someone living for today, even if we wish we could be monogamous with them. Our lives don't work that way. Besides, in a few days I go back to Midgard, you go home to Nexus. Long distance relationships rarely work. I'm not stupid enough to think it would work for us." She turned to the other girls. "But that," she said, indicating my groin area, "belongs to me until I leave."

"Pfft," said Alison, and splashed water in Miriam's face.

The rest of them followed suit, and Miriam ducked under the water. When she emerged, and the water settled down, Aline restarted the episode, and we soaked while we watched.

Before getting out, I called Jeeves to bring me a spare belt. The girls all pulled themselves out first, and stood there dripping and naked, watching me use the scooter to get myself out.

They all laughed when I fully emerged from the water, with briefs around my ankles and socks still on. They deferred to Miriam as she removed the sodden socks, and briefs. Fortunately, the grav that held me off the base unit, allowed things to be pulled through the field, so I didn't need to move my leg.

I scooted over to the shower, and was washed by Miriam, Alison, and to my surprise, Aline. The others washed themselves. Drying off was a group affair.

Jeeves came in as we finished. He handed me the belt, and departed without a word.

We all started pinging the underwear dispenser for what we wanted, and Miriam brought mine over, and gently dressed me.

When she finished, I slipped the belt on around her waist. We talked her through the setup procedure, and she selected a very stylish cocktail dress as her first belt to suit change. The others did likewise. I chose a dinner suit, and changed as well. We moved into the Rec Room as a group, getting comments from the others there, some of whom changed their suits to join us. Miriam was the last in, having dropped her uniform into her suite.

I pinged her to bring it with her later, so I could scan her in it, and make a suit definition for her.

By nine forty five, I was ready for another pain shot, but rather than advertise the fact, I took my leave of the group, and went to my own suite, before asking Jeeves to give me one. I patted Angel for a little while, having coaxed her up to the upper levels of her kitty castle so I wouldn't need to bend.

I had Jane add the special gloves to the scooter's hiding place. I practiced bringing them up to my hands, and back down to storage. Now as long as I had my scooter nearby, I had the ability to do things like dressing myself, without needing help. As helpless as I was, I was no longer as helpless as I was. I chuckled to myself.

Miriam came in a short time later, carrying her uniform. I had her put it on, scanned her in it, and made up a suit definition for her, while watching her strip it off again. I pulsed her the definition, and she activated the suit. She went into the bathroom to see herself in the mirror, and came out laughing. I suggested she go get her dress uniform as well, and she ducked out and back really quickly. We duplicated the whole process.

I used the facilities in the bathroom, and manipulated the scooter to lay myself out on the bed. It came to a rest by the wall.

Miriam pulled my briefs and sock off, changed her suit to a belt, and pulled off her own underwear.

It wasn't easy to keep her from knocking my bruises, but we managed to find out that everything worked as it should.

Twenty One

Around two the next morning, I woke in a lot of pain, and called Jeeves for a shot.

Miriam was asleep beside me, and Angel was curled next to my neck as usual. Jeeves came, shot me, and left.

I lay there feeling bruised in both person and spirit. While the girls had cheered me up the night before, and our love making had been interestingly experimental to keep me from accidental extreme pain, my overall mood was down.

I had a habit of rushing around without due caution. Each time I did, the damage I took to my body was worse. I needed to start using some healthy paranoia to stay safe. I needed to work on making myself feel better as well. I needed to keep a positive mental attitude, but that was hard to do when you ached constantly. I needed... I sighed.

"Sitrep, Jane," I said quietly.

"The jump into London system was uneventful," she said through my PC. "We're two hours out."

"Fifteen minutes out, contact Repulse and have them move away. Then contact Guam and release the tow. Once Guam is on her way, I want the four Guardians docked as we planned. To anyone watching us enter orbit, we should look like one big ugly ship."

"Confirmed."

"Dock us if they'll allow it, but keep us buttoned up until someone requests to leave. Once the airlock opens, I want all the security droids posing as human, and placed to cover the entire dock area out to the longest gunshot possible."

"Confirmed."

I lay there wondering what could possibly go wrong here. When I ran out of possibilities, I fell asleep.

I dreamed of purple smoke, with unidentifiable shapes moving through it.

I woke again around six fifteen, and called Jeeves in again. Miriam stirred next to me. Angel stood, stretched, and leapt off the bed, presumably looking for breakfast.

Miriam grinned at me, and I had to stop her from rekindling the activity of the night before. She pouted at me, but I didn't share her mood.

All I remembered of my dreams was purple smoke, and it was becoming a red flag to avoid at my peril.

There were only two things I wanted to know. How was I going to screw up next? And what shit was the cosmos about to dump on me now?

"It's not you," I said to Miriam. "I'm sore, tired, and wondering what else is about to go wrong around me."

She hugged me gently, and moved out of my way so I could get myself up. She followed me into the shower. The grav pad in the shower took her a moment to get used to. I was carefully washed, and was able to wash her upper parts. Back on my scooter, she carefully dried me off, and pulled on my briefs and socks. I shifted into 'slinky red', and she into fatigues.

I had no appetite for food, so I headed up to the Bridge, while Miriam sought out the Dining Room. I could see immediately we were docked at a station.

"Sitrep," I said to Jane, when I was seated in my chair.

"We docked at four thirty, and are still buttoned up. You have emails to look at."

I pulled out my pad, and settled in a lounge chair in my Ready Room instead.

Jane had highlighted one from the British sector government. It contained a schedule for the next three days, beginning with an informal cocktail party at two today, and a formal dinner at seven tonight. Tomorrow there was an awards ceremony at two, with my attendance being expected. As the commander of the British troops, I was required to stand in the official party for the medal presentations. In the evening was another formal dinner. The following day was marked as 'be free for Her Majesties' pleasure'.

I asked Jane who else had received official emails, and apparently everyone had received their own.

I then asked her what the time difference was, expecting we were going to be very out of sync. I was surprised to find that the city of London was on Earth normal time, the same as every station and ship was. The planet itself had a rotation so close to Earth's, making the normal leap year adjustment kept the sync aligned. I wondered what the odds were of it happening, and if the British sector had deliberately begun here because of it. No time for history lessons though.

The next email was from Marshall Bigglesworth, who'd asked senior officers to a meeting at nine.

There was an invoice from the local 'tool man', which I looked down before paying. I could understand him wanting payment before delivery, as it was a sizable total. It completed what I'd sent Annabelle to get on Dallas. All the team had their own combat suit except for Annabelle, including

George and Alison. We now had another forty one combat suits, plus twelve specials for Jane to use, bringing us to a total of sixty three, including mine. The power backpack for the suits was also listed, and I noticed Jane had ordered twelve instead of one. There was also Pulse Rifles and Meson Blasters. The last items had to do with components for building an Armoury.

I paid it, and asked for immediate delivery. I had a response straight away, indicating a half hour before arrival. I pinged Annabelle she was getting a delivery in half an hour, and would need the team down at the main airlock to receive it. Jane began organizing cargo droids.

I told her to move all the security droids out into a circle at maximum gun range as soon as the airlock opened. The combat droids were to be formed up in a V formation around the inside of the airlock, with just enough of a gap at the top of the V to allow entry of the delivery, and movement in and out. I also instructed her to take control of her twelve combat suits, and have them stationed at the airlock all the time it was open. This was to be a permanent arrangement for whenever we were docked.

A screen popped up showing her existing suit running down the Cargo Bay towards the still closed airlock.

I kept on with emails, until one stopped me. There was a bounty payment in from Earth sector on the four assassins who'd almost killed me.

I stopped dead.

I hadn't thought this before. But they had almost killed me this time. Only the intervention of a higher power had kept me alive. And not necessarily for me either, but because

I was part of whatever they were up to. If it hadn't been for Kali, they would have killed me, in spite of the extra protection I was wearing.

My mood darkened.

I continued on until I was interrupted by the girls trooping in. Miriam smiled at me, but Alison, Amanda, and Aleesha looked serious.

I put my pad down, and sighed. They settled on chairs around me.

Alison looked me in the eyes.

"Okay Jon, spill it. What really happened to you?"

I sighed again.

Amanda's hand went to her gun.

"I told you what happened," I said, before she could whack me on the foot again.

"Who were you talking too," asked Amanda.

"Them," I replied, indicating the two figures on the conference table.

Actually now I looked at them, I could see they'd moved back to the top end of the table on either side of the damage, where I'd found them originally.

"And they are?" asked Aleesha.

"Kali and Ganesha."

Alison's eyes went wide, but the others didn't seem to know the names.

"Who are they when they're at home?" asked Miriam.

"Indian Deities. Kali the Destroyer, and Lord Ganesha. Two you don't mess with."

"Gods?" asked Amanda.

"Same order of being, but I don't use the 'g' word."

"They can't be nice beings to put us through what they did," said Aleesha.

I shrugged.

"We each went through what we needed to, even if we don't understand why we needed to experience it."

"Pig's arse", said Amanda forcefully. "None of us needed to think you were dead for fifteen long minutes. I wouldn't wish that on my worst enemy."

The others nodded.

"I don't know why they did it that way. They have the power to simply interrupt time. But they let time go on while we talked. I was brought up to believe that such things always have a reason." I looked at Amanda. "Maybe it was as simple as convincing you keeping your distance was a mistake."

"Bullshit," she said.

"Maybe so, but, how about this. We share dreams. Who do you think is most likely making that happen?"

"Oh."

"Yes. So maybe they want us close together to make the shared dreaming more reliable or something."

Amanda looked troubled.

"Sis," said Aleesha, "he could be right. We share this link for some reason."

"Why did I have to go through it?" asked Alison.

"You got too close to him," said Miriam.

Alison looked shocked, and then guilty. I had wondered about that. She'd tried to initiate sex a lot more than I would have expected. Maybe sleeping together before the Avon battle had been a mistake, and after, she let herself feel more than was there.

"Why me?" Miriam added.

"You didn't go through what they did," I said.

She looked about ready to explode at me.

"You weren't there," I went on quickly. "For you, it was second hand until you got to me, and you arrived after I revived."

She subsided. None of them looked happy.

Alison and the twins went blank. Pings, I thought.

"Annabelle wants us at the airlock," said Amanda. "Do you know why?"

"Yes," I said, and grinned at her.

"And?" said Aleesha.

"Go and find out," I said to them.

The three of them left without a word.

Miriam sat there looking at me for a full minute. She rose, pecked me on the mouth, and left as well.

I went back to emails, after pulling up a screen of the airlock opening, so I could watch the combat suits arriving.

It wasn't long before I knew I'd made BA's day.

Twenty Two

Just before nine, I materialized outside the meeting room.

I say materialized, because I'd followed Darius, Chet, and Annabelle, in chameleon mode. They'd asked where I was, and been told I was already off the ship. This was technically true, since I was at the bottom of the ramp waiting for them.

Once we arrived, I shifted back to 'swanky red', since they were in Dress uniforms. I startled them all, but they quickly laughed it off. We went in.

There were five people already there.

Admiral Bentley I knew. Beside her was Marshall Bigglesworth. The other three were General Patton, General Price, and to my surprise, General Harriman.

He laughed at my surprised expression, came over, and shook hands.

"You didn't expect to see me, did you?" he said.

"No Walter, I didn't. Does this mean my Liner is here somewhere?"

"Yes Jon, it does. It's being moved to dock with your Carrier as we speak. I received the invitation to come a lot earlier than everyone else to enable me to get here in time. As it happens, your Liner is a lot faster than anyone knew, so I've actually had a mini vacation waiting for you all."

Annabelle and I both grinned. He and Annabelle hugged.

The other Generals came over and shook hands with me, and lastly, Marshal Bigglesworth shook my hand.

He motioned for us all to take seats. The room appeared to be some sort of VIP lounge.

The others sat, and watched me lower myself into a seat. A butler droid slid a pouffe under my leg as soon as I was down.

Another put drinks beside each of us.

"This is an informal gathering," said Bigglesworth, "before we get caught up in the official events. Since we've all been in contact during this crisis, I thought it a good idea to actually meet, and see if we can make this a regular event. For too long I think, the sectors have been too insular. As we found out the hard way, our sectors are vulnerable if we stand alone." Everyone nodded to this. "We may not be able to convince our governments of this, but among ourselves, we can keep up a dialog, so in future if something like this happens again, we know where we stand, and who to contact for help if we need it."

"I agree with that assessment," said Price. "Sci-Fi sector was clearly unprepared for what happened to us, and without help, we would have fallen to the aggressors. We were lucky Admiral Hunter decided to help, and the British fleet arrived in time to bolster Avon's defenses. Without either, we were lost."

"I agree also," said Patton. "The situation in Miami caught us completely unprepared, and demonstrated the sad truth that our mainstay ships are old, and out of date, just like some of our more junior flag officers have been trying to tell us for years." Chet went red. "I'm pushing for modernization, but I agree we need to have closer ties, in the event something like this happens again."

"I also agree," said Harriman. "Without Admiral Hunter's forces, Midgard would have swept through our sector in a matter of weeks. Unfortunately, we suffered from a government unwilling to spend on defensive purposes, and when pirates took advantage of our weakness, we were reduced to relying on sheer luck to save us. Now we have a government obsessed with fear of threats, and while they have been spending to restore our forces, we still don't have a force that could have protected us from Midgard's. We'll be negotiating with Admiral Hunter for the contracting of his forces should the need arise. But they are his forces, not the Australian sectors. We need allies. I don't for one second believe the pirate threat has been diminished significantly. It's simply been moved for now, as it periodically moves when one area makes an effort to remove them. They could decide to hit any one of us now we've been revealed to be vulnerable. We must stand together, even if our governments won't make it official."

Jedburgh cleared his throat, and all eyes turned to him.

"Chet and I are here because junior officers believed in a man who gave insane orders, and followed those orders, bullying their people into following those orders. The orders were only insane to the likes of us, who haven't fought a major war in our lifetimes. Who haven't thought beyond the established protocols for so long, we've forgotten the cardinal rule of war. Adapt or die. We built ships for a war against other sectors, while the real enemy is pirates and radical groups. We built and trained for a slug war between capital ships using pulse weapons, and ignored what the little systems had developed. We learned to our cost that if you specialize too much, the enemy will throw at you what you can least respond to. We need to completely rethink war in our time, and start to restructure our fleets to cover all the bases."

They all turned to me.

"Age, wisdom, and beauty, before young wrecks," I said.

They all laughed.

Bigglesworth turned to Bentley.

"I'm not sure why I'm here," she said.

"You played a pivotal role in the conflict," said Price. "You all did. For too long the senior flag officers of all our sectors have been ignoring the two and one stars who have been telling us what reality is, instead of what we thought it was. The last major war was over a hundred years ago, and we've grown complacent. We fight brushfires here and there, but this is the first time for way too long that we faced a major threat. We came up wanting, and it cost too many lives all round. You're here," he made eye contact with Susan, Annabelle and Chet, "because the burden fell on you, and you carried it. So we want your thoughts."

"I'm just a battlewagon driver," said Susan.

Bigglesworth burst out laughing.

"There's nothing 'just' about you, Susan. Admiral Hunter delegated a lot of responsibility to you, for tactical fleet movements. You showed you do more than drive a ship. Why do you think I've been trying to promote you? We need your innate ability. For now, I'm content to leave you where you are. But you will be called on to use that second stripe of yours from now on. So talk to us."

"Since you asked," she said, "I think the situation is worse than you all think. None of our sectors have the experienced officers needed to mount any form of major campaign. We triumphed this time because we fluked pooling our talent, and for once, practical reality biting our bollocks, dictated the sectors co-operate. Sheer luck, or maybe it was divine intervention, put the right people in the right places, at the right time. But it could just as easily have been a total disaster. I think we need to co-operate more openly in the future, to the extent that our senior officers train together. If something like this happens again, we need to be able to form a unified command, with the best officers across the sectors heading up each branch of the command. To do that, we need to know who they are, where they are, and have a means of getting them together rapidly. We also need to ensure that the resources necessary are not only available, but they also can get where they're needed rapidly."

She ran out of breathe. Hallington continued.

"We have the people," he began. "But some of our brightest are still junior officers. Two of my Commanders recognized what we needed after spending one day with then Captain Hunter. Being Lieutenant Commanders at the time, we didn't listen to them enough. The cost was two Fleet Carriers out of commission, too many Cruisers destroyed, and too many lives lost. None of our Captains have any real combat experience. None of our ships, save the new ones, are capable of doing what their missions are. Between us, we lost two Admirals, and a lot of Captains. The Commanders survived because they have more battle skills than our more senior officers do." He indicated me. "The only thing any of us did right in this whole mess, was to listen to this man. Those who ignored him, died. We need to bring forward the best of our people to replace the dead wood driving our ships at the moment, and then train them all to work together."

He stopped. There was silence.

All eyes turned to Annabelle.

For the first time I'd ever seen her, I thought she looked scared. I saw her get a grip. As junior officer in this company, and only recently promoted to flag rank, talking to this group as an equal was obviously daunting to her, where nothing else was.

"I left the Australian Militia," she said, "precisely for the reasons outlined here today. I joined Jon when I saw he had the makings of a first class General. Even when he's reacting to something unexpected, he thinks ten moves into the future. He plans when others are partying. I've watched him wrestle with things so far outside his training and understanding, and every single time he came to the right conclusion, and made the right decision. With the exception of General Harriman, Australian sector has no talented officers. Those of us who are, were effectively bullied out. A lot of it was politically based, by a government who didn't want to hear about threats and inadequacies. Our current government, while trumpeting the threats, are actually worse than the previous one as far as addressing the problems are concerned. I've travelled extensively in the last few years. Much of all our best talent are now Mercs, or as said, junior officers. I've gathered the best of the ex-Australian infantry teams to me, and I regretted not centralizing us, since we needed them all with us over the last week. We let them go, and we paid the price for doing so. Not just my teams, now spread along the spine, but all the real talent from all our sectors. We need to repair the damage."

She ran out of steam, and they all turned to me.

"This was a wakeup call," I said. "Something big is coming. You were all tested. You know what the problems are. The governments will never do what we need them to. It's up to you to deal with the issues, repair the damage of a century, and prepare your sectors for the real threat."

"Ragnarok?" suggested Jedburgh.

"Two isolationist cultures, mine and Midgard's, have prophecy of the end of the world. Both seem to be saying it's very close now. One of them sought to prevent it in a way most would consider to be the madness response. The other sent me to deal with them."

"Sent you?" asked Price.

"Why else would I be here? At home I'm sixteen years old, and not considered an adult yet. But I was brought up with prophecy from the moment I had my first nightmare about the coming darkness, which is the first sign. I was encouraged to build computers and simulators when other kids were playing ball. They didn't dissuaded me from playing combat games, and studying military history. I wasn't aware of it, but now it seems fairly obvious. I was identified by prophecy at an early age, and trained without obviously being trained. I can't say for sure, but it feels like I was sent. As if those who know prophecy, knew I had to be out here, now. Otherwise, why was I even allowed to leave home two full years early? It never occurred to me at the time, because I was so happy to get my first trip out system. It's only been two months, but I feel like I've aged ten years."

"Not aged," said Annabelle, "but you perform at the level of a twenty year veteran."

The others agreed with her assessment.

"So what are you saying?" asked Bigglesworth.

"I'm saying, this was a warning. When the real threat comes, we have to be ready, or nothing will survive. If we don't combine our strengths and eliminate our weaknesses, we will be lost."

"Any idea what the threat is?" asked Hallington.

"The Keepers call it the Darkness. My nightmares begin with a single black dot, which becomes millions, and blots out the stars. Who or what it is, I've no idea. I'm not sure if the Keepers even know."

"Timing?" asked Harriman.

"Not this year, but I don't feel like it's more than ten. I may know more in ten months' time."

"Why ten months?" asked Bentley.

"Outback has an isolationist policy, which is relaxed for only five days each Earth year. I'm here because I was in hospital when that five day window last expired. I have to wait another ten months to go home, before I can confront the Keepers about prophesy."

"Wont they communicate before then?" asked Price.

"No. All coms equipment is turned off. Any attempt to land on the planet is met with force. We take our isolation seriously."

"I want to be there when you go home," said Harriman.

The four stars looked at each other for a moment.

"Jon," said Jedburgh. "Each sector will be sending a representative with you, unless you object."

"I won't object, but the Keepers aren't going to talk to just anyone. Or even let them listen. Whoever goes will need to be trustworthy and discreet. And even that may not be enough. Depending on how much they know, anyone who hears the full prophecy may need to be able to cope with some big shock, and be capable of knowing how much to tell others. We may find out, but be sworn to silence. The Keepers are a downright secretive bunch."

"Let's face that when we have to," said Patton.

"Fine. Let me know nearer the time who's going, and I'll send transport to pick them up. I've tasked my AI to build me a new fast courier ship, specifically to break the speed records. So I should be able to solve the fast movement of key people problem Susan mentioned."

"We'll probably all be interested in buying them," said Price. "Keep us in the loop for anything else you develop as well. I assume that's why you appropriated the Midgard shipyard? So you can develop and build your own ships?"

Most of them looked surprised at this, but Bentley was laughing.

"You didn't know?" she asked generally.

All except Price shook their heads.

"I knew he had another station on the way," said Harriman. "But not a shipyard."

"We jump into Midgard in the middle of the night, take out their fleet, and he leaves me holding the bag while he goes off to chase some intermittent scanner contact. By morning, he arrives back at the jump point with a giant shipyard in tow, and claims it was abandoned, and he couldn't leave it there as a navigation hazard."

They all joined in laughing.

"When General Wellington arrives a little later," she went on, "he claims it was sitting there all on its lonesome, and followed him home like a kitten."

The laughing intensified. I waited for them to get a grip.

"What's this about another station?" asked Hallington.

"The Midgard official he talked to," answered Bentley, "was so terrified of him, he literally kicked the location of Midgard's Orbital station out of the person who knew. On the way there, he finds a Mining station, which was moved back to Midgard to be a base for General Wellington. When the Orbital station was found, his AI took over the station computer, and tricked most of the people into evacuating. He sent his Marines in to take out the rest. Then he had it towed to the Azgard jump point as well."

They all looked at me.

"Spoils of war," I said.

Jedburgh snorted, and Harrington looked worried.

"What?" I said. "You all keep putting uniforms and rank on me, but I started out as a Privateer. I built the ships you like by salvaging everything I could after each battle. The station and the shipyard are simply bigger hulls. Maybe it's not what career military do, but I never considered myself to be career military. I see myself as a temporarily seconded Mercenary Privateer. Once I can shuck these uniforms for good, I'm the head of Hunter Security, and Hunter Trading, and salvage is part of my business."

"Besides," interjected Annabelle, "If what we think is coming is, he needs a decent base and support facilities."

"Fair enough, I think," said Patton. "I wouldn't tolerate anyone in the ranks doing any such thing, but this whole situation requires its own rules."

"Agreed," said Price and Harriman together.

"So what do we do in the meantime, while we wait for you to be able to go home?" asked Bigglesworth.

I chucked.

"First, you decide if you take me seriously or not."

They all looked at me seriously enough.

"Well, you all have a piece of the military puzzle for this end of the spine. It's up to you to do something about it. This is the first step. Let me know how you get on, and I'll try to fit in with you if I can."

The Marshall and the three four star Generals looked at each other, and then nodded to each other.

"I'm afraid you don't get off so lightly," said Bigglesworth with a grin. "Your task in all this is to gather together the best of the Mercenary forces under your command. You get to go home now, but none of us have any doubt that a suddenly created Mercenary fleet is anything other than a call to create an independent force the sectors can call on in times of need. So take time for a rest, heal yourself, and then get to work. Admiral!"

I nodded to them, but wasn't game to say anything. What he said did make sense. Annabelle was grinning at me.

"Is there anything else you'd like to add, Admiral?" asked Patton.

"Yes, I need a butler to bring me a pain shot."

For some reason they all found this incredibly funny.

Twenty Three

After my pain shot, things settled down to a more general professional discussion.

Rank vanished, and all sorts of subjects of interest were visited. At one point, Price turned to me.

"I've been wanting to ask you, what did you do to Admiral Dingle?"

There were chuckles around the room, but everyone looked at me for an answer.

"Nothing I know about. Why do you ask?"

"Dingle was one of our most promising officers coming up through the ranks. He was a very effective Cruiser driver when he made Captain, so we fast tracked him. But when he received his star, he completely changed. Competence vanished, and was replaced with arrogance and self-importance. We couldn't un-give him Warspite once he was appointed, because he never actually fouled up. But that ship wasn't half as effective at anything, once he had command. Granted she was old and out of date, but she was still the flagship of our fleet, and he was only one of two one stripe Admirals we had serving."

"Sounds like he rose to the level of his incompetence," I suggested.

"You'd think so, except for his performance under you has been back up to the standard for which we promoted him in the first place. I wondered what you did to get it out of him, where the rest of us failed."

I paused, thinking.

"My first contact with him was in the middle of the night, when I told him if he left his ship where it was, it would be in small pieces before the day was out." They found this quite funny. "I had to show him a vid of the station jumping before he accepted it was possible, and Warspite just about ran me down moving." The laughter intensified. "I gather Vonda took a piece out of him not long after, but I never did find out what she said."

"That still doesn't explain the change in him," said Patton.

"Vonda wanted to replace him, but I convinced her he was better off where he was. We didn't know Repulse was coming at the time, so we had two objectives. We needed a target the enemy had to take out first in order to focus them where we wanted them, as well as a station for them to take as a forward base. I convinced Vonda that Dingle was the right person for the job of sacrificial lamb, someone who would die gloriously, unaware of what he really was."

"You weren't really thinking of sacrificing a Battleship, were you?" asked Jedburgh.

"Not as such. But at the time, I couldn't see any way in which Warspite could survive. As it was, she almost didn't, and we provided Midgard with two main targets instead of one. We simply didn't have the Point Defense to save her, with her being the only main target. As it happened, we ended up with much more Point Defense than we'd first thought, but right then, Warspite had to be the focal point of our defense, and her survival wasn't likely."

The others nodded.

"As far as Dingle is concerned, it could have been a number of things which shocked him back to competence."

"List them," said Price.

"First off, we simply ordered him to prepare to defend the jump point against the expected fleet, told him what they would fire at him, and gave him a time of three seconds to train for, to fire on the first down jump. As far as he knew he was going to be facing the full fleet alone."

"Hell," said Harriman. "That would have given some flag officers a heart attack."

"The battle itself could have been the turning point for him. He wasn't a happy Admiral after, having his ship almost destroyed around him. He wasn't impressed when I asked him if he needed a tow." They all laughed. I turned to Price. "I guess the next thing was, having just about lost his ship in action, you didn't relieve him of command. Instead, his ancient, out of date ship, received what he'd probably been pushing for since taking command, and came out of the yards a completely new force to be reckoned with."

"You're right," said Price, "he was a constant pest with requests for Warspite to be upgraded. But he never presented them with arguments that made any sense. We always assumed it was his self-importance driving him."

"So suddenly," I said, "his ship is given a new lease on life. On the jump into Azgard, Warspite was the vanguard, even though we all jumped together. His new missile system was very effective, and even though the tactics were new, he was fighting a kick-arse ship now."

The nods all round showed they agreed with my assessment.

"It's hard to know when the change happened, or why, but that's what I think led to it."

"Could have been having a very competent commander to emulate as well," said Chet.

"Vonda certainly was an effective leader," I replied.

They all smiled.

"I wasn't meaning General Wellington," said Chet.

I looked at him, not understanding what he was saying. Smiles became laughs.

"Jon," said Price, "I probably shouldn't really say this, but Vonda told me, had she been in operational command, Avon would have been taken. She's a very capable General, which is why I sent her, but the situation needed an Admiral, and we didn't have one with the experience, or the stones, to get the job done. Had she managed to defend Avon, she was adamant the entire attack force would have died jumping into Azgard. I wasn't asked to promote you to Vice Admiral, I was told it was essential she be relieved of the command, because she wasn't up to the job, and you were. I couldn't relieve her then, but as the same rank, she could defer to you without any problems for the lower ranks, especially since managing ships is an Admiral's job, and managing troops is a General's job. You probably weren't aware of it, but from Cobol on, she effectively delegated the war to you, and was trying to stay un-noticed in case junior officers wondered why the senior officer wasn't the one giving all the orders."

I looked at him for a long moment.

"She'll make a good Governor," I said.

"She will, and she knows that."

We were interrupted by butler droids bringing in lunch platters. I was relieved the conversation had been stopped at that point.

The group broke up after lunch, so we could all prepare for the party in the afternoon. I trailed Annabelle back to BigMother, in chameleon mode. The Americans had headed for Guam, docked on the opposite side of the station.

Angel was happy to spend some time playing with me, especially as I wasn't sure when I'd be back next. I made a point of explaining it to her, and suggesting it was a good time for her to have some quality sleep.

Precisely at one thirty, a shuttle touched down on the Flight Deck, and was taken below, where we were waiting for it. Both Jane and Jeeves boarded with us, the latter with a supply of pain shots for me, so I wouldn't have to seek them out. Jane had done some work on Jeeves, changing his appearance to the Hunter Dress Uniform, without insignia. His orders were to see to my needs exclusively.

We were transported down to the planet, landing on the Palace roof. A grand staircase wound down the middle of the building, emerging into a huge vestibule area, with many rooms leading off it. We were directed to the main ballroom.

Although not yet two o'clock, we were announced, in order of rank. There was a receiving line of mainly politicians, whose names I promptly forgot, with Marshall Bigglesworth on the end. After shaking my hand, he waved a butler droid forward, and instructed it to take my party to our designated location. On the way in, I'd not seen this being done with anyone else. I was about to ask him, but he very slightly shook his head, so I nodded and followed the butler.

It led us over to the only clump of lounge chairs in the room. I lowered myself into the central chair, and a medical pouffe was placed under my leg. Jeeves dropped a ginger ale on the table beside me. Alison took the chair next to me on one side, and Amanda the other side. Jane stood behind me, as if to protect my back from any threat.

I told the rest of the group to go mingle, and after some reluctance, they did. Jeeves gave me a pain shot soon after. With the edge removed, I let myself sink into the comfortable chair.

People began to seek me out, and the chair opposite me was kept occupied. I tried to keep conversations general, and avoid saying anything which someone might later use against me. While I had no experience of this kind of event, I'd read enough as a kid to know the politics going on behind the scenes was likely more important than the event itself. Politics of any kind was something I was very keen to avoid.

Sometime around three, I had a break in the conversation flow, which gave me a chance to look around the whole room. A movement above drew my attention, and I saw a pretty girl standing on the next level up, watching things unfold below her. She appeared to be about my age.

Our eyes met. She smiled at me, and suddenly turned and fled.

I wondered what had spooked her.

I looked around, and found both Amanda and Alison with big grins on their faces. Neither would say anything though.

The afternoon wore on, the conversations became repetitive, and I felt an intense need for some sleep.

The party wound down at five, and I was shown to a large suite where I could rest before dinner. I wasn't sure how many rooms there were in this suite, but the girls all followed me in, and vanished. I eased myself down on the bed, moved the scooter over next to me, and promptly went to sleep.

Twenty Four

I awoke at seven thirty, to a combination of pain and Jeeves calling my name.

I lay there for a moment, bothered by more unremembered dreams of purple smoke, until I suddenly realized I was now late for dinner.

Jeeves gave me another pain shot, and I pulled myself off the bed using the scooter. I needed the bathroom badly. By the time I felt refreshed, I'd lost another fifteen minutes, and set out after Jeeves to wherever dinner was being held.

I was the last one there, predictably. But instead of being told off for being tardy, I was greeted with booming applause.

I looked around the large Dining Room, seeing an oblong space, with a long table down the middle. There were only two empty seats, one at each end.

A palace functionary indicated the seat at the end closest to me. I eased myself into position ready to sit, but before I could do so, another functionary at the other end of the room said, "All stand for Her Majesty."

I remained where I was, still on my scooter, while the rest of the table all rose.

The young girl I'd seen during the afternoon entered, took her place at the other end of the table, nodded down the table, and sat.

"You may be seated," said the functionary.

I eased myself into my chair, and the functionary nearest me deftly moved me under the table without banging my leg, while a second positioned a pouffe for it. The table itself was wide enough that no-one was near enough to bang my leg. Once again it made me a bit isolated, but it was better than having people kicking my leg accidently. Jane took the scooter from the room.

Nearest to me were the Generals and Admirals. At the other end were senior British and London government officials. In the middle was everyone of consequence who fought the war.

While a good distance away from me, my main sightline was the Queen. As the courses came and went, I concentrated very hard on not looking at her.

Conversation went on across me, but I let it go without my input. I'd had enough sleep to keep me going, but not enough to feel rested.

And truth to tell, I didn't really want to be here. I'd have preferred to be back in my bedroom, on my way home, doing releases for all the dead I didn't pull the trigger for, but gave the orders which killed them. Their weight seemed overbearing. I'd missed the celebration on Dallas, and was now wishing I was missing this one as well.

It seemed almost obscene to be celebrating at all. How many ships had I killed? How many people? It wasn't any wonder I'd been dead for fifteen minutes. I deserved it. A spiritual person killing in the magnitude I'd done? I wasn't sure why I'd woken up.

Or maybe that was the point. Living was my penance now.

Still not hungry, I'd pecked my way through the first few courses, and was now moving my dessert around my plate.

"Are you okay, Jon?" asked Walter.

I looked up from my plate, which I hadn't really been seeing, and looked at him.

"Sorry, what?"

"Are you okay, Jon. You don't look like you're all here."

It felt like most of this end of the table were looking at me.

"I guess I'm not. It's sinking in how many people I'm responsible for killing, and finding something in my belief system which allows it, has proved to not be a happening thing." I sighed. "I'd just as soon be in my bedroom and heading home, than anywhere trying to celebrate."

"You're missing the whole point, Jon," said Darius. I looked at him. "We celebrate survival, not what it took to survive. We give credit where it's due, for those who made that survival possible. We celebrate life and its continuation."

"Well said," added Walter. "Jon, take some time when you return to Nexus. Go and find a beach somewhere, and sit on it for a week or two. You've had a rough two months, and done the impossible at the same time. You're exhausted as well as physically damaged. The last thing you should be doing at the moment is think."

"Not much else I can do."

"Not so," said Patton. "You're mobile. Try a combat range on your scooter. Hell, I might find one and come try it with you!"

My end of the table all laughed, and I joined in reluctantly. He had a point. I could try the assault courses on my scooter. It would keep me busy, and perhaps give me a new skill set.

I made an effort to finish my dessert.

The others around me made more of an effort to keep me in the conversation now, so the mood I'd been falling into wasn't allowed to progress any further. All the same, I didn't recall anything which was said.

As everyone was enjoying their coffee, and talking about how good it was, I sat back and looked around the table. My eyes went up one side, and came to rest on the Queen, who I suddenly realized, I knew nothing about, not even her name. In fact, I hadn't been aware British sector had a Queen. Something must have happened recently. I thought I should've been asking someone. But then, did it really matter? I was here for another couple of days, wasn't getting involved in anything local, and probably would never be back. I had enough to worry about besides the British monarchy.

I was suddenly aware the Queen had locked glances with me. I went bright red, and looked away, making myself scan down the other side of the table. Damn that blush suppressor, I thought. I should do a complaint. So I did. I went into the menus to find software support, filled out the bug report, and sent it off. I turned the override back on, which eliminated the red on my cheeks, but when I looked up again, the Queen was still watching me. This time, she smiled at me, and turned away to say something to one of the people near her.

When the dinner finally broke up, I was very glad to be out of there.

By eleven, I was back in my bedroom, patting Angel. Most of my team had elected to stay planet-side, since the following morning was free, and none of them had spent much quality time dirtside in a long time.

Jeeves gave me another shot at eleven thirty, and I went straight off to sleep.

Pain woke me again at three thirty. Jeeves gave me the next shot, but I was too restless to go back to sleep.

I hauled myself out of bed, leaving a curled up puss behind, and scooted down to Custer's gun ranges. Once there, I activated the suit on the scooter to mount my guns on my suit, and started into the combat courses. I had three guns to choose from, while keeping control of the scooter and my balance on it. At first, I found it almost impossible to keep control and fire a gun at the same time. However, like everything, practice makes perfect, and after a solid hour, I began to get the hang of it. I found I could hold myself on using my arms wrapped around the handle bars, and shoot using both hands, while controlling speed and direction with my PC. As another hour went past, my score improved from really dismal to approaching average. Hardest was the Long Gun, as I couldn't sight it properly. So I concentrated on bringing my score up with just the gatling stunners. When I was finally into the eighties range, I called it a session, scooted back to my bedroom, showered, and stretched out next to a still sleeping Angel.

Pain once again woke me, but I'd had another four hours sleep this time, without dreams. Jeeves gave me my overdue pain shot, before I moved myself. I felt lethargic, and the thought of the medal ceremony to come today, almost had me go back to bed and hide under the covers. Still, it was for the British troops, all I had to do was be there.

I found Angel scratching her kitty castle, and gave her a good rub up the wrong way, which had her purring loudly.

I sat in my living room and waded through emails. The Avon 'tool man' had sent me an upgrade for my suit. The message with it made it clear this was a beta version, and would only work with three belts merged. He'd run with my suggestions, and introduced a layered approach to the suit reaction. The suit would now form three distinct layers when it went into a defensive mode. The outer layer would emulate combat suit armour well away from the skin, the middle layer would concentrate on moving the momentum of the hit downwards, while the inner layer retained the original purpose of being body armour, preventing actual damage to the person.

The outer layer, in theory, would take the damage potential of the hit and channel it to the deck, while the middle layer dealt with the residual momentum. If the hit was too much for the outer triple boosted suit to handle, the middle layer would take over the outer layer role. It was hoped the combination would not only prevent momentum knocking over the person being hit, but also prevent any bruising.

While I can't say I looked forward to having this tested, I uploaded the upgrade and checked the suit integrity value. It was now even higher than before. I emailed him back my thanks, and should I be a target again, I'd let him know how it performed.

I couldn't see I'd be any worse off, even if the layered approach failed to work.

In any case, I was determined to avoid placing myself in locations where I'd be shot at again, if I could help it.

Chameleon mode worked really well, and I intended to do a lot of sneaking around from now on. Even when I regained some mobility, the scooter would come in handy, since the faster you were going, the harder it was to hit you. Something else for me to practice - speed scooting!

At eleven thirty, as I was beginning to think about some lunch, Alison walked in with Marshall Bigglesworth.

"Don't get up, Jon," he said quickly, as I reached for my scooter. "I wanted to go over the ceremony this afternoon with you. Your aide told me you were up here, so I took the opportunity to come look at your flagship. I hope you don't mind, but she showed me around. It might be old, but I really like what you did with her."

"Thank you, sir."

"Call me James, Jon. We're the same rank you know."

He chuckled, and seated himself next to me. Alison remained standing.

"Not really, James. The Americans added my fourth star, but retired me the next day. So it's not really earned, being retirement promotion. Sci-Fi is the only force I'm still active with, so technically I only have three. I wear four on my Hunter uniform because it's expedient to do so, not because I feel I've earned it."

"Let me guess, you had problems justifying being the boss when other people you employed out-ranked you?"

"Yes, exactly that. I wore an infinity symbol as a rank, before the Americans drafted me after the first pass through Midgard. At least now wearing four stars I was given, solves any problems in the future. Once Sci-Fi release me, I can go back to just being a Merc group leader."

"Maybe so, but forget that bollocks about not earning your fourth star. I've repeatedly watched the combat feeds of every action you've had since leaving Dallas the first time. Your General Smith was right, you're a natural General. And we needed one in an Admiral's role this time. You let Smith do the infantry work. You left Wellington on Cobol to do the General's work, while you moved on to the next objective. You did it again on Azgard. You told them what you wanted, and let them do it according to their own expertise. That's what four stars do. Get used to it. Four stars is what you were made for, and now you're here, you may as well accept it."

His grin was impossible to ignore, and my own mirrored his after a moment.

"So," he went on, "this afternoon. Her Majesty will be reading the citations. I'll be on her left, you'll be on my left. Her aide will hand her the medal, she will present it to the recipient, who will bow to her. They'll then move to face me, shake, salute, and move to you for the same."

"Why am I there?"

"I'm there as commander of the British Fleet. You're there as the combat commander of the campaign. If General Wellington was with us, she'd be on the podium as well. All you need to do is shake each person's hand, and return their salute."

"I can do that."

"If something else comes up, our aides will ping us. It's not normal, but with a young inexperienced Monarch, such things can happen."

"I wondered about that yesterday. Last I heard the British sector had a King. Since I left Outback, I've had no time for events outside my own doorstep, so it was a bit of a shock to see an obviously young Queen at the table last night."

"We had a disaster here about four months ago. The Queen was the only Royal not in attendance, because of an illness, and so was the only one to survive. At this point, we're still not sure if it was simply an accident, or an assassination by the Republican movement. As you can imagine, the security around Her Majesty is the tightest it's ever been now."

"Didn't the Royal family wear belts?"

"You mean those suits you and other mercenaries wear?" I nodded. "No, it wasn't thought appropriate for them, and the King himself was adamant he wasn't wearing any kind of body armour, as it sent the wrong signals to the people."

"Only if it's done badly. There's no reason why anyone should know anyone is wearing a suit belt. When used with clothes, you simply have the belt appear as a belt, one which goes with the outfit being worn. Do you wear one yourself?"

"No, fleet hasn't yet addressed the issue. However, I'm pushing it given what happened to Darius and Chet recently. As I understand it, casualties would have been a lot lighter had everyone been wearing a suit belt."

Get it done.

"Sir... James, it strikes me as the two biggest targets here at the moment, are the Queen, and yourself. Both of you should be wearing suit belts. Let me arrange them for you now."

"Are you sure no one will be able to tell?"

"No-one can, at least not to casual inspection. If they get close enough to touch, the difference should be obvious, but neither of you should be allowing people close enough for that. The first anyone should know is when they shift to full defense mode in reaction to the proximity of a weapon, or some other threat."

"Okay. How long will it take to get them?"

"Should be here before we finish lunch." He nodded.

I pinged the local 'tool man', and ordered eight new belts, with three boosters each, to be delivered unpacked as two combined belts of three, and two of two. I asked for imme-diate delivery to BigMother. The invoice came back immedi-ately, and I paid it.

We sat down to lunch, Alison joining us, with rank put aside. Jeeves came in with the new belts as we were finishing eating. Once again, I'd failed to eat very much.

I gave one of the two belts to Alison, and told her to merge them.

"Why, Jon?" she asked. "I already have a fully boosted suit."

"You and Annabelle are the most vulnerable of the team on the ground, since you rarely wear combat suits. Annabelle nearly bought it on Azgard, with what you have now. While I was getting new belts, I thought I'd give you both the same protection I have."

She nodded, and we watched as her belts merged into one. Being seen in her underwear by the Marshall for a few moments, didn't seem to faze her. I gave her the second two, to give to Annabelle before the medal ceremony.

I passed the first of the three's to James, and we talked him through the setup process. Once complete, I pulsed him chameleon mode in case either of them had to hide at some time. I also talked him through scanning uniforms, so he could make his own suit fatigues. For now though, all he really needed was the combat protection mode, and I made sure he changed the suit to hair trigger activation.

I gave him the remaining three belt for the Queen, and had him promise to have her wearing it as soon as he could get her alone before the ceremony. He felt sure this was possible. Lastly, I showed him where the menus of clothes and accessories were, so the Queen could easily choose how she looked.

Now nearly one, we headed for the Marshall's gig, to return to the Palace.

Twenty Five

By one forty five, I was standing to the left of Bigglesworth, on an ornate rostrum in a room obviously designed for award ceremonies.

When I say standing, I was still on my scooter, as there was no way my left leg could have taken my weight at all, without me passing out. All the same, I was beginning to regret being here. Up until now, I'd not really simply stood around in the same place. I'd been moving from place to place, at each end of which I'd been seated. But for the first time, I now had to stand in one place. As the minutes passed, I was feeling less and less well. It's funny how pain has a way of making itself felt, when you move the least.

Those due for awards were lined up in ranks in the middle of the room, lowest rank at the front to highest at the back. Susan Bentley would be last. Local dignitaries and British Flag Officers were seated on the right side, from my perspective, and all others on the left, including my entire team.

Generals Price and Harriman were standing on the other side of where the Queen would stand. I pondered why, but didn't come up with anything beyond they were there for the same reason I was.

Precisely at two, the Queen was ushered in with all due pomp and ceremony. Marshall Bigglesworth welcomed everyone, and said some words about the campaign, and the role of the British forces in it. I wasn't really listening.

A military aide to the Queen passed her the first citation and called out the first name. The recipient marched forwards, and braced to attention before the Queen. She read the citation, had the medal passed to her, and passed it over with a few words to the recipient. After bowing to the Queen, he moved to face Marshall Bigglesworth, they shook, saluted, and moved in front of me for the same.

This was duplicated dozens of times, with my part being automatic. I used my left hand to hold me upright, and my right for shaking and saluting.

By two thirty, the knuckles on my left hand were white, and I now bitterly regretted not getting an early pain shot. But there was nothing for it, I had to stand there, and function as if nothing was wrong.

Susan Bentley marched forwards on the quiet chime of three, to receive her Distinguished Service Order. By this time I was needing my right hand to hold me up, and removing it was becoming increasingly difficult. I was glad this was the last award, and I'd be able to sit down soon. Susan bowed to the Queen, shook and saluted with Bigglesworth, and moved to stand in front of me. Her eyes narrowed in alarm as she took in my condition, and she shot a rapid glance at Bigglesworth to see if he'd noticed. Apparently he hadn't, for which I was glad. We shook rapidly, and her body in front of mine hid how desperately my right hand returned to holding me up, after our salute.

She marched away, and I waited to be dismissed.

Instead, John Slice was called. He startled where he sat in the middle of my team, rose, and marched forwards. He braced as all the others before him had. The aide passed the Queen another citation.

"Wing Commander Slice," she said, "volunteered to defend Avon, was called back to service, and seconded to the Sci-Fi Space Force, where he distinguished himself at the battle of Avon, and went on to play key roles as the fighter force commander for the multi-sector fleet. Wing Commander, you are promoted to the rank of Group Captain, awarded the Distinguished Flying Cross, and retired once again from the British Fleet, with our gratitude and thanks."

They shared a few words as his medal and new rank insignia were passed over. He bowed, and was about to step back when General Price spoke.

"Group Captain," he said. Slice turned to face him. "The Sci-Fi sector thanks you for your service, and awards you our Distinguished Flying Cross as well."

He was passed another medal, they shook, and saluted, which he repeated with Bigglesworth and myself, before returning to his seat.

The Queen' aide called Eric Neilson next. A look of shock on his face as he stood, dressed in Hunter Dress, was replaced with passive calm by the time he braced before the Queen.

"Lieutenant Commander," she said, "it's our understanding that you neither volunteered to fight at any time during the recent war, nor were asked to serve, drafted to serve, or in any way required to serve. You simply fought. When Marshall Bigglesworth became aware of your presence and contributions at Avon, you were recalled to official service. We understand you have been accepted into Hunter Security, and promoted. Your promotion to Lieutenant Commander is officially recognized now by the British Fleet, and at the end of this ceremony you will be replaced on the inactive list. You are awarded the Distinguished Flying Cross."

She passed him his British insignia and medal, they shared a few words, and he bowed and prepared to return to his seat.

"Lieutenant Commander," said General Price. "The Sci-Fi sector also awards you the Distinguished Flying Cross."

Eric repeated the whole process Slice had just done before him, and returned to his seat.

I was in serious trouble by now. My entire left side was aflame. I'd almost missed getting my right hand back on the scooter in time to keep me from falling off. I hung on like grim death, hoping no one was noticing.

266 Squadron were called next. They were also informed they had been recalled to active service with the British Fleet when they arrived at the Midnight Cobol jump point to form the blockade there. Their promotions within Hunter Security were officially recognized, and they were each also awarded the DFC. Lacey was also awarded the Distinguished Service Order for his leadership and successful defense of the Australian sector.

This time it was General Harriman who stopped them leaving, duplicating their British awards with the Australian equivalents.

Lacey was the last to shake my hand, and he was visibly shocked by how I looked. He saluted me first instead of after the handshake, making it as quick as he could. Our handshake lasted longer than normal as his strength guided my hand back to the scooter. He returned to his seat, and I stood there waiting for the final dismissal.

The next name I heard was Brigadier General Smith. I startled, not expecting any of my team to be called, lost my grip on the scooter, and blacked out.

Twenty Six

I woke up on a bed, with Jane and Jeeves standing over me. Marshall Bigglesworth was behind them, with the Queen standing next to him. I was relatively pain free, so I assumed Jeeves had given me the long overdue pain shot.

"How long?" I asked.

"Only a few minutes," said Jane.

"You blacked out," said Bigglesworth, "but Colonel Jane caught you before you reached the floor. Why didn't you say something to me, or ping me you needed a break? We could have interrupted things after Susan Bentley."

I looked at him. It hadn't occurred to me.

"I'm sorry," said the Queen. I must have looked shocked at the whole concept of a Queen saying sorry, as she smiled. "We should've taken your condition into account, and built in a break in the proceedings to allow you to sit for a while. The ceremony has been paused, and we'll resume when you're able. Your official presence is no longer required, so you can sit out the remainder comfortably."

"Why do we need to resume at all?" I asked. "I thought we were finished. I guess I didn't say anything because I was expecting to be dismissed at any second."

"Not finished just yet, Admiral," said Bigglesworth with a grin.

Jane left the room, and returned with a grav chair very similar to my own. She looked a question at me, and I nodded. She plucked me from the bed and sat me down on the chair, without giving my leg as much as a twinge. Thanks be to pain meds.

The Queen and Bigglesworth left, and Jane pushed me back into the Ceremony room, through the general entrance. A lot of anxious faces smiled as I was pushed in, obviously looking better.

Bigglesworth entered, and recalled the room for the Queen's entrance. She came in, and returned to where she'd been before.

The whole team were called as a group, in order of rank beginning with Brigadier General Smith. They were all surprised to be called, and as a group, formed a line according to rank across the room, in front of the Queen.

She thanked them for their service, and stepped back to allow General Price to continue the proceedings.

"Smith's Alpha-team," he began, "were in the wrong place, at the wrong time, when they literally dropped into the beginning of the Midgard war. They were merely going home, after helping to end the Pompeii civil war. At first, they had no choice being there, and simply fought to survive. But as I understand it, when choice was offered, the response was, 'We go in at the shit end'!"

There was general light laughter across the room. The Queen even smiled. I wondered how he'd found that out.

"And so they did. It's a rarity to find a Mercenary Unit more professional than sector Marines, but Smith's Alpha-team is just that. They formed the core of a fighting force which successfully defended a station from boarding, and retook key stations from the enemy during the advance back to Midgard. Each member of the team is awarded the Meritorious Service Cross. Brigadier General Smith, you are further awarded the Distinguished Service Order. Congratulations."

He passed out the medals in rank order from lowest to highest. They saluted him as a group, bowed to the Queen, and forming up facing me, saluted me as well. I saluted them in return, and shared the pride they all showed. They filed back to their seats.

Annette Bronson was the next to be called. The Queen also thanked her for her service, as did General Price, before she was passed to General Harriman, who awarded her the DFC.

George was next. He was thanked by the Queen, and awarded the DFC by General Price.

I sighed in relief. That was everyone. I could get some sleep now.

Jane was called, by the rank of Colonel, which her insignia showed her to be if you didn't know her actual rank.

The Queen thanked her for her service, and passed her on to General Price.

"Colonel Jane is a special case. Without her, the defense of Avon would have failed. Without her, our offensive would have fallen at the first hurdle. Without her, Sci-Fi, American, and Australian sectors, would have fallen to the Midgard forces."

The room was silent, and looking puzzled.

"Colonel Jane was the key to solving a technical issue, which I'm informed, literally pushed the balance of the war in our favour. Admiral Hunter made the intuitive leap which enabled us to perfect a true anti-missile missile system. But it's Colonel Jane who makes it work."

He smiled around the room, enjoying the confused looks he was seeing. I grinned at him.

"Your Majesty, Ladies and Gentlemen, Colonel Jane is an Artificial Intelligence, perhaps uniquely the first to, we believe, achieve sentience, and the lynchpin in the defense of all our sectors."

The bombshell dropped into a shocked audience.

"Hunter Security has recognized her with rank. The Americans rewarded her with a Unit Citation, but the Sci-Fi sector awards her the Distinguished Service Order in her own right."

I clapped this announcement loudly with a huge grin on my face, and a few seconds later, my team followed my lead enthusiastically. After a brief hesitation, the Americans joined in, and soon the whole room was clapping her.

General Price handed her the medal, they shook and saluted, and she returned to stand behind my chair.

Now I can get some sleep, I thought.

The Queen's aide called my name.

Jane pushed a shaken me before her, and left me there. The Queen smiled at me again, obviously seeing confusion on my face.

"Admiral Hunter. We're aware that the American Space Force promoted you to full Admiral before retiring you. Were you a British citizen, and in the British Fleet, we would also be promoting you. Alas, you aren't. However, we respect this rank and regardless of any other rank you hold, any future role you hold where British Forces are within your command, will have those forces acknowledge you as a full Admiral."

She paused and looked first at me, then the room as a whole.

"While the British sector no longer has close ties with the Australian sector, the ties once forged when Australia, back on old Earth, was part of the British Commonwealth, have never been abrogated. Consequently, I am able to award a member of the Australian sector military forces with British gallantry awards. Admiral Hunter, you are awarded the Distinguished Flying Cross for combat achievements unheard of before. You are further awarded the Distinguished Service Order for outstanding leadership and bravery under fire."

She paused again, and her grin widened, obviously reacting to my look of complete non-comprehension. Her aide handed her another citation. I looked at it stupidly, wondering what else was even possible.

"Admiral Hunter, for your actions at the second battle for Avon, where you evacuated all personnel from your station, and flew it into battle solo, ensuring that British Forces also present were kept away from the primary danger, and for your total disregard of your own safety in what has been described as an insane act of courage in preventing the enemy from reaching Avon, you are awarded the first Victoria Cross in over one hundred years. Congratulations, Admiral."

The room went crazy as she held out her hand for me to shake it. I was having trouble breathing she could see, such was my complete and total shock.

As she passed me the three medals, she leaned over towards me, and said quietly, "Hold it together for just a little longer, and then you can sleep until dinner time."

I bowed my head as low as I could, seated as I was. She returned to standing where she'd been, while Marshal Bigglesworth regained control of the room.

General Price stepped forward, and Jane appeared behind me and eased my chair around to face him. She remained standing behind me now, as an aide normally would.

"Vice Admiral Hunter, you are promoted to the rank of Admiral, and placed on the inactive list, effective immediately. You are awarded the Sci-Fi sector Distinguished Service Order, Distinguished Flying Cross, and the Meritorious Service Cross. Congratulations."

He held out his hand and I shook it.

"Admiral, Sci-Fi sector consider the single decisive factor in winning the Midgard war, was your leadership of the campaign, where you put your own safety below the safety of those under your command. The Avon system is in your debt. We believe the promotions and medals you have received are insufficient recognition for your actions and achievements. To this end, with the agreement of the Australian sector, ownership of the Midnight system is transferred to you, without sector obligations. Congratulations."

My jaw fell open in total shock. The room went crazy behind me again. It took Bigglesworth several minutes to regain control.

General Price stepped back, after handing me the medals and the ownership plaque, and once again shaking hands.

General Harriman stepped forward, and Jane moved my chair slightly.

"Vice Admiral Hunter, you are promoted to the rank of Admiral, and retired from the Australian Militia, effective immediately."

He grinned at me, knowing I'd never been comfortable with him drafting me in the first place.

"Since you weren't present at the Midgard blockade, and were not formally active with the Australian Militia during the war, the Australian sector is unable to duplicate the medals you have just received. However, since the forces which were at the core of the defense of the Australian sector in the Midnight system were yours, freely offered without being asked, and being your personal assets put at risk for the safety of the sector, the Australian sector has been looking for a suitable reward for your selfless acts. With the agreement of the Sci-Fi sector, ownership of the Bad Wolf system is transferred to you, without sector obligations. Ownership of the Nexus 618 system is also transferred to you without sector obligations, with three conditions, which require your agreement before the transfer can be finalized. Congratulations."

The room was dead silent now, everyone as stunned as I was. Harriman handed me two ownership plaques and shook my hand. The room burst into applause.

When the room settled down again, the Queen had the last word.

"All hail the hero of the Midgard war."

There were three loud cheers, the last of which threatened to tear the ceiling loose. Or so it seemed to me. The walls did seem to bulge outward as well. But maybe I wasn't seeing very well.

Bigglesworth dismissed the gathering, and I was mobbed by my team and Miriam.

Walter accompanied Jane and I back to my suite, where the rest of the team were politely turned away.

"Well, Jon," he said when we were settled in lounge chairs, "it wasn't easy, but I got you what you wanted."

I shook my head, not believing what I'd just been through.

"What are the conditions for Nexus?" I asked.

"Australian sector retains ownership of the third asteroid ring, which is currently being mined for the sector. We rely on a lot of the specific minerals found there, which aren't available in such quantity elsewhere. You agree to unrestricted access to the third ring by Australian sector ships, both government and private." I nodded. "You also agree to unrestricted and untaxed access to all Australian sector jump points for ships of all kinds, subject to the third condition."

"Untaxed?"

"Yes, Jon. With the exception of activity in the third ring, you can impose what taxes you wish in your space. Without sector obligations means you owe no tax to the Australian or Sci-Fi sectors of any kind. Nor are you bound by either sector's laws within your own space. Effectively, you now own your own mini sector. It doesn't contain a habitable planet, but you'll have two large stations in it, and the beginning of your own industry with your shipyard. You'll need to organize a sector like structure for your space, including its own laws. Do you want to be King?" He laughed as I sat there stunned. "You agree you won't tax access to the jump points, nor impose any restrictions on access to the

Australian systems. You also need to agree to provide adequate security for your space, given Australian sector security is at stake if you fail to."

"I can agree to all of that."

"Good. When we return to Sydney, there'll be an official ceremony where the agreement for Nexus is signed. I'll inform them of your agreement to the conditions, so everything will be ready when we get there. You should also think about things like non-aggression pacts and sector alliances. You'll be returning with a fleet which is capable of destroying the whole sector, and a lot of people will want you bound with treaties to ensure you remain a good friend of the Australian sector."

"I can't see any problem there. Beyond having a place for a base, I had no other ambitions."

"One other thing, and I'll let you have a nap before dinner. I still want to move my HQ to your new station, once it's ready for habitation. Will that still be possible?"

"No problems at all. Talk to Jane after she moves me to my bed. We've done preliminary plans for the new station, and allocated the Australian Militia part of the main docking ring, and a whole space scraper. Jane will give you the plans. You can buy the space or rent it, and fit it out however you wish. It will adjoin Hunter military space which will also have its own space scraper. If you send the plans off to your people now, work can commence as soon as the station gets there, and the base upgrade is complete. It's an old station, and is going to need a major upgrade to bring it up to modern standards. I have the credits to do the work, it'll just take several months to do."

"Great. I'll leave you to your nap then. See you at dinner. And don't worry about being on time, we'll wait for you."

He turned and left. Jane plucked me out of the chair, and deposited me lightly on the bed. I was asleep before she was out of the room.

Twenty Seven

I dreamed I was King Arthur, seated at the round table, surrounded by my knights, most of whom were females in armour instead of silk gowns.

We ate meat off the bone, drank wine from ornate goblets, and caroused all night. As dawn lit up the sky, everything vanished in purple smoke.

I jerked awake. Jane was standing over me.

"Dinner time, Jon," she said. "Do you want the chair or the scooter?"

"Scooter," I said.

She brought it in, I pulled myself off the bed, and went into the bathroom. I felt the need for a shower, and wished there was a spa and the time to soak. The shower had to suffice. I came out in Hunter Dress.

A pulse came in from Jane. It was a new Dress uniform definition, with my new medals on it. I went back into the bathroom to look in a mirror.

"How did you know the order to place the medals?" I asked her.

"I asked Patton and Bigglesworth. Patton was loathe to admit it, but the Victoria Cross is the older established award, so takes precedence. The Victoria Cross was created in 1856, while the Medal of Honour was created in 1861. The others are also ordered in order of creation date, and merit."

I had fourteen medals now, although twenty if you included the multiple awards. They were arrayed in four lines of four ribbons each, with the Victoria Cross and Medal of Honour on a line above them.

I felt seriously overdressed.

Jane led me to a room I hadn't seen before, Jeeves following behind. It appeared to be some sort of sitting room, where I found the other flag officers enjoying pre-dinner drinks with the Queen. The only one missing was Susan Bentley.

"How do you feel?" the Queen asked me, as I seated myself.

"Better, thank you Majesty."

"We're all here now ma'am," said Bigglesworth.

I noticed the difference in pronunciation. The last word sounded like 'mam', where I'd have said 'marm'. I made a mental note in case I needed to use the word myself.

"Admiral Bentley sends her apologies, but we had a report of pirate activity in the Birmingham system a few hours ago, and she's taken her fleet to investigate."

The Queen nodded to him.

"The reason I asked you all here," she said, "is to tell me how the military sees the future of this end of the galactic arm. My governments tell me one thing, I'd like to hear both the military side of things, and what the other sectors are thinking. This is purely off the record. My father taught me never to blindly accept what I'm told, especially when it sounds like what I want to hear."

She held up a hand as several mouths opened to speak.

"No, not now, after dinner. I mention it now so you may think about what it is I should be hearing."

She turned to me.

"I see you chose to put our highest medal first on your uniform."

Her smile invited anyone to challenge her statement.

"Actually," said Patton, "the order is correct. While of equal value, the Victoria Cross is the older award, and therefore should be placed first."

"Are you all aware it's never happened before?" asked Harriman.

There was an expression of surprise around the room, indicating most of them didn't.

"I did some research for my own interest," he went on. "The Victoria Cross has been awarded to an American before, as has the Medal of Honour been awarded to a Britain. But Jon here is the first person to be awarded both."

"Yes," agreed Bigglesworth. "In fact the press have only just realized this themselves, and have asked me to arrange a press conference so they can take pictures of Jon with both medals. I told them he wouldn't be agreeing to that. I agreed to ask him if he will allow an interview with a single reporter, who will agree to share the interview with all media channels. Jon?"

I sighed.

"I told Amy Allen when she came on board my ship, there would be no interviews with me, ever. But I guess I'll have to make an exception in this case. You can tell them I'll do a very short interview with her in the morning, and she can take a single image for use by all."

"Is your reluctance because you still have the head bruise?" asked Hallington.

It was still a yellow colour, and as my other bruises went, the least of them now.

"No. I simply don't feel comfortable being news fodder."

They all laughed.

"Like it or not," said Harriman, "You've been feeding the newscasts for two months now. The newsies aren't going to leave you alone until you stop doing newsworthy things."

I looked upwards.

"Make it so!" I said to those watching from above.

The laughter intensified. I shook my head, and laughed with them.

A functionary came in at that point, and announced dinner. At the same time, Jeeves came in, and quietly gave me my next pain shot.

We followed the Queen through to a private Dining Room, where she sat immediately. I was last to stand at my place, and we all sat together. A functionary pushed me under the table while another placed the necessary pouffe. I sent the scooter to an unused corner of the room.

Dinner was the finest I'd ever had, and amongst good company. While it was oddly formal because of the presence of the Queen, I was glad to be there. While not back to eating a full meal yet, I ate more than I had been.

We moved back into the sitting room. Talk turned to the future of the sectors as the Queen had requested, while coffee was being served. She asked probing questions and received direct answers. We outlined our concerns about prophesy, and the inadequate state of all the militaries at this end of the arm.

"Are you talking alien invasion?" she asked at one point. "Or another nut job uprising?"

All eyes turned to me.

"We don't know," I replied. "I seriously doubt the latter would be worthy of prophesy, and as we all know, so far, we've never encountered any evidence of aliens existing."

"Doesn't mean there isn't though," said Jedburgh. "In spite of the lack of evidence, we know only about a portion of the Galaxy. Despite all of our technological achievements, we haven't been able to discern enough about the other galactic arms, or the central core of the galaxy, to determine anything conclusive. But to assume there's no other intelligent life in the galaxy, would seem to be like sticking your head in the sand and wishing away the man about to kick your butt." He paused as he noticed we were all looking at him intently, as funny as the joke was. "My daughter is almost rabid about this stuff," he finished apologetically.

Everyone smiled or chuckled.

"All we really know is," I said, "this arm of the galaxy has only us. At least so far. We don't even know if we've discovered all the jump points there are along the arm, nor have we been able to penetrate the radiation system which blocked our advancement into the core systems. For all we know, there are jump points between the arms, in systems which we cannot reach yet. Maybe we haven't met aliens yet simply because they don't yet know we're here, or haven't yet found a way to reach us."

Patton stirred.

"One of our scenarios, which the Joint Chiefs keep up to date, is the possibility of alien invasion. It was first proposed five hundred years ago, and about every fifty years, some Commander is tasked with dusting it off, and updating it. I personally think these prophecies are more likely to be about some cosmic event than an alien invasion. But all the same, my job isn't about pandering to my own beliefs, it's the defense of the sector, and I think it's high time we all dug out every threatening scenario we have in the archives, and update our response protocols."

There was a mutter of assent all round. Discussion continued.

The Queen took it all in, and in the end, all she could promise was to take our concerns seriously, and to see what could be done at the government level. The Monarchy was more active in government than it had been in the middle past, but there were limits.

As the gathering broke up, the Queen turned to me.

"I'll see you for lunch tomorrow, Admiral."

It wasn't a request.

We all bowed as she left, although mine was little more than a deep nod. There were handshakes all round, and promises to keep in touch.

By eleven, I was back on the roof, to take a shuttle back to BigMother.

I found Miriam waiting for me on the bed, naked.

As it was almost due again, Jeeves gave me another shot, and left us to discover more ways of enjoying each other's company, without my screaming in pain.

Twenty Eight

I woke at four for another pain shot, and went straight back to sleep.

Miriam was lying next to me, looking at me, when I woke again. She kissed me.

"Last time for a long time, Jon," she said with a sad look on her face. "We head home this morning."

I reached for her, and we spent another hour alternating frantic moments with tender ones. She helped me into the shower.

By eight, after a pain shot, we were down in the Dining Room, where I found Amy waiting for me to be ready for her interview. The whole team was present, so I held her off while everyone ate, and had a chance to congratulate me individually on my awards of the previous day.

"When are we moving on, boss?" asked BA.

"No fixed time in mind," I replied. "I have to be at the Palace again for lunch, so call it a free day, and unless something comes up, we'll head for home tomorrow morning."

"Suits us," said Annabelle. "We've been invited to the SAS barracks for lunch."

"Enjoy," I said with a smile.

I didn't eat.

Miriam ate quickly, and we had a private goodbye moment in my living room, before she left for the Flight Deck to launch her Excalibur.

I went back into the Dining Room, and waited until everyone was leaving before nodding to Amy. We went up to my Ready Room. I laid out some ground rules, and we did a short interview. After, I posed for some seated images, which showed me in Hunter Dress, with medal ribbons prominent. I immediately changed back to 'slinky red', which didn't have the ribbons, and felt more comfortable.

Angel interrupted us finishing up, and reminded me she'd had no quality time with me in the last day, so I spent the rest of the morning following her around and patting her wherever she demanded it. Fortunately this only involved getting down to floor level twice. Part way through, I alternately tickled her and watched the Guam, Starman, and Stiletto, depart towards the Washington jump point.

When Angel tired of the attention, I explained I needed to go again for part of the afternoon, and I'd see her when I returned, whenever it was.

The Royal Gig arrived on the Flight Deck at eleven fifteen, was taken down to the Launch Deck, where I boarded it with Jane and Jeeves.

By quarter to twelve we were being shown into the same sitting room as the previous day. Before the Queen arrived, Jeeves gave me another shot, and went to stand with Jane in an unused corner.

Precisely at twelve, the Queen entered, waved me not to get up, and took a seat opposite me. She beamed a grin at me.

"Finally," she said, "I have you all to myself."

I had no idea what to say to that, so I said nothing, and allowed my face to look surprised. She laughed.

"I don't bite you know," she went on. "Well, actually I do, but let's not go there."

She grinned at her own little joke, and I felt obligated to do likewise, even though I had no idea what she talking about.

"This is purely social, so we can dispense with the formalities. You're Jon. I'm Liz."

She saw my eyes opening wide, and continued to laugh.

"Elizabeth the fifth, if you want to be completely accurate, but in private, I'm just Liz."

"Yes, Majesty," I said.

"Jon, stop it. We're the same age. I'm Queen, and you're the Hero. You own your own sector now, so might as well be a King. I don't see any point in us being formal in private."

"Since you put it that way..."

"I do," she interrupted me, and laughed again.

A ping came in from Bigglesworth. I held up my hand to her, and pointed to my head.

"Are you with the Queen?" he asked.

"Yes," I pinged back.

"Something's wrong. The SAS barracks isn't answering pings, and there are troop movements I know nothing about. One report says there are ship movements around one of the outer planets. But I can't get any hard information."

"We may have a problem," I said to Queen Liz. "Marshall Bigglesworth is telling me now. Hold on while I find out more." She nodded.

"What do you want from me?" I pinged him back.

"Protect the Queen. Stay with her until I give you the okay. If the worst happens, you are authorized to take any action to ensure her safety."

"Understood."

"Are you armed?"

"Yes."

"Good. You are authorized for lethal force if need be."

"Also understood."

"If you need to get her to safety, do so. The Palace isn't a very secure location, so if you need to, take her to your Carrier."

"Will do."

I turned to the Queen.

"Marshal Bigglesworth is concerned there's something happening he's not being told about. He fears the worst I think. Are you wearing your belt?"

"Yes, he was most insistent about that."

I sent a request for control access to her belt.

"Please okay the request for access to your belt, so I can make some changes, and check your settings."

She paused.

"Do you trust me?" I asked her.

"Yes," she said without any hesitation.

She authorized my access. I checked to see if her suit was on hair-trigger, and it was. I pulsed her over 'slinky red' and activated it. The suit formed over her clothes.

I turned to Jane.

"Scooter."

She brought it over, and I pulled myself up. I immediately activated the scooter belt to bring my guns up. Both gatling stunners went to my upper arms, and the Long Gun to my right thigh.

"Team coms," I said to Jane.

"Confirmed. Active."

"Team coms are active," I said. "General Smith, sitrep."

"Thank heavens, Admiral," she responded. "We're holed up in the SAS barracks. Troops have us surrounded. We're secure for now, but only have side-arms, and no outside communications."

"Combat suits on the way. I fear we might have some sort of coup in progress. Standby for instructions."

"Understood."

"Wing Commander."

There was no answer. I tried each of the pilots, including Slice and Eric, but none of them replied.

"Jane, let's assume the worst. Sitrep with BigMother?"

"Troops approaching the dock."

"Have the security droids enter the ship, seal both airlocks, and undock."

"Confirmed."

"Launch the Pythons, and dock them at a side airlock to receive combat suits and droids. Move combat suits for the team there, with half of your special suits, and one hundred combat droids. Outfit for stunning, but have them take heavy weapons as well. If the gloves come off, I want General Smith to have all the options. Drop them on General Smith's position. If coms fail, take what action you feel is appropriate to meet up with the team and the SAS forces. General Smith has the command."

"Confirmed."

"Send my combat suit to Gunbus, and launch her. Put her in position for a fast pickup from the roof if we need it."

"Confirmed."

I paused, and took a breath.

"Now I understand," said Queen Liz. "Before I only saw the boy in you. Now I see the man, and especially the Admiral."

I ignored what she'd said.

"Move over next to me, Majesty. Jane, place yourself to cover her if anyone comes through that door." I indicated the main entrance.

They both moved as I asked.

"Problem, Jon," said Jane. "I can't undock BigMother. The station won't release the docking clamps. They're in the station airlock, and firing into our outer airlock. They must intend to take the ship."

I sighed.

"Fine. If they want to play rough, we'll play rough. What do you have at the airlock?"

"Six of my combat suits, and fifty combat droids. The other fifty are still on their way from the other airlocks. The remaining combat suits are in the bay being converted to an armoury."

"Return the fifty to the airlocks. If they can't get in the front door, they'll try airlocks or the Flight Deck next. Secure all ways of entering the ship. Use all the combat suits we have, not already allocated."

"Confirmed."

"Secure Angel. I want her in her carry cage, next to an air supply. Have air backpacks taken to her location as a backup, just in case."

"Confirmed."

"Okay, let's deal with problem one. Have your combat suits take out the people in the airlock. Then move your force into the station, and remove any opposition. Leave half the force to guard the airlock, and secure the station operations areas. Release the docking clamps, and back the ship away from the station when you can."

"Confirmed. Airlock opening. Combat in progress."

I stopped for a moment to think. I put combat sensors in primary mode, searching for nearby weapons.

None of this made any sense unless the Queen was taken or killed.

There was no movement nearby. Actually, in itself, this was a bad sign. It meant the Palace staff had abandoned their posts. Including the security forces. Unless the security forces had been lured away, like...

I immediately sent Susan Bentley a priority email urging her to return. I told her I suspected she was on a wild goose chase designed to keep her away while a coup took place.

Movement. My proximity alert showed weapons incoming.

I snapped both of our suits into full protection mode. My suit changed in a way I hadn't seen before, making me look like I was wearing hugely thick body armour.

I seized both gatling stunners from my arms, and looped my arms under the hand holds for the scooter, using my elbows against the undersides to keep me in place, raising my guns towards the door.

Jane was suddenly likewise armed. I didn't know how she did it, because I hadn't seen her with a gun since we'd arrived at London. She must have figured out a way for her suit to hide them.

We waited, proximity alarms showing where the movement was.

As the door burst open, both of us began firing. A dozen armed men went down as they entered. Another dozen behind them opened fire on the three of us. Our suits took the fire without problems, and they went down under our gunfire as well.

The firing stopped. I changed our suits back to 'slinky red'.

Queen Liz went over to the first fallen man. She kneeled down, and took a long look at his face.

"What is this?" she asked. "This is the Duke of Norfolk!"

"You might want to rethink such appointments," I said, "when you get a moment." She looked at me strangely and straightened up. "Jane, we're leaving. Gunbus to the roof please."

"Confirmed."

"Majesty, step up onto the scooter behind me, and put your arms through underneath my armpits and loop them up around my shoulders. Please don't touch me anywhere below the shoulder level."

She did as she was told. The feel of her pressed up against my back felt good.

"Hold on tight, and don't let go for any reason."

"Okay."

"Jane, pick up the Duke, and take point. Once on board, put him in the brig. If he's the leader of whatever this is, having him in custody might be an asset."

"Confirmed."

She picked him up as if he weighed nothing, and I followed her out of the room, and up the staircase as fast as I dared. Jeeves followed me. At the top, we started taking fire again from a platoon of troops already up there, and we stopped to mow them down. They were ordinary troops with no body armour of any sort. Ideal for handling civilians, but not for Jane and me.

Gunbus came down like a dropship, and stopped to one side of the roof, with her ramp extended a meter above us. I kicked the scooter up enough to scoot into the open Cargo Bay. The ramp retracted, and the airlock began to close behind us, as Jane and Jeeves jumped through after me. Jane took Gunbus up as fast as she'd come down.

I scooted us up to the Bridge. Queen Liz dropped off the scooter, and sat in the Coms chair. I eased myself into my chair, which had the leg support already in place, and sent the scooter to a corner. Jane came in a minute later, and took the XO's position, as she normally did on Gunbus. As I looked beyond her, I saw the figure of Kali in its position, although it was supposed to be on BigMother's Bridge instead. Ganesha's was also there.

Gunbus burst through the top of the atmosphere into space, and the scanner became fully active again.

Dull red dots further out in the system, lit up the scanner and HUD.

A channel opened.

The vid showed a middle aged man with Admiral's stripes, on a uniform I didn't recognize.

"Ah," he said with a grin. "Our beloved Queen, with the boy cripple, who plays at being an Admiral."

His grin became predatory as he looked at me.
"Well boy, surrender or die!"

Twenty Nine

I stared him down.

In response to his supercilious predator grin, I gave him my Admiral's look.

"To whom do I not have the pleasure of addressing?" I asked him.

The grin slipped, and annoyance showed for a second.

"You are speaking with High Admiral Thaddeus Abbott, of the pirate Battleship Unassailable."

"Oh? High Admiral is it? Does that imply there's a Highest Admiral you report to?"

I gave him my smug look.

"Don't banter wit with me, boy. Surrender or die."

"Funny, I was about to say the same thing to you."

His grin slipped again, for just a moment. Then he laughed.

"You and whose army?" he challenged me with. "We'll be taking back the Carrier you stole from us, and eventually our Corvette as well. The Carrier can't leave the station, so all you have to fight with is that puny so called Heavy Transport."

"I'll match my puny transport against your Battleship any time you like, Mr. Abbott." I emphasized the Mr.

The grin slipped completely, and rage replaced it.

"You choose to die then. Pity. We wanted the Queen alive so she could dissolve the British nobility once and for all, and then abdicate. My Republican allies have promised to allow me to base in this sector, while we retake what was once ours. No matter, a dead Queen kidnapped by a love sick boy will do just as well. My fleet will be in orbit shortly. Prepare to be destroyed!"

The channel closed.

"Smarmy git," I said. "That went well."

"How did that go at all well?" asked Queen Liz.

"We now know there's a Republican coup in progress, and they have allied themselves with pirates. The question is, your Majesty, what do you intend to do about it?"

"Do? What can I do?"

"Act like a Queen for a start. Do you abdicate, or fight? Choose."

"Fight!"

"Then act like a Queen under attack. What are your orders?"

She looked at me for a moment, stood, and drew herself erect.

"Jonathon Hunter, I call you to service in the British Fleet, with the rank of full Admiral. Do you accept this commission?"

"I do."

"You are ordered to put down this coup, and deal with this pirate rabble. Use any resources available. Appoint anyone you trust to command, with commissions in the British Fleet."

"Yes, Majesty. Please take your seat, and buckle up."

She did so, and I took a moment to think. I wasn't given any longer.

"Military transport approaching the Flight Deck of Big-Mother, rear entrance."

"Take us there, Jane."

"Confirmed."

I checked the scanner. We had maybe ten minutes before the pirate fleet arrived, and it would take five to reach Big-Mother. I pulled up details of the fleet. One Battleship, two Cruisers, four Destroyers. One of the Cruisers and two of the Destroyers were British Fleet.

"You have mutineers, Majesty."

I pointed out the British ships to her.

"Destroy them please. Destroy them all."

"Yes, Majesty."

I put team coms on the Bridge com system so Queen Liz could hear.

"General Smith."

"Sir?"

"The team has just joined the British Fleet, by Order of her Majesty, Queen Elizabeth the fifth. You are ordered to put down the coup, using any means necessary. Stun if possible, but heavy weapons are arriving with the combat suits if needed. Be sure a target is an enemy before you take terminal action. At this point, we don't know who is friendly, and who is not. Once your area is cleared, you will retake the Palace. I assume the Houses of Parliament were also taken, so assume this is the case and act accordingly. Think like a coup leader and retake any place you consider they may have gone after."

"Jane is in battle on the Orbital station as we speak. I'll be busy with an enemy fleet up here, so you have the command on the ground. If you encounter any superior officer who won't take your orders, stun and detain. At least one Duke is a ringleader, so make no assumptions about who may or may not be involved. Marshall Bigglesworth got the alarm out to me in time, but I've not heard from him since. He's either down, or somewhere being jammed. One objective is to ascertain his fate, and if needed, effect a rescue. We're operating under the direct command of the Queen, for as long as the situation requires. Do you understand?"

"Yes, sir. I have General Hobbs with me now, and he's been listening in. The SAS will take my orders, and are preparing to move out now. The Dropships are coming in as we speak."

"I sent six of Jane's special suits."

"Understood."

She started bellowing orders.

"Hobbs?" I said to Queen Liz.

"Two star, very reliable."

I nodded, and turned my attention back to the Orbital station, which was coming close now.

"Jane, sitrep."

"Battle is still occurring around Station Operations. Big-Mother is secure on the station side, and the airlocks are closed. Still unable to undock."

"Military Transport?"

"About to touch down on the Flight Deck."

"Can you identify who it is?"

"Mercenary unit. Hell's Sword."

Great, another dark merc unit. I brought up a screen from a Flight Deck cam. The transport touched down, and combat suits emerged.

"Analysis of their combat suits?"

"Bottom of the range," she said, with a smirk.

"Any tactical difference we can exploit?"

"Main differences are how much damage they'll take. Their sensors are nowhere near as good either. In fact, I just jammed them. They have no sensors or coms now."

A smile came over my face. The Queen had her first look at the expression Alsop hated so much.

"What's the difference in terms of how much gravity they can take, and still move?"

"Basic suits can still move in five gees. Ours can take ten gees. They're gathered outside a single airlock, preparing to enter."

"Unlock the airlock, back our forces out of weapons range, and let them in."

"Let them in?" said Queen Liz, a look of amazement on her face.

"Yes. Jane, once they're all inside, turn up the gravity to eight gees."

"Confirmed!"

"If you have to, go as high as you need to immobilize them completely."

"Confirmed."

Gunbus slowed as we came near the station.

I took manual control, and brought us around the rear of BigMother, and we looked down the Flight Deck.

The Military Transport was sitting square in the rear entrance, and as we watched, the last combat suit disappeared through an airlock. It closed behind the suit.

"Mercs immobilized," announced Jane. "It only took five gees too. Suggests the suits were old."

I grinned at her.

Now for the transport. I opened a channel.

"Gunbus to Hell's Sword."

"What have you done to my team?"

"Neutralized them. Stand down, and you get to live, otherwise I'll blow you where you are."

"You wouldn't dare. You'd damage your own ship."

"Not really. You don't have shields. One torpedo will tear you apart enough you won't be leaving in a hurry."

"Huh! You wouldn't."

"Are you basing this on what you see on your vid, or have you actually viewed my Mercenary record?"

"You're a kid. What record could you possibly have?"

"Fine. With luck, you'll still be alive to look it up."

I closed the channel. I looked at Queen Liz, and raised my eyebrows several times quickly. She grinned.

I took a careful bead on the middle of the transport's engine, and fired a single torpedo. The back end of the ship exploded, spraying ship fragments in all directions. I backed us away, and turned to see what the pirates were doing.

They were in a V formation with the Battleship in the middle, and now less than a minute to orbit. I moved us away from the station so I'd have room to maneuver if I needed to.

"SAS barracks secure," said Annabelle over team coms. "Moving out now."

"Fighting continues on the station," said Jane. "I still can't undock."

"Bugger it," I said. "Get those Meson Streamers which almost killed me, and cut her loose from the station." I looked at the Queen. "Sever the station side connections." She nodded approval.

"Confirmed."

A channel opened from the Battleship.

"Last chance to surrender, kiddies. Bad enough having a girl in charge of the government, without a boy pretending he can protect her from us."

"Jane," I said deliberately into the open channel, "take aim at the Battleship. Full broadside. Target the Bridge."

"Confirmed."

The High Admiral of pirates laughed. The rest of his Bridge crew laughed with him.

"What do you intend to fire at me boy? Your anti-fighter missiles can't hurt my shields, and you know it. The only missiles you have which are any threat are on your Carrier, which can't fire while docked."

"Do you have a parrot?" I asked him.

"Parrot? What are you babbling on about?"

"All good pirate captains should have a parrot. And a wooden leg. I ask because I'd hate to kill an innocent parrot."

He laughed hysterically, and his crew followed his lead.

It took him a minute to calm down.

"No boy, I don't have a parrot. You've been reading too many kids books."

I grinned at him.

"Maybe so. And I'm relieved to only be killing vermin."

His mirth changed to malice in an instant.

"Target that ship," he ordered.

"Mr. Pirate," I said. "You're wrong about something important."

He laughed again.

"And what would that be?"

I looked at Jane.

"Fire."

Thirty

Three hundred missiles launched downwards from Big-Mother, arced around her hull, and headed for the Battle-ship.

"Launch."

Four white dots appeared on the scanner, as the four Guardians disconnected from BigMother. They moved into a position flanking Gunbus, and we moved to intercept the pirate fleet. For a moment I seriously thought about launching Custer as well. But she didn't have the offensive firepower to help much, and there was no way we could move to her safely. Besides, Gunbus made a smaller target to hit.

"Launch the Hives."

Twelve Hive clusters detached from the upper hull, and moved into flanking positions as well.

"Missile launch," said Jane. "They have the Mosquito system!"

Seven hundred tiny missiles had launched, showing they had a single Mosquito launcher on each ship. As we watched, most of my missiles were destroyed, and only a handful hit the shields of the Battleship. The fact of any getting through at all suggested they were using only a single medium level AI to control them.

"Guardians to attack the Destroyers one at a time. I want them destroyed to remove their Mosquito launchers. Hives to co-ordinate with torpedoes."

"Confirmed."

My ships moved. I bucked Gunbus away from the first pulse salvo coming from the Battleship. The enemy formation changed to line abreast, and then fell apart as each ship moved differently to counter the speed my ships were moving to intercept them at.

Pulses crisscrossed the area. I had to concentrate on keeping Gunbus clear of them.

Part of my mind went into staying clear of the pulses. The rest of my mind analyzed the best course of action.

Abruptly, I flipped Gunbus end for end and started heading away from the fight at full speed. Pulses followed me, so I had to continue juking erratically.

"What are you doing?" asked Queen Liz.

"Getting you to safety Majesty."

"You want me to be known as the Queen who ran away?"

"You want to be a dead Queen?"

She glared at me for a moment.

"No, I don't want to be dead. But I also don't want to be the Queen who ran away."

"Trust me."

"To run away?"

"No, to know when running is the only rational thing to do, and when fighting is the proper logical choice."

A pulse almost got us, as my attention had wandered from the battle behind us.

"Don't jog my elbow Majesty, please."

The Guardians and Hives were firing on the first of the Destroyers, using guns, missiles, and torpedoes. They were all taking hits from the other enemy ships, but shields were holding for now.

She glared at me again, but didn't say anything more.

I dodged another set of pulses, and we kept on running away.

A channel opened.

"And so the boy coward runs," gloated Mr. Pirate Abbott. He laughed, until something caught his eye. "What the hell was that?" he asked someone off screen.

"That," I said, "was one of your Destroyers turning into confetti."

The Guardians and Hives turned their attention on the next nearest Destroyer. Shields were down round the eighty percent mark now.

There was a bellow of outrage from his pirate-ness, followed by orders.

The Battleship turned away from pursuing us, and started towards the fight behind it.

I flipped Gunbus again, now heading more up than back. First I wanted an angled line so the pulses still coming from some of the Battleship's guns would have the hardest time hitting us, while at the same time, I wanted to position Gunbus for the attack I had in mind.

A second Destroyer exploded. The Guardians started shooting at the next closest. Shields were now in their seventies.

The Battleship entered range of the Guardians about the same time I reached my turning point. All her guns now began to fire at the Guardians. The drain on their shields increased, but the enemy ships were trying to fire on all of them, where my ships were only firing on a single target until it was destroyed.

The third Destroyer staggered and went dark, as a missile salvo mostly hit it. There weren't enough Mosquito missiles being launched now to fully counter the Guardian's full broadsides, and the missiles still coming from BigMother. Their AI obviously couldn't cope. The Guardians shifted target to the last Destroyer.

Gunbus was halfway to its target now, hopefully forgotten. I grouped up all the main guns, both the fixed forward ones, and in the side turrets, and waited for target lock on my target.

My finger itched next to the trigger, and my thumb hovered over the torpedo button.

"What's that dot close to us," came the bellow through the still open channel.

I had target lock now.

The last Destroyer exploded, and the Guardians, with shields now down in their thirties, opened fire on one of the Cruisers. The Hives followed suit.

At the longest range for accurate firing, I pulled the trigger, and began pumping out torpedoes. I kept at it as long as I dared, and then pulled Gunbus right to turn back the way I'd come, aiming for a narrow miss of the Battleship's side.

I waited one second too late.

Just as the turn began, a pulse from the Battleship tore down Gunbus' left side, and opened the ship to space from front to back, as if a hand had simply ripped the side off her.

Our suits snapped into space suit mode, and connected to the nearest air connections.

Jane was gone. Her side of the console was ripped away with the hull.

Everything went dead, and Gunbus pin-wheeled, completely out of control.

I looked at Queen Liz. Her eyes were closed, but I could see she was still breathing. Most likely fainted.

Just as well, as she was going to miss the next bit.

I desperately wanted to miss the next bit.

I sat there, unable to do anything, the view spinning crazily, as Gunbus followed her torpedoes into the Bridge of the Battleship.

Thirty One

We got lucky.

Gunbus hit rear first, crashing into the now destroyed Battleship Bridge and it's under areas, like someone doing a flop over a high jump.

I sat there stunned for several minutes. Pain was shooting up my leg, and when my wits returned, I could see the leg support had been torn off my chair, and my leg had dropped into a more normal position.

The knee was now bent, which mainly accounted for the pain. The doctors were obviously wrong in their prediction of no knee movement for five days, but this wasn't the way I wanted to find it out.

The Queen was still in her seat as I was, bent over to one side, and still breathing, although apparently out cold.

The Bridge itself was a wreck, although in the best condition along the right side.

A warning message popped up. I was on suit air. The ship was dead, including life support. However, I had more time than I expected. Merging three suits seemed to also merge and improve the basic air time. I had about half an hour to find an alternate source.

I looked around for my scooter. Gone. It must have been sucked out when the side was ripped away.

I called for Jeeves. No answer. I couldn't recall if he'd followed us onto the Bridge or not.

I sat for a minute, and tried to think of options.

Medical was out, since the care units required ship life support.

My combat suit was down in the Armoury. It should be able to keep one of us alive for hours if need be. There might also be air backpacks down there. I honestly didn't know if there were or not. They might have been transferred to Custer when we'd made the move, or left there. I'd have to hope they were left behind.

I took stock of myself. My suit was functioning perfectly. I'd not taken any injury, in spite of the damage to my chair. My gatling stunners were gone. But the Long Gun was still on my right thigh. I plucked it out and checked it. It was fully charged and interfacing with my PC correctly. I took the bolt off the holster, and plugged it into the gun. I had no illusions. I was on board an enemy ship, and the chances were high someone would be looking for survivors of the crash area. I doubted they would be looking for prisoners. If I had to shoot, I wanted to be able to put them down properly. I holstered the gun.

So, Cargo Deck. The immediate problem was how to get there. I was going to have to walk, or maybe crawl. Worse, I was going to need to carry Queen Liz. I couldn't leave her behind in case something happened to prevent me getting back. I had no idea what the condition of the ship was below me. It might be a one way trip.

Or no trip at all, if I couldn't move.

Suit.

That was Kali. I thought about it.

The obvious thing was to merge space suit mode with protection mode. The suit changed as I activated this. It became more bulky, and stronger. I straightened my leg, gritted my teeth and held it straight, while I changed the suit leg to a solid unbending brace. I eased my leg down again, now perfectly straight. The pain spike subsided.

The next step was to put some weight on it. I eased out of the chair and gently put my left foot on the deck. I almost passed out, but didn't. I waited for my vision to clear.

Suck it up! I had to walk, or we'd both die here. I stood, letting the wave of pain wash over me, although my weight was mainly on my right foot.

Embrace the pain.

Kali again. Easy for her to say. I took a deep breath and deliberately invoked meditation mode. I embrace my pain. I embrace my pain. I embrace my pain. It became a mantra I repeated over and over, drowning out all other thoughts. I moved towards Queen Liz, still unmoving in her chair. Fire burned up my left side with each touch down of my left foot, but I slowly moved across to her.

I unbuckled her from the chair, and pushed her upright. Next problem, how to move her without any ability to bend my knees? Fortunately, she wasn't a large girl. I pulled her up towards me, and held her up once she was on her feet. I twirled her around me, putting my back to the chair, and allowed myself to fall back into her chair, right leg bent, left leg outstretched, guiding her over my right shoulder. I shifted both hands to circle around under her butt, and lifted her over my shoulder properly. It wasn't a classic fireman's lift, but it was close.

I took a big breath and stood up, shrieking as agony took my left side. In space, no-one can hear you scream – it didn't leave my suit. I stood there muttering my mantra, letting my breathing settle, as the meditation energy I was invoking calmed me down.

I took a step towards the door, right foot forward. Then a left, followed by a quick right. I could manage a hobble, so hobble I did, getting to the doorway, now missing its door.

"Small steps", I said to myself.

Each step would get me further, just take them one at a time.

I moved slowly to the top of the stairway, and looked down. It looked relatively intact. I eased down a few steps, and allowed myself to sink to the top step, sitting with left leg outstretched, and right supporting me. I let the Queen down next to me.

I began the long rump-walk down to the Cargo Deck, sliding her down beside me. Each step was a jolt for her, and she was going to have problems sitting down for a while if she survived. For now, the jolting didn't wake her up.

Half way down I received a fifteen minute warning pop-up. It had taken me as long to get this far. The Battleship hadn't been destroyed, so I had no idea how the space battle had ended, as it surely must have by now. Someone must be coming to find out what happened to us.

I put it out of my mind, and concentrated on moving us faster down the stairwell, bringing us both one step at a time. Oh what I'd give to have an access shaft right now. Mental note if I lived long enough, have access shafts put in all ships from now on. Stairs might be better exercise, but it simply wasn't a focus at the moment. I giggled and caught a hold of myself. A ship with no power wasn't going to have a useful access shaft, just a hole to fall through. My mind wasn't thinking too well it seemed. I wondered why we had gravity at all for a moment, but had to assume the Battleship still had power, and its gravity field was holding us now. I returned to my mantra.

Down we went, slowly but surely.

At last, with five minutes left, we reached the bottom. I was exhausted now, and inflamed. The only thing I felt was pain. Pain is good, I said to myself. It means I'm still alive.

I stood again with no small amount of trouble, and grasped Queen Liz by her right arm, and pulled her along after me as I made my way into the Armoury.

Two minute warning.

The combat suit was on its side, having been thrown out of its charge slot. I connected to it, and powered it up. The back opened. I used my remaining strength to push her Majesty roughly inside as fast as I could. The back closed, and I checked on its life support. Good for five hours. She at least should be rescued. I switched her suit to 'slinky red'.

One minute warning.

I looked around for the air backpacks, but couldn't see any. There was only the single combat suit in the Armoury, with its Heavy Pulse Rifles, which were still in their charge racks.

Life support failure.

I sat next to the Queen, and let my last few breaths flow through me, stopping the mantra, and simply entering a deeply meditative state.

Give yourself to me.

Kali again. I looked around to see if I was in my Ready Room again, but no. I was gasping my last in the wreckage of Gunbus.

Give yourself to me!

"I give myself to you," I parroted, my eyes losing focus.

My pain stopped.

My breathing stopped.

My heart stopped.

Thirty Two

I burst out of myself as some sort of incorporeal entity, flowed out of the wreckage of the ships, and into space.

I looked around.

Time had stopped. Nothing moved.

Jane was not far off the side of the Battleship. She looked like she was firing her guns behind her, perhaps using their slight recoil as a propellant. I was relieved to see her okay. It might be a droid body and expendable, but she, it, she, was my friend.

I moved to a position where I could see the whole battle site. Four Guardians were visible. All four were damaged, but only one was extensively damaged. There were the hulls of one Cruiser and one Destroyer, both appearing dead.

I looked back at the Battleship. It appeared to be functional. I moved inside and sought out an area where there should be live people. Towards the center, I came across the CCC. Everyone there was down. They looked like they'd been asphyxiated. I continued through the ship and found the same everywhere. Curious. There was no apparent cause of life support failure. There were many damaged areas, but all of them were closed off from the rest of the ship, so no particular hit had caused the crew to die.

I moved out of the ship and headed towards the station. BigMother was a short way away from it. Custer had undocked, and was on her way towards the Battleship. I moved through her, but no-one was aboard. I moved on to Big-Mother, but only Angel was there, and she was safely in her carry cage, being held next to an air connection point in my suite by one of the butler droids.

The Mercenaries were still flat on the deck just inside the airlock from the Flight Deck. Outside, the captain of the Military Transport wouldn't be looking up my record after all.

On the station, the battle for Operations was still in progress, but Jane was almost through mopping up. I went back to check BigMother. The docking clamps had been cut, not released. But she hadn't been let loose in time to join the battle.

I headed down to the planet.

Amanda and Aleesha were inside the Palace, blazing away with their combat suit stunners. Pulses hung in the air leaving their guns on a line towards hapless troops. A line of bodies extended behind them, mainly alive, although one had its face smashed in. British troops were spread out through the building. BA and Annabelle were in the Parliament building, with more British troops. I found the other team members scattered across a number of other government buildings, all acting as lead combat suit for at least a platoon of troops.

Bigglesworth was in his office at the Admiralty, firing a gun across the top of his desk, unaware Aline in her combat suit was about to remove his problem for him.

George and the other pilots were at the RAF hangers. They were all down, but appeared to be alive. It made sense to stun all the pilots before you brought in a fleet to attack the planet. Royal Air Force might be an obsolete name for a space travel age, but the name was traditional, and like so much else which was traditionally British, had been retained along with the Monarchy.

I couldn't help anyone, so I launched myself back up into space.

With nowhere else to go, and no concept of why I was in this form, apparently timeless, I returned to Gunbus. I found Jeeves in my suite, pinned under some debris. I had no way of telling if he was still active or not. I found the Duke of Norfolk still in the remains of the Brig. His body had been torn in half.

I returned to where I'd left my body.

I discovered a figure approaching where I'd left myself. I circled around it, discovering it was a suited man, wearing an air backpack, who looked disturbingly like his pirate-ness. He was carrying a handgun, and it was pointed in my general direction.

I didn't know what else to do, so I tried to re-enter my body.

Time started up again.

My heart gave a beat.

I took a breath of almost unbreathable air.

Pain smashed at my consciousness.

Thirty Three

My suit generated an air connection and smoothly connected me to the combat suit's external air connection point.

In seconds, it regenerated its ability to sustain me for another half hour, and disconnected. It shortened the time Queen Liz could last by that amount, but it kept me alive a bit longer.

I pulled myself back to my feet, and faced towards the oncoming figure.

A channel opened between our suits.

"So boy," he smirked at me. "You're still alive."

"Damn right I am," I responded. "But how are you? Your Bridge crew are dead. Were you the only one to have a suit belt on? Did you run out as soon as you saw the torpedoes coming? So the coward makes sure he lives when his crew are all dead!"

"I took steps to ensure I survived, yes. Anyone in my position would do."

A phrase came to me from an old flat screen.

"I have given a name to my pain, and it is Abbott!"

"What?"

"You heard me arse-hole. I choose to call my pain your name, because that's all you are. Pain for other people. You're a parasite on society, and give true parasites a bad name."

His face went bright red, his gun jerked, but before he could fire, I drew my Long Gun and fired first. The shot took him in the forehead, and he went over backwards, his own shot coming nowhere near me. I holstered my gun, and hobbled over to the gun racks, where I pulled a Heavy Pulse Rifle down.

In my weakened condition it was almost too much for me to manage, but I swung the muzzle towards my enemy, and lined him up.

He was just getting up, bringing his gun around at me again.

I fired the Pulse Rifle. The pulse took him in the middle of the chest, and he went flying backwards to crash into the wall behind him.

I hobbled after him, keeping the Pulse Rifle lined up on him. He was struggling to rise from the floor, as the next pulse hit him.

I debated hitting him again. If he had a standard suit belt, one more pulse would probably shred it. If it was boosted, he could take it.

He stirred and fired at me again, the shot taking me in the left arm, and bouncing off harmlessly.

I gave him another pulse. His suit held together, but he passed out. He'd taken three bruise-worthy hits now, so he was going to be sore when he woke up in a cell.

A stun pulse came from behind me, hitting Abbott in the middle of the chest.

His suit shredded.

His body explosively decompressed.

I looked at the mess in surprise. He must have had some sort of skin break somewhere to cause it. Too bad.

I turned to look where the stun shot had come from. Jane was standing there. She holstered her guns, and started over towards me. I dropped the Pulse Rifle.

"Why did you do that?" I asked her via PC coms.

"He had it coming," she responded.

"How so?"

"While I was out there, I had the chance to access the ship's computer. Even his own people hated him. As far as anything good about him is concerned, he's been running on empty for a long time. He was seriously overdue for someone to take him out."

"So you happened to the crew?"

She grinned, and nodded.

"How were you able to take the computer over? Wasn't there another AI?"

"There was, until the Bridge was destroyed. It must have been on the Bridge, because after Gunbus crashed, the ship's computer was wide open to me. I took it over, and turned off the life support."

"Do we have engines?"

"No. One of the Guardians destroyed them to stop the ship from escaping. If I'd realized I had access to the computer a few seconds earlier, I could have saved us some trouble. But Custer will be here in two minutes, so you won't be on suit air for much longer."

"Good. Can you control the combat suit with the Queen still in it?"

"Yes. She's unconscious, but doesn't appear to be injured."

"Okay, let's move to where Custer can get to us. You'll need to give me some support."

She moved over beside me, and I put my left arm around her shoulders. We shuffled along with me holding my left leg out in front slightly and hopping each step. The combat suit followed along.

Outside of Gunbus' hull, she had to lift me over a lot of the debris.

We waited for Custer at a point where the ramp could extend to us. She came in slowly, stopping with the ramp extended. Jane lifted me off the ground, and jumped up to it. She carried me to the top, where Jarvis was waiting. He gave me a pain shot. The suit took the medication, and delivered it to my skin.

After giving it a minute to work, I put my left foot down on the deck, and found I was able to manage a hobble. By the time I arrived at the rear hatch, the airlock was closed and the bay aired up and warm again. I switched to 'slinky red'.

We started towards Deck One. I definitely need to get an access shaft put in.

Thirty Four

With the Queen extracted from the combat suit, with her suit returned to a belt, and her laid out in the XO's bed, I was assisted into my chair on the Bridge.

"Sitrep," I said to Jane.

"You better listen to team coms from a little while ago first."

"General," said Amanda, "can you move a team to the RAF hangers ASAP?"

"Why?" answered Annabelle.

"George and the other pilots are over there. Stunned I think."

"How do you know that?"

"Jon just had another out-of-body experience. Aleesha and I experienced it with him."

"BA?"

"Boss?"

"See to it please."

"Sir!"

"What happened to Jon?" Annabelle asked next.

"Gunbus was shot down, crashing into the Bridge of a pirate Battleship."

"Is he alright?"

"They both are."

"Both?"

"The Queen is with him."

There was a loud sigh.

The recording ended.

"The pirate fleet was destroyed," went on Jane. "Two British ships, a Cruiser and a Destroyer, are intact and under my control, but will both need towing, as they're extensively damaged. Three of the Guardians have minor damage, the fourth has hull breaches and extensive internal damage. We were lucky none of the breaches were against magazines. The Battleship will need towing, but other than no longer having a Bridge or the areas underneath it, it's in reasonable shape. BigMother is free from the station, and undamaged, although some holes along the Flight Deck will need some minor attention, as will the mess you left need some cleaning up. Angel is trying to get out of her cage."

I laughed.

"Let her out please. Tell her I'll be back soon."

"Don't go back too soon. That is one seriously pissed off puss." I laughed even harder. "The Mercs are still flat on the deck. What do you want to do with them?"

"Can you introduce a gas into the suits?"

"Sure. Make them sleep?"

"Yes. Once asleep, restore the gravity to normal, remove them from their suits and Brig them. Ah, we do have a Brig on BigMother, don't we?"

"We do."

She laughed at me. I still don't know everything about my own ship yet.

"Do that. Take their suits somewhere you can dump them for a while. The Brits might want them."

"Confirmed."

"Can you retrieve Jeeves before we head back to Big-Mother?"

"You know where he is?"

"My suite, jammed under some debris. I have no idea if he's still functional or not. And while you're there, there's a dead Duke in the Brig. Can you bring the remains back here? He'll need to be formally identified."

Her avatar nodded, and hurried out.

"Combat suit is now charging," Jane went on through ship coms. I nodded. "The station was taken. Some minor damage to combat droids, but repairable. All those involved in the coup are in the station detention cells now. Mopping up on the ground is still in progress, but the fighting has ended. No casualties to our team. The pilots were only stunned, and have been moved to a hospital for checks."

"Good. Does anyone need me?"

"Yes."

"Who?"

"The nearest doctor."

"Ha-ha. I'll go down to the Medical Bay while we wait for your avatar to return. Once back on board, take us back to BigMother. I'll lie down when we get there."

I hobbled down to the Medical Bay, changed my suit back to a belt, and was looked over by one of the doc-droids. It pronounced me undamaged. It had no explanation for the movement now available in my left knee, but other than the original bruising, I'd not hurt it any more for all the movement and pressure on it. It did suggest I continue to keep it straight for another few days. I shifted back into 'slinky red', added the leg brace back on, and hobbled up to see if the Queen was awake yet.

She was still out when I went in, and with nothing else to do, I sat on the end of the bed.

She stirred a few minutes later, and bolted upright, with a wild un-Queenly yell.

I grinned at her.

"Where are we?" she asked.

"My Frigate."

"I'm sorry. You were right."

"What about?"

"Running away. I should never have disagreed with you on that."

"Hindsight is always easy. If I'd pulled away a second earlier, we wouldn't have been hit."

"I think I fainted when the side of the ship vanished. Please don't tell anyone."

"I won't. You were knocked out in the crash."

"Is that why my arse hurts?"

I chuckled, and grinned at her.

"Ah, no."

"Why then?"

"We both went down five decks worth of stairs, arse first."

"Whatever for?"

"We only had a half hour of air in our suits, and the only working life support was in my combat suit, down in the Armoury. It took me all of that half hour to get us down, and the only way of going down stairs I had, was on my arse. I wasn't in any condition to carry you, so you went down the same way, one step at a time."

"Oh. You made it then?"

"Obviously."

"What's been happening?"

"I don't have a full account, but the fighting is ended. My team and your troops took out those staging the coup. The Duke died in the Brig, when we crashed. The pirate Admiral survived, and tried to take another crack at us. He's red paste all over the wreckage of my Cargo Deck."

"I'll buy you a new ship, since it's my fault you lost it."

"With luck she can be fixed. When they put the Battleship in for repairs, they can remove Gunbus and see if she's repairable."

"Battleship?"

"Jane captured it after the crash destroyed the AI they had on board. Its engines were destroyed, so before I can take it home with me, it needs some work."

"Before you take it home with you?"

"Sure. Privateer Law. I'll put in a claim for the ship, having captured it from pirates in a battle."

"What on earth will you use a Battleship for?" She held up her hand at me. "No, don't tell me, I don't think I want to know."

"Oh, I think I have a few ideas." I grinned at her. "By the way, two of your ships survived. They'll need tows to a shipyard, but should be repairable."

She sighed, remembering mutineers. At least she didn't have to deal with trials for them. She had a full circus on her hands with any of those in the coup who'd survived.

"Recovery complete," said Jane. "Moving to BigMother."

"Come onto the Bridge," I said to Queen Liz, "and let's see who we can contact."

I hobbled out, and she followed me.

Once on the Bridge, we were able to contact Marshall Bigglesworth. Arrangements were made for the Queen, to meet us on BigMother.

Back on BigMother, we took the long trek up to Deck Two, where I showed her to one of the VIP suites, and suggested she get some rest while her people did their jobs.

I went to my suite, calmed down a not at all happy puss, and discussed with Jane what I wanted done with the Battleship and Gunbus. I intended to get some sleep, so if the opportunity to get them both into a shipyard became available while I slept, Jane would know what to do. I also gave some instructions for adding an access shaft to Custer.

I showered and changed into boxers and t-shirt, and went to bed. Angel curled up by my neck as usual, and I was fast asleep before the lights dimmed.

Thirty Five

I woke up abruptly, oddly feeling very refreshed, while pain still washed my left side.

It hurt, but not nearly as much as it should've. My eyes had hardly registered Amanda and Aleesha sitting next to the bed, before Jeeves was there giving me a pain shot. It was Jeeves too, I could tell. He'd obviously had some work done, but still needed a bit more.

"Welcome back," said Aleesha, after Jeeves had departed.

Amanda had the look of someone either pinging, or emailing.

"What's up Doc?" I said with a giggle.

One of my favourite twentieth century cartoon sayings from when I was a kid. Aleesha gave me a piecing look, as if wondering about my sanity.

"Why the vigil?" I asked her.

They looked like they'd been staked out waiting for me to wake for some time now.

"It's eleven, Jon. We weren't sure when you'd be waking up. The doc said to let you wake naturally."

"Doc?"

"Umm, you've been asleep for forty four hours now."

"What?"

The force of my exclamation made her lean back a bit.

"The Doc who came up to look the Queen over, also looked you over. He was shocked at your overall condition. In his opinion, you were malnourished and dehydrated. He put you into a deeper sleep. You had a hydration module on you for about twelve hours."

I suddenly became very aware of my bladder.

"Welcome back, sleepy head," said Amanda.

"Help me into the bathroom," I said.

I rolled myself to the side of the bed, and swiveled to bring my legs over the side. Amanda held a hand out, so I grasped it, and she gently pulled me to my feet. My left leg seemed to be able to move properly, and there was no additional pain when I put the foot down.

She helped me hobble into the bathroom, where I shooed her out. Fifteen minutes later, I hobbled out wearing 'slinky red'.

The twins looked me in the eyes with a steady gaze.

"What?"

"We have to make sure you eat a full meal before you do anything else," said Amanda.

"No distractions," added Aleesha.

I waved them out before me, but they were having none of it. They followed me to my Dining Room. I stopped to pat Angel on the way, after coaxing her half way up the kitty castle so I didn't have to bend too far.

Jeeves had Chinese food for four people on the table waiting for us. I sniffed the aromas, and was suddenly very hungry indeed. I loaded up my plate and dug in. The twins followed suit.

"Sitrep," I said between mouthfuls.

"The coup was successfully put down," said Amanda, "but you knew that before you went to sleep."

"George and the others are fine," said Aleesha. "Just stunned."

"I knew that too," I said. "Stop alternating, and one of you tell me the rest."

Did I get up on the wrong side of the bed? Or was finding out I'd lost nearly two days enough to make me crabby? I decided I had good reason to be crabby.

The twins looked at each other. Amanda opened her mouth to continue.

"I know that too," I said before she could say something.

"What?" they asked together.

"You saw my out-of-body experience with me."

"That was weird," said Aleesha. "Time stopped, and yet we saw everything you did."

"The weirdest part was seeing ourselves frozen in time like that," said Amanda.

"Tell me what I don't know."

"They confirmed it was Admiral Abbott you and Jane killed. He's been top of the British sectors' most wanted list for a decade. You can expect a lot of bounty payments for removing him. Someone in the media managed to get aboard Gunbus with the forensics team, and take a vid of him splashed across the wreckage. It made headline news. Apparently he used to be a bigwig here until he went pirate, after which all the admiration for him turned to hatred. The celebrations for his death were unbelievable. Half the planet wasn't at work the next day because of too much partying."

"Gunbus?"

"I'm sorry, Jon. She was too badly damaged to be worth trying to fix. It wasn't like Custer, where the hull was mainly intact. She had most of the left side missing, and the entire hanger was crushed where she crashed down on the Battleship. It was just as well your Excalibur was on BigMother, or it would have been completely destroyed as well."

I sighed deeply. It was likely I had a new record to add to my list. Shortest life of a capital ship. She'd been less than two months old. Damn, that hurt more than my side did. Belatedly I realized that record went to some Americans, who'd died in Miami, within days of being launched. It didn't help. I'd killed a friend by a second's bad judgement. I shook the feeling off.

"Battleship?"

"At the local shipyard, getting the makeover you told Jane to organize. She's been adjudicated to you already. Oh, and the salvage droids found your scooter and guns floating in space. They're in your Ready Room."

"Jane, send them down please."

"Confirmed."

"You haven't told him the other big news here, sis," said Aleesha.

"What big news?"

"It turned out the coup wasn't organized by the Duke of Norfolk. They found the bodies of him and his family on Norfolk, apparently slain several weeks ago. The family were supposed to be on holiday, while the Duke was attending to matters on London. When the authorities there went looking for evidence of the Duke's treason, the trail led them to the bodies of the whole family. They genetically tested the imposter, and found he'd been surgically altered to impersonate the Duke. No-one understands why the impersonation was done as yet. Unfortunately, the only two who probably knew, died on the Battleship. As yet, they haven't identified the imposter."

"Eat your dessert, Jon," said Amanda. "You have a meeting at the Palace at two."

"Not another medal ceremony, I hope."

They laughed.

"No," said Amanda. "We had it yesterday. We all received British medals this time, since you apparently drafted us into the British Fleet."

"Huh? I did no such thing. Annabelle yes, I had to commission her, so she could command the ground troops. She was the only flag officer down there I knew I could trust. But the rest of you were just seconded under contract as far as I knew."

"Well someone obviously didn't think so," said Aleesha. "We're all on the inactive list of the British Fleet now, with the same ranks we have in Hunter Security, or their equivalent. All except George, who is kicking himself he let himself be ambushed, and spent the whole time out cold. Lacey looked like he wanted to kill someone when he woke up and found out what they missed. Most of the local defense pilots felt the same. Those on the ground, and on the station. I believe the security around pilots is going to be increased as a result of how easy it was to take them all out."

"Actually," added Amanda, "I think we were promoted, since their fourth officer's grade, which is what I understood us to be, is Captain, and we were commissioned as Major's instead."

"Odd. I expected some confusion from my rank system, but not that. I expect you want to be Lieutenant Colonels now?"

"Hell no," they said together.

"Too much responsibility," added Aleesha.

I grinned at them.

We finished our desserts. The three of us had emptied the platters. As we were getting up, Jane came in with my scooter and guns. The scooter didn't look like it had any damage, but I ran a diagnostic to be sure. Its suit still worked, including the hidey hole I'd built in. I also ran diagnostics on all three guns. Everything working as it should, I had Jane place the guns in the hidey hole, and stepped up onto the scooter. I didn't technically need it now, but scooting was definitively preferable to hobbling. At least for the next couple of days. No doubt I'd get an earful from a Doc in due course about exercise during the rehabilitation period. I could hardly wait.

Out in the Living Room, Angel was belly up on her kitty castle, so I stopped to tickle her. She purred and carried on, so it turned into a full pat-the-kitten session. At last, she lost interest, and went to sleep.

The twins led me out, and down to the Rec Room, where it seemed everyone else was waiting.

I was mobbed.

Thirty Six

The Marshall's Gig arrived at one thirty to take us all down to the Palace. I'd had to tell them all my story, and had heard all of theirs.

I asked why everyone was going, and was told there was a dinner in the evening, but only the one shuttle being provided. It didn't sound right to me, but I held my tongue. Jane was along as well, I noticed, but I assumed she was my actual bodyguard while away from the ship.

We landed on the roof, and I scooted down the stairs at the head of group. Marshall Bigglesworth met us at the bottom.

"Dress Uniforms, please," he said.

Everyone shifted their suits except me. I looked at him for a good thirty seconds, and he stared me down.

"Oh no," I said. "Not again. No more medals."

"Jon," he said, "I promise you're not getting another medal. Dress uniform, please."

I sighed. Something was up, but I wasn't going to get a straight answer out here.

I shifted to Hunter Dress, since I didn't have a British Dress uniform. Bigglesworth didn't comment, even though he would have known I should've been in British Dress. Technically, I was still an active British Admiral.

He led us in. The center section of the ceremony room was laid out with chairs, all empty and waiting for us. The left and right sections were already full of people. Generals Harriman and Price were in the front row of the right section, as was Admiral Bentley. Presumably her fleet was in orbit now. The rest of the row were all Generals and Admirals as well, but I knew none of them.

My seat was in the center of the front row. I stepped off my scooter, and sat, left leg only slightly bent, and positioned comfortably in front of me. Jane took the scooter to a corner of the room, came back, and sat next to me. Annabelle was on my other side, with the others positioned by rank.

On the dot of two, a functionary announced the Queen, and we all stood, while she entered, and sat when bid. Rising and sitting were both awkward for me, but I managed.

"Admiral Hunter, please," said Bigglesworth from his place beside the Queen. "Front and center."

I glared at him, feeling betrayed. Both he and the Queen were keeping their faces straight, but their eyes were gleaming.

I hauled myself out of the chair once again, and hobbled over to stand before them. Bracing to attention wasn't an option.

"Admiral," said Bigglesworth, "if you need your scooter or a chair, please let Colonel Jane know, and she'll bring it to you."

I nodded.

"Nice to see you on your feet, Jon," Queen Liz whispered to me. "You look a lot better than when I last saw you."

I nodded again, not game to say anything.

"Admiral Hunter," she said in her Queen's voice. "You placed your life and assets on the line, in defense of the Monarchy and me personally, without being asked or ordered to. Your people have been thanked by a grateful

Queen, planet, and sector. We are in your debt. How may we reward you?"

For a moment I thought it was just a rhetorical question, but she stood there waiting for an answer.

"Release me from service, so I can go home," I said.

"Done," she said. "Admiral Hunter, you are placed on the inactive list, effective immediately. However this is not enough. Can you kneel?"

"Kneel?" I parroted, feeling confused.

"Kneel," she repeated.

Totally at a loss to understand why, I made an effort to go down on my right knee, trying to keep my left leg extended behind me so it wasn't bent too much. I couldn't hold it, and had to bend the left knee half as much as the right to keep from falling over. I wobbled, trying desperately to keep some balance, and had to place my right hand on the floor in front of me to stay upright. My left leg complained about its treatment, but didn't feel to be taking damage.

I raised my head as much as I could to see in front, but I could no longer see the Queen's face.

There was the noise of metal scraping on metal.

"Jonathon Hunter," she said, "I appoint you Knight Commander of the Order of the British Sector."

Metal touched me on each shoulder, and I saw the end of a very old sword flash though my limited vision range.

Shock took my thoughts away. I desperately wanted to wake up now, as surely this was a bad dream having a go at me.

"You may rise, Knight Commander," said Bigglesworth.

I struggled to get up, but found I couldn't. I pinged Bigglesworth for help. He reached a hand down and pulled me to my feet.

I swayed precariously for a moment, but found some balance. He stepped back, and left me standing there.

My eyes opened wide as I saw not a medal, but what could only be called regalia, passed to the Queen, who seemed to cover me in it.

I looked at her, my eyes pleading for this to be over. She grinned at me for just a second, and it was gone behind her Queen-on-duty face.

"Sir Jonathon Hunter, we have one other presentation to make. The Dukedom of Norfolk is vacant, due to the unfortunate circumstances of the past few days. A family line which has faithfully served the Crown for hundreds of years, is ended by murder, treachery, and treason. As you have demonstrated all the traits needed to warrant your selection, we appoint you Duke of Norfolk. Congratulations."

Shock became poleaxed shock. I stood there, unable to move, unable to think, while more regalia was put on me, and the Queen handed me a plaque of patent. She held out her hand, and I reluctantly shook it.

"I present to you," she said to the room in her Queen's voice, "His Grace, Sir Jonathon Hunter, Duke of Norfolk."

The room went crazy around me.

Thirty Seven

"So, how does this work?" I asked a short time later, sitting in the Queen's sitting room.

"How does what work?" she asked in return, apparently playing dumb.

"This Duke thing?"

Those present laughed. The Queen looked towards one of her aides.

"A Dukedom is more of a ceremonial appointment than anything," the aide said. "In the old days, a Duke was Lord of a Duchy, and ruled it as a vassal of the Crown. He taxed those who lived within the borders, and in turn paid tax to the State. As the Monarchy lost its powers, so did the Dukes. Most of them don't have estates attached now. They represent the Crown for a specific area of influence, as do all titled Lords and Ladies. When the British sector was established, most of the Dukedoms were assigned planets of the same name. So the Duke of Norfolk, your good self, is the highest ranking Noble for the planet Norfolk."

"What duties are involved? I hadn't planned on coming back anytime soon. So I'd rather not have duties requiring me here much, if at all."

"The Dukes advise the Crown about issues to do with their Dukedoms. They play a ceremonial role in the local parliaments. The Duke of Norfolk has always played a role on London as well. We see no problems associated with your not being here. There are other Dukes who will be delighted to take on the roles you aren't here to perform. And on Norfolk, duties can be delegated to the local Earls, who'll also be delighted."

"Sounds like it wasn't a good decision to appoint me."

"The appointment," said the Queen, "was my decision, and my choice. It has some downsides, but ultimately, the Crown needs loyalty and reliability close to it at the moment. I trust you. So do many others now. You'll be called on periodically, but not for everyday matters which can be handled just as well by others."

"You'll be sent information about your role in the British sector," added the aide, "once it's been finalized."

I nodded.

"Besides Jon," said the Queen, "you have title to systems now, and you need to consider how you run them. There are plenty of corporate owned systems, some even owned by individuals, but no-one else owns more than one. And all of them owe allegiance to a sector. Your space is unique. You're already a Duke. If you call your space a Duchy, and run it as such, you'll find yourself accepted far more readily than as someone setting themselves up as a King, or some sort of Despot. Think about it."

"I will. It's all a complete shock to me."

"I know. We anticipated that. It's who you are."

I waved away what I assumed was a compliment.

"Your Battleship will be completed in the morning, Admiral," said Marshall Bigglesworth. "I think you'll find your new title works in your favour as far as calming the fears of those who don't like seeing real power in the hands of an unknown individual. Mercenaries were the way things went for good reasons at the time, but no-one really likes seeing a

Mercenary company capable of being able to hold a planet for ransom, for example. It's how pirates began. Mercenary companies becoming too powerful. If you set up a Duchy, having your own defense force is expected. But a powerful fleet in the hands of an individual, is something to make politicians nervous. Especially having a battle fleet. No-one can fault how you came by your fleet, but everyone will be happy when it has a defensive purpose, and constraints in place."

"To that end, Your Grace," said someone new, "we have documents here for you to consider."

"What sort?" I asked.

"Non-aggression pact, and Alliance. Obviously these cannot be signed until your space has a structure, and a name."

I looked at him for a moment, wondering what I'd dropped into now. Diplomacy wasn't my strong suit. It was looking like I'd need to have a crash course in it. Or find a good diplomat to hire.

"Thank you, I'll look at them on the trip home."

"I'll pulse them to your aide. Once you agree to terms, we can arrange a signing ceremony at a convenient time and place."

"Does the ceremony need to be here?" I asked.

"No Jon," said the Queen. "We seek Alliance with you, so you can specify where the signing takes place."

"No doubt the Australian sector and Sci-Fi sector will also wish the same Alliances," said the official who'd first mentioned them.

"Hmmm. Perhaps we could use my new station once its upgrade has been completed. That will be several months from now, so it gives time for due consideration. I'll think about it, and let you know."

"We look forward to it, Jon," said Queen Liz. She looked around the room. "Now, if you'll all excuse us please."

The room emptied, leaving us alone.

"Now Jon, follow me. Afternoon tea awaits us on my private balcony."

She led me upstairs and around into her private apartment. I scooted behind her through an ornate sitting room to, as she'd said, a balcony, overlooking a private garden. Here were two very comfortable chairs, with a small table between them. We sat, and a functionary offered us tea, and various kinds of cakes.

I hadn't had tea in years. In fact, I remember giving it up as a young teenager, when I figured out the reason I put so much sugar in it, was I didn't really like the stuff. However, it wouldn't be very diplomatic to refuse tea with the Queen. So I loaded in the sugar, and found the blend to be very enjoyable. The Brits really did know about tea. I'd have to think about importing some of the better blends.

We said nothing for a while, while functionaries fussed around us. After a while, she went blank as if receiving a ping, after which she waved them away, and we were left alone.

"I have two personal gifts for you Jon, a way of saying thank you for my life."

She held up her hand to silence me before I could say anything.

"First of all, you sent me a belt which saved me first from injury when we were attacked, and then kept me alive when my own foolishness deprived us of air to breathe. You prevented me from being taken, forced to disband the nobility, and abdicate. You kept me alive at serious risk to your own, even though you were barely able to take care of yourself. I owe you, Jon."

I opened my mouth to say she didn't. But she held her finger to my lips to silence me.

"I do Jon. Stop being so selfless all the time. Anyway, my first gift to you is this."

She threw a feed to the wall behind us. I saw a shipyard, where the airlock doors were opening slowly. Once fully open, a ship emerged. It looked familiar.

"Yes," she said. "I'm giving you a new Gunbus. All your things from the old one which could be salvaged, have been put aboard. Including your kitten's things, and the two figures on the control panel. It also has a set of butler droids, and two top of the line combat suits. By the way, before you go, I want to meet your kitten."

"As you command," I said with a grin on my face.

"Really?" she said with a grin. "Then follow me."

She led me back through the sitting room, hobbling not scooting, and into what must be her own bed chamber. It was so large, you couldn't call it a bed room.

"So," she said with an impish expression. "Your second gift, is me!"

My jaw dropped. She pushed me down into a chair, and proceeded to do a very sexy strip tease for me. I cancelled my arousal override. My suit changed shape slightly to compensate.

When she stood naked in front of me, she pulled me out of the chair, and kissed me full on the mouth, her breasts pushed against my chest. The kiss lasted until we both gasped for air.

"Now Your Grace, let me see how that suit comes off."

One does not say no to a Queen.

Thirty Eight

Precisely at seven that evening, I was guided into the main Dining Room, where I found the rest of my team already seated.

I'd showered and been given a pain shot, which was somewhat late, given we'd not wanted to be disturbed for quite some time. I'd never experienced quite a mixture of pleasure and pain before. It was disturbing on one level, and enjoyable on another. Her Majesty had turned out to be a tiger in bed. Tigress in bed. Actually, bed hadn't figured all that prominently, as we'd discovered ways of avoiding me bending my knees.

I'd had a twinge of concern cross my thoughts at one point. I'd only just said goodbye to Miriam, and here I was in someone else's bed. But Miriam had known she couldn't hold on to me. Long distance relationships with no known next meeting point, were not likely to last. And after all, one didn't say no to the Queen of the British sector. One said "Yes Ma'am", and frequently.

Amanda nudged her sister as I entered, who nudged Alison. They all looked at me as if I was the cat which ate the canary. I popped up a hollo mirror only I could see, in case there was obvious evidence showing of what I'd been up to for the last few hours. I was in Hunter Dress again, and my arousal override was back on. Hollo mirrors weren't as good as regular ones, so there was nothing I could pinpoint, although I did seem to have a grin plastered on my face, and maybe that was enough for them to make assumptions.

I took my place at the table, sending my scooter to a corner, and promptly had to rise again, when the Queen entered. Her eyes flicked to mine, momentarily. It was long enough for Aline to catch, and the other three caught her look.

I wondered what all the fuss was about.

Dinner was as good as the last one I'd had here. But this time I felt a good deal more comfortable. I chatted with those around me, and remembered nothing but the touch of a set of lips against mine, and several other things one doesn't mention in polite company. Or in any company, if one wanted to keep one's head on one's shoulders.

After dinner, coffees stretched out, and a sort of torture set in, being so close to her, and not being able to touch her once again.

On the way back to BigMother, I was asked when we were leaving. I didn't know, and told them it depended on when the Battleship came out of the shipyard, and how long it took Jane to figure out how to dock it with BigMother.

I did tell them to be ready for a Royal inspection at ten in the morning. I didn't tell them the whole reason was so Liz could meet Angel. I hadn't asked why she hadn't met her last time she was aboard, and while I was asleep. She wanted to come aboard, it was the reason given. If it wasn't, I'd find out in due course.

BigMother hadn't re-docked with the station. As we flew past the front section, I noticed the docking clamps which had been cut off the station, were now gone. So she could now dock, but hadn't. I guess my order to undock was still in effect. We were parked far enough away from the station not to interfere with ship movements, but close enough for short shuttle rides.

I thought about that on the way down the lift. It might be a good idea to not dock BigMother in the future, or only dock long enough to unload and load, before undocking and orbiting further away. If the shit was going to hit the fan again sometime, I wanted my combat ships out where they could be most useful, not tied up at a station. Perhaps I could use Gunbus as an executive shuttle. Shuttle being the operative word. There was no way I wanted to go up against a Battleship again in something as small as a Corvette. Lesson learnt. Not only wasn't I paranoid enough, even now, I seemed to be getting gung-ho as well. Stupidity kills on the battle field. It almost had.

Back in my suite, I gave Angel some attention, and went to bed.

I woke up alone the next morning. Even Angel was absent. By six fifteen, showered and kitten patted, I was in my Ready Room, reading emails. Rather surprisingly, I hadn't needed a pain shot. The ache I knew all so well was there, but it wasn't really outright pain anymore. My bruises were yellowing now.

Amy had sent a copy of all the reports she'd filed with the media in the Australian sector. Me, big hero. Hero unavailable due to injury. Hero's forces put down coup. Me getting knighted. Me getting Duke'd. It all came over like a bad soap opera.

Then there were the stories coming from home. Surprise and happiness an Australian should be knighted and appointed as a Duke. Surprise and outright hatred an Australian should sell out to the British Monarchy. Shock that the Australian government had given away systems to an individual person, let alone a kid, especially when they'd refused the mining industry ownership of Nexus since the sector was established. More shock over said kid having a battle fleet which could destroy the whole sector. Calls for the government to take back the systems. Calls for non-aggression and alliance treaties with the new mini-sector. Calls for close military ties to ensure the Australian sector's security. Calls for the Prime Minister to resign.

My eyes glazed over. I didn't need other people's drama. It's why I pay no attention to the media at all. Never have, never intend to.

Politics though, I was going to need to learn how to play that game. Oh joy.

A headline caught my eye and stopped me completely.

OUTBACK FILES TO JOIN HUNTER'S RUN.

I pinged Amy to join me as fast as she could get up here.

She came in five minutes later, looking like I'd roused her from sleep. It was a good look for her, but I doubt she would have agreed if I'd mentioned it. Which I didn't.

I threw the headline to the wall.

"What is that?" I demanded.

"What it says. Outback filed a petition yesterday to leave the Australian sector, so the system can join your new mini-sector. Outback's status has always been something peculiar. They pay their sector tax, but have never participated in the sector government. They pay less tax than any other system, as they've never required anything from the sector. And as the first planet colonized in the sector, the sector constitution left them out of many things which bind the other systems. You should know all that."

"What the hell is Hunter's Run?"

She grinned at me.

"It wasn't me! Honest. Someone in the Sci-Fi sector wrote a story about your trip to Pompeii to rescue the team, and called it the fastest run through that section of space ever done. Someone else picked it up and called the stretch of space through Midnight and Bad Wolf, Hunter's Run. When your ownership of the systems broke, everyone referred to the systems with the name. I think it stuck."

"Bollocks it has!"

"Then you won't want to hear the latest reference."

I sighed.

"No, but tell me anyway."

"You're being called the Duke of Norfolk and Hunter's Run."

I put my head in my hands.

"Speculation is rife," she continued, "on how you structure the new mini-sector. King Jon the first is running at five to one. Duke Jon is at three to one. The next closest is Field Marshall Hunter, the military dictator, at nine to one."

I bashed my head on the desk three times.

"What are you going to do, mini-sector wise?" she asked.

"I haven't decided, and frankly, you're the last person I'll be telling."

"I promise not to file anything until you say I can. I'm contracted to you at the moment, so you do have a say in it."

"I don't know, so there's nothing to tell you. And if you report anything at all, I'll boot your arse out the nearest airlock!"

"Yes, Your Grace."

She grinned at me.

"Anything else I need to know about?"

"The government is tearing itself apart on the Outback issue. But those in the know are saying they really don't have a choice. Outback has the right to leave the sector. Asking was only a courtesy on their part. What most of us journalists want to know though, is how the Outback government even knew about any of this, let alone issuing instructions and filing petitions, given they're non-contactable for another ten odd months. As far as everyone knows, they don't even have an operable receiver on the whole planet at the moment. Or so they tell anyone who asks."

"That is a good question. I'd like to know myself. So Australian sector will allow Outback to leave the sector?"

"The smart money is on yes, but it's going to cost the government big time if they do allow it. It's one more hit on a shaky government. They came into office on the tails of the pirate threat, promising sector defense and stability, and promptly did almost nothing, leaving us at the mercy of Midgard. We dodged that bullet purely because of your forces, the use of mercenaries for sector defense leaving a very sour taste in a lot of mouths, on all sides of politics. The government can't win on this issue. And that will make the Prime Minister a very unhappy man. You better watch out for him at the negotiating table. He'll need to look strong to stay in power, and yet, the need to negotiate with you at all, will be perceived as his fault for giving away the systems in the first place. Makes a politician dangerous, being in that position."

"I'll keep it in mind. Why is giving away the systems a problem? Bad Wolf is practically useless to anyone, and Nexus only has a single ring being mined, which I'm not getting control of. So they gave away mostly empty space, useless rubble, and a few gas giants. What's the big deal?"

"It's the principle of the thing. Never give away territory. The trouble was, the war was kept away from the sector through your actions, and the reward had to match the potential sacrifice. They had no choice, and everyone knew it. General Harriman made enemies though, in proposing it in the first place. Once he suggested it in government circles, it had to happen, as there was nothing else of significant magnitude to reward you with. And as you said, they didn't give away anything important. All the same, politicians don't like being boxed into a corner, and forced to do anything. Remember that."

"I will. I guess I may need to call on your advice."

"I'll add it to my bill."

She grinned at me, and I reluctantly grinned back. I waved her out, and she left.

I went back to emails.

The answer to the Outback question was in an email from David Tollin. His email was encrypted, and I had to get Jane to sort it for me. I threw his vid to a wall.

"Sir Duke Jon," he began with a grin. "Congratulations. I think. Everything is running smoothly on Hunter's Redoubt. Your new stations passed through with no problems, and should be in position in Nexus by now. Your AI's have begun refitting work to Hunter's Haven, although not much can be done without funds. I've setup accounts for all three stations, and for each ship of yours doing trading runs using the AI as captain. If you can drop a few hundred million into Hunter's Haven's account, I can get the material for the refit flowing."

"Regarding your mini-sector, with your permission I'll set up accounts at the sector level. We can talk about how best to structure the sector when you arrive back, but for now, you need accounts separate from your own. You will need them for tax collection, and accounting purposes. Start thinking about how you want to fund your sector, and what sort of administrative structure you want."

He paused, and looked serious all of a sudden.

"No doubt you've heard about Outback filing to leave the Australian sector and join your new mini-sector. This is true, as far as it's known. What isn't known, is a closely guarded secret. I'm sorry to say I've been keeping a few things from you. The day after you left Outback, a Keeper arrived on the Orbital from Gaia. He had sealed instructions from the government, after having called a special session before the Door opened. They were to be opened only when certain events had occurred."

"Jon, we could have brought you back, while you were unconscious in hospital, after Wanderer was attacked. The Keeper called the attack and your hospitalization a sign. He forbade us from bringing you home in a Care Unit, or telling you anything about this. I'm sorry, I know this'll distress you.

It made me really angry at the time, and I took a piece out of the Keeper. It made no difference to him."

I stopped the vid.

So, I was sent here after all. It had never occurred to me I could have been taken home while the Door was open. For a moment it made me very angry to find out all of my suffering of the last two months could have been avoided, and deliberately wasn't.

I'd always known I had something to do with Prophesy, but for them to just cut me adrift like that? Just how cold blooded were the Keepers? Just what sort of game were they playing?

I sighed. My anger dissipated. The answer was always, wait another ten months. Less than ten months now.

I started the vid again.

"Jon, this is where it gets really weird. The instructions were to be opened when word was received of two events happening close together. Knowledge of the two events was date coded as well, so we only found out the events were significant on the days they happened. The first was your being given ownership of Nexus, Bad Wolf, and Midnight. The second was your being appointed Duke by the British Queen."

"Jon, they knew! There's no other explanation. If we ever needed something tangible to say you are entwined with prophesy, this is it."

"Only the Keepers know what prophesy actually is. No-one knows if this is prophesy unfolding, or not. But whatever the Darkness is, I think we can say for certain now, it's coming. In any case, when news of you gaining ownership of systems reached Outback, I was called back to Outback Orbital, as it was another pre-instruction I be here when the instructions were opened, which happened when we heard you were now a Duke. Inside, we found the petition to leave the Australian sector, and another one to join 'Hunter's Run'. We didn't know the name existed until media sources pointed it out to us when we asked them."

"Jon, regardless of the Australian sector's decision, we are instructed to join your mini-sector immediately. When the Door opens, the government will defer to you. Effectively, you are the government of Outback now!"

I stopped it again, and sat there in a state of total shock.

None of this made any sense at all.

After ten minutes sitting there with a non-functioning mind, I restarted the vid.

"I'm heading back to Hunter's Redoubt as soon as I send this off to you. I used one of your fast freighters, which is run by your AI, and only has life support in the Bridge area. Not comfortable, but the fastest way to get about in a hurry. Outback's administration on Outback Orbital will handle all contact with the Australian sector government. My job is to prepare your mini-sector to become an official entity. I'll do some options for you to consider, and send them as soon as I can. The faster you get a structure in place, the better. Until you do, all sorts of things can't happen, which need to as soon as possible."

"I can see you sitting there as stunned as I was. I'm sorry I don't have any real answers for you. But I can pick up one end of the burden for you. I suggest you return to Nexus as fast as you can get here. Pick me up on your way through. See you then."

The vid ended, and I just sat there.

Every time I think nothing more can possibly be done to me, it turns out I'm wrong.

Hooley, bloody, Dooley.

Thirty Nine

It took me a while to get it together, and respond to David.

I told him to do whatever he thought was needed to be done, and I'd be there as soon as I could. I reminded him the shipyard could build droids, and all he had to do was ask Janine, the AI, to build what was required. If he needed to source materials, he was to go ahead and do so. I transferred five hundred million into the Hunter's Haven account, as I wondered where the name had come from, since it hadn't been me naming either of my stations. For now, it would suffice.

I also transferred one hundred million into the shipyard account for resources. It was going to need an upgrade at some point as well. The life support system was completely inadequate for a start, being manually looked after. Its building systems were far too manual as well. Before it could function as a modern shipyard, it would need to be modernized.

By eight I'd waded through a lot of bounty payments, real estate advertisements, porn links, and general junk. One of the real estate ads informed me for a measly fifty million, I could own my own island on Gold Coast. I took a moment to look at it properly. It was an interesting idea. What was a better idea, was renting one to use for a holiday once I was able to shuck everyone else's responsibilities I kept having dumped on me.

Get back to Nexus, start the mini-sector ball rolling, sit on a beach, and watch the twins skinny dipping. Sounded like a plan to me.

As if the thought evoked their notice, I was pinged by Amanda.

"Come down to breakfast, Your Grace."

The giggle on the end told me how seriously she took the title.

I scooted to the access shaft, dropped down a level, and missed the handrail. I twirled in the air, bounced off the wall, and dropped like a stone. I regained control only meters up from the Cargo Deck at the bottom. The scooter bounced, and I shot back up again, once again missing the Deck Two handrail, and banging my head against the top of the shaft, before starting down again.

This time I managed to grab the rail on Deck One, and slide myself out. I leaned against the wall and placed my forehead against it for a minute.

"Are you coming or not?" pinged Amanda.

I was really tempted to answer that, but thought better of it in time.

This time, I scooted down the stairs.

As usual, I was the last person there. I left my scooter in a corner, and hobbled over to my chair. I'd no sooner sat down, than a streak of white shot in the door, did a circuit of the room, and shinned up my left leg to plop down in my lap.

Meow.

There was a general titter of laughter as I patted the puss.

"Any word on when we can leave, boss?" asked BA.

"Eager to be away are we?" I asked generally.

There were nods all round. I felt the same. We'd been here too long, even in spite of me sleeping a lot of it away.

"The Queen is here at ten. Once she leaves, assuming the Battleship is out of the shipyard by then, we can be off soon after. By the way BA, I meant to ask how your new toys are."

"New toys? You mean the combat suits? Absolutely first rate!"

The grin told me more than the words. There were nods around the table as well. The pilot's looked puzzled.

So was I. I hadn't actually been referring to the suits.

"Jane," I subvocalized, "did we get the special backpacks with the new combat suits?"

"Negative," she responded through my PC.

I pinged the local 'tool man' to ask about them. He pinged back immediately saying they'd been harder to do than thought, and the order had been completed only the night before. I pinged him back I was sending a shuttle to pick up the order, and asked Jane to send an avatar with the shuttle.

I pinged the shipyard to find out about the Battleship. The response was more expansive than I'd anticipated, and made me realize I'd not checked up on the Guardians before now. All the Guardians were still at the shipyard, but would be ready to go in about an hour. The Battleship would be ready by noon.

"Battleship will be out by noon," I said into a silent moment. Silent except for the chomping of food. "Give it an hour to dock all the ships, and assuming Her Majesty is gone by then, we can be off."

"Good," said Annabelle. "Can I see you after breakfast?"

"Sure, when you're ready."

She nodded, and went back to eating.

"BigMother will be ready for docking by noon as well," said Jane through my PC.

"Ready for docking?" I asked sub-vocally. "What have you been up to now?"

"I've had to make some changes to allow the Battleship to dock under BigMother. The middle two rear docking pods needed upgrading to be able to support one battleship instead of two Guardians. It means Custer won't be able to dock underneath either. I assumed you still wanted to be able to dock BigMother at stations, so the Battleship will stick out the back a ways. The changes to the Battleship included a docking airlock in the topside, to match the one Custer uses. The Guardians by the way, are still there because I ordered docking ports on both sides, so they'll dock with our Cargo Deck airlocks, and allow another ship to dock on the other side of them. Between the docking ports is now a life supported corridor, allowing people to walk through from an outside docked ship. So we dock two to the sides, and two underneath. The new Gunbus also has a new airlock on her other side, so she can also dock to both sides."

"I'm glad you thought about all of that."

"Someone had to."

"True."

"What's all the nodding about, boss?" asked BA.

"Jane was updating me with ship modifications. Oh, BA? After breakfast, take whoever wants to go down to the Launch Deck with you. There's an order coming in on a shuttle, which will need transfer to the Armoury."

"What sort of order?"

"Some new guns."

"Do we need more?"

"I thought so."

"Okay, will do."

Annabelle met my eyes, and I gave her the double eyebrow raise. She smiled.

Angel launched herself off my lap and hit the floor running, shooting out the door, bound who knows where. Maybe she'd heard her own breakfast being opened or something.

I rose, hobbled over to my scooter, mounted, looked at Annabelle and nodded, and scooted out. I went up the stairs this time, rather than risk being found at the bottom of the shaft in a heap. In my Ready Room, I settled into my chair behind my desk, and carried on with emails.

Annabelle came in a short time later.

"You want to go collect your other teams," I said to her, before she could seat herself.

She grinned at me.

"Yes. Can I?"

"Take Custer. It'll be good experience for George to captain her for a while. Act like an Admiral for him, but let him make as many of the decisions as you can, as well as flying the ship. That ship needs a full Commander as captain, but he hasn't the experience yet. Maybe this trip will give him some."

"I seriously hope not." We both grinned. "Who can I take?"

"Abigail and Alison are needed here. Anyone else who wants to go, can."

"I'll find out. Can I take combat suits in case we need them?"

"Sure. Take what you need. Be a good test for George if he remembers to make sure Custer has enough food to get you wherever you need to go and back. Actually, regarding that, I'll drop some funds in the ship account in case you need to buy anything. Any idea how long it'll take to return to Nexus?"

"Maybe a month, but I won't know until I contact each team and find out exactly where they are, and any time constraints they have if they currently have contracts. I've let them run independently for a while now, so I've not been in touch as much as I should've."

"Sounds like the sort of adjustment you make between being a Colonel, and a General."

"Very true. Do you want me to continue to act as a General? I was thinking there wasn't really much need now the war is over."

"I'll be thinking about roles on the way home, along with a lot of other things. Now I have my own mini-sector, the need for a properly organized military is even more important than as a Mercenary unit. So I can see a permanent role for a General. You may end up overseeing station security forces as well. There's only so much an AI and droids can do as far as interfacing with humans, so we'll need some security people. The General could supervise each station security head, as well as the Colonel in charge of each combat team."

"Sounds feasible."

"Are you interested?"

"It comes with the star. I always wanted the star, so I knew what I was wishing for. Besides, I'm getting too old for leading troops into battle. Azgard nearly killed me, and I've been thinking about it ever since."

"Look out for good people to recruit. You heard the Marshall. They think my role is to bring all the best of the Mercs under my control. I'll need you to tell me who they are, and do the recruiting."

"Isn't that a two star's role?" she said with a laugh.

"Find me a decent one star to lead the troops into battle, and I might just give you the second one."

I grinned at her. She grinned back.

"I'll go tell George to warm up Custer, and see who else wants to come along."

I waved her out, and she left. I pinged Lacey to come see me.

I dropped a million into Custer's ship account. If they needed to buy food or ordnance, it should be enough. If they needed more, then something big would be going down, and I'd probably need to join them.

Lacey bounded in about fifteen minutes later.

"Sorry sir. The squadron was out doing a fly around. We were going stir crazy sitting here doing nothing, so I decided we should get some flying in, while you were entertaining the Queen."

Come to think of it, I hadn't seen them at breakfast.

"Sorry to call you in. Are the others still out there?"

"Yes. George is teaching the others the finer points of the Excalibur."

"Ah. He's about to be called in then. Custer is going off on a mission as soon as the Queen leaves."

"Should I call them all in?"

"Up to you. But I called you here to give you orders."

"Yes sir."

"I want 266 to fly point for BigMother on the way home. I'd suggest a V formation on Camel, about half an hour ahead. Use your discretion though. I want anyone coming towards warned away from us, and the other side of jump points cleared before we come through. Use your AI to communicate with Jane, to co-ordinate the jumps. I don't want a repeat of that idiot who collided with us on the way here. I want to get home in a hurry, but we'll use a cruising speed, not top speed, so it'll give you time after the jumps to reestablish a lead zone."

"We can do that, sir. I'd best get the lads to land then, as we'll all need to transfer our gear to our ships."

"Okay, better have them wait until the Queen departs before you launch again. Get a butler to organize the transfer of food and drink as well, and make sure you all have more than double you think is enough. Who knows what may waylay us on the journey."

"You do seem to have that sort of luck, sir."

I looked at him to see if he was joking, but apparently not. I nodded to him.

"I'll get on with it, sir."

He stood, saluted, and left.

Forty

By ten I was standing on my scooter down on the Launch Deck.

The Queen's shuttle was on its way down. Everyone was here, but milling about waiting.

BA came up to me, kissed me full on the lips, and hugged me, scooter and all.

"What was that for?" I asked her when she let me go.

"I've always wanted to be able to use a Meson Blaster, but it was never feasible to lug around a tripod for it when you're running in a combat suit, and without the power unit in the tripod, one couldn't be fired. Now I can. Annabelle told me it was your idea, so thank you. The backpack won't upset the balance of the combat suit at all, and integrates so well, the only thing you notice is the power levels being much higher. I gave it a serious workout. I can carry two Meson Blasters now, while running flat out, and fire the inbuilt stunners at the same time. Seriously bad-arse!"

We high fived.

"I was thinking about what would happen if the team went up against another team with similar equipment. It seemed like an innovation which would give us an edge. For a while anyway."

"That it will."

Her grin was Cheshire cat level. The shuttle appeared on the lift.

"Ranks please General," I said towards Annabelle.

She barked a command, and everyone formed up behind me.

A cargo droid pulled the shuttle towards us, and stopped it so the Queen could step down in front of us. Another cargo droid pushed a set of stairs into place. The hatch opened, and Queen Liz stepped out, followed by her entourage. General's Harriman and Price followed along after, with aides in tow.

Annabelle looked ready to give another command, but was beaten to it by the Queen.

"No protocol, please," she said. "This is a social call, not a state visit."

"Social call?" I said.

"Yes Your Grace, social call. In fact, I'm here on false pretenses." She indicated a lady behind her, who was carrying a bag. "I'm actually here to make sure you get a proper medical checkup before you leave, and get yourself into who knows what kind of trouble next. This is Dr. Whiteman, my personal physician."

I looked at her dumbfounded. Behind me I could hear sniggers being suppressed. I looked around sharply, and a sea of respectful faces stared forwards.

"Come along, Your Grace, your quarters please." She turned to Annabelle. "Could you give a tour to the rest of my entourage please?"

"Of course, Your Majesty."

She looked towards the group, and waved a hand towards the launch bays.

The two General's came up to me before I could be hustled away.

"I offered General Price a lift," said Walter. "Hope that's okay."

"Sure," I said. "Follow us up, and pick a VIP suite each which doesn't have a name on the door. Have a butler droid bring your stuff up for you. Your aides should be able to find spare suites further along the deck."

"Come along, YOUR GRACE!" bullied the Queen.

I scooted towards the access shaft, and they followed along after. At the shaft, I checked they all knew how to use it, and gently wafted myself up to the Cargo Deck. I was the first in, and the last out. But I wasn't taking any chances with missing the exit rail.

The others boarded a trolley, and I scooted along next to them. I did think of scooting a different direction, but I doubted I could hide long enough for it to matter. It was a big ship, but not that big.

We all made the jump up to Deck Two successfully, with me again bringing up the rear. The Queen looked to be enjoying herself.

I waved the Generals on down the passage way, and entered my suite. The Queen and the doctor followed me in, the doctor shutting the door behind us.

"Please lock the door," the doctor said to me. "I don't want us being disturbed."

I did so, sending it a lock code through my PC, but wondered why. No-one was going to disturb us anyway. If I was wanted, I'd be pinged.

Angel sat up from where she'd been sleeping on her kitty castle. Queen Liz and the doctor hurried over to her, and

Angel was delighted to meet them. After a good pat, the doctor turned back to me.

"Bedroom?" she asked.

I sighed, and pointed it out. She waved me to go in, and followed me.

I spent the next fifteen minutes in my briefs and belt, being prodded and poked, tested, and investigated.

"You're bruising is coming along nicely," she said. "Try not to damage yourself again before they heal. You should have full movement of the knee again within a few days. Make sure you eat properly, and drink enough."

She went over to the door.

"He's all yours, ma'am," she said as she went through, leaving me sitting on the bed in my briefs.

Queen Liz came straight in, and closed the door after her. She stood there looking at me, with a grin on her face.

"Actually," she said, "my false pretense was a false pretense."

She laughed, and came over to me, pushing me back onto the bed. Her suit changed to a belt. She pulled off the skimpy top she was wearing underneath, and then the lacy knickers. She practically tore my briefs off me, jumped onto the bed next to me, and straddled over me. Without thinking, I checked her for hairpins, but didn't see any. I relaxed, and switched off my arousal override.

"I just wanted to give you a proper send off," she said huskily.

We just made it to the Dining Room for lunch, before everyone else started without us.

Aleesha opened her mouth to say something, and Amanda clamped a hand over it before she could. They silently did their communion thing together for a moment, and then pretended to be interested in their drinks.

The presence of the Queen put a bit of a dampener on the usual lunch atmosphere, but for all that, it was an enjoyable meal, in spite of an intense effort on both our parts not to make eye contact and exchange cheesy grins. All too soon it was over, and the Queen and her party were departing.

I watched the shuttle disappearing up the lift with mixed feelings. She was a really fun person to be with. But she was Queen, and I needed to be somewhere else. It would never work. I sighed.

I turned to head to the Bridge, and Annabelle caught my eye.

"You can leave now if you want," I said to her. "How did George go with preparations?"

"He remembered the food and the beer, but not the drinking water."

We both laughed.

"Keep me informed of where you are, please. Daily report. If I don't get one, I'll assume you're in trouble, and come after you. Always have Jane encrypt your emails too. And don't let anyone send unencrypted ones which give away your whereabouts or anything else important. Given recent events, let's assume hostile intent is following us all the time now."

"Yes sir. Good attitude. See you in about a month."

The 266 pilots had already disappeared, heading for their ships.

The rest of us made the jump up to the Cargo Deck, where those going on Custer climbed on a waiting trolley. I watched it heading away. The last time I'd watched my friends go, I'd thought they'd died not long after. This time, I was sending them off. Part of me hoped it wasn't going to be a one way trip for them. I told myself to get a grip. They had a well-protected Frigate, for divine's sake. In any case, this was something I was going to have to get used to, sending people off on missions without me.

I found myself alone, and scooted for the access shaft upwards.

When I arrived at the Bridge, I found more people there than I'd expected.

The two Generals were in the VIP seats. Jane was at the XO's console, instead of her normal place next to the helm position. Abagail was at the Coms console. Amanda and Aleesha were on each side of the helm. Angel was on her pad, and the girls were tickling her. Aline was next to Amanda. Alison was next to Aleesha. Amy was in her usual seat at the rear. On the other side from Amy, was Walter's aide, but I couldn't recall her name. The man next to her, wearing what seemed to be a combined smirk, sneer, and frown, was presumably General Price's aide. Slice and Eric made up the full company, seated in front of Amy.

I sat in my captain's chair, and felt really glad to be back in it.

"Sitrep," I said to Jane.

"Custer is away, and moving to the Washington jump point. The Battleship is about ten minutes out, waiting for us, as are the Guardians. Gunbus is on the rear right Flight

Deck. Apricot One is on the left side. Midnight Orchid is above us for the moment, waiting for a place to dock. I had a new set of side airlocks put in her, so she can dock side on. Nascaspider is docked to her. There was a last minute request for us to take some cargo to the Australian sector, so I sent Zippy to collect it. It'll take two trips for her, but she'll complete the second one before we make the Verse jump point. I'll dock her to the forward main cargo airlock, and offload onto the Cargo Deck. By the time we dock all the ships, it'll be the only airlock left."

"Move us out," I commanded her.

"Confirmed."

BigMother turned and started towards the Battleship, clearly seen in the distance. Price's aide's expression took on more of a frown.

When we arrived, I nodded to Jane.

"Let's get the Hives bedded down in their new home Jane."

"Confirmed."

The twelve Hive clusters, docked on the top hull of Big-Mother, all launched. Jane threw vids up which allowed us to see them head around the ship, on both sides, and enter the side of Unassailable through six docking ports on each side of her.

It took Jane half an hour to line up and dock all seven ships.

The Battleship was down the centerline. She was connected to the same airlock Custer had just left, and to two support docks at the rear. She stuck out a long way behind us, being a good quarter longer than BigMother. I'd have to consider if I kept the name of Unassailable for her, or re-named her. It was a bit pretentious, even for a Battleship.

Two of the Guardians were docked alongside her. The other two were along BigMother's sides. Midnight Orchid was docked to the side of the one on the right, and Nascaspi-der was now docked to the Guardian to the left.

"What did you do to the Battleship?" asked Walter.

"I redesigned her to be a drone Hive carrier. BigMother was designed for standard fighters, and can't really carry enough of the drones. As a dedicated Hive carrier, the Hives can launch and dock without separating into separate ships."

"Seriously?" asked Price. "What else did you do to her?"

I threw the specification to a side screen, and told Jane to get us moving to the Verse jump point.

"I left her original guns alone, but the inside was substan-tially gutted. The only remaining life support is Deck Three. It has a CCC, Ready Room, and Conference room layout, pretty much the same as what we're sitting in now. Deck Two here is duplicated there, with accommodation for one hun-dred troops as well, with the normal Armoury, bathrooms, spa baths, and gyms. There are five airlocks, two in each of the sides, and one topside with an access shaft."

"Along her sides has been put two hundred capital mis-sile launchers in groups of twenty five, and six Hive docking ports for a full length storage and maintenance deck. The rest of the side space has as much Point Defense as could be fitted on. She has a full length Cargo Deck with the stan-dard forward cargo airlock. The access shaft to Deck Three goes to the Cargo Deck to allow people to use the Cargo airlock to access stations, but seals to maintain air integrity, as that deck will normally be kept in vacuum when people don't need to use it."

"The power plants were substantially augmented, and the engines overhauled and updated. She matches BigMother for speed now, and if we fire up her engines while docked, we should be able to increase BigMother's speed by twenty five percent."

"That's totally outrageous!" said Slice, in an awed tone.

"Isn't it just?" I said with a grin. "The destroyed Bridge area was replaced with a Mosquito firing system, with ten launchers. The idea was to make her into an all-purpose assault ship, with drone carrier being her primary role. It frees up BigMother to be a command ship with a conventional fighter capacity, and to be a central docking hub for her fleet."

I popped the specs screen off, and looked around at all of them.

"Its four hours to the jump point, so do whatever you feel like doing. I'll be in my Ready Room if anyone wants me."

Forty One

The Generals followed me in, with their aides following behind.

I changed direction from my desk to the conference table. The two figures were still at the end of the table, but I noticed the table itself had now been repaired.

"Nice figures," said Price's aide, now with a definite sneer, looking towards that end of the table.

"Gifts I was happy to receive," I said, in a tone which indicated he was out of order.

"My temporary aide, Commander Pyne," said Price. "My normal aide went down sick just before I was due to leave on this trip. The Commander's last assignment was captain of a Destroyer, but he's getting some administration experience now, in the hopes we give him a Cruiser next."

Pyne opened his mouth, but Walter cut him off.

"I don't think you ever met my aide officially, have you Admiral?" I shook my head in the negative, looking at her. I'd seen her a number of times, but didn't know her name. "Lieutenant Colonel Petersen."

"Gloria, when I'm off duty, Admiral," she said with a smile.

She was a petite redhead. I idly wondered if the red hair was natural, and had to mentally slap myself back into the present. I smiled back at her, and waved everyone to the table. It occurred to me, I'd never actually noticed her rank before. It was always her dazzling smile I remembered. Concentrate.

"Let me guess," I said. "You have documents for me, and want to talk about Non-aggression and Alliance treaties?"

Both Generals grinned at me.

"Let me get my aide up here to join us."

I pinged Alison to be here five minutes ago. She walked in a few seconds later, so she must have assumed I'd call her when the Generals headed in after me. I introduced her. As a Major, she was low rank at the table.

"The British have already been talking to you?" asked Walter.

"Indeed. Alison has their documents for me to look over, when I get a chance on the way home."

She nodded to me. I hadn't actually checked before if she'd received them or not.

"So send her yours," I continued, "and I can look them all over together. But it'll be a while before anything can be signed. I need to sort out how I organize the mini-sector first, not to mention a name for it. I told the British we could hold a signing ceremony on my new station, once its upgrade is complete. About two months I would think, give or take."

The General's both nodded. The three aides took on a blank look as they pinged and pulsed each other. We sat and waited for them to finish.

Alison nodded to me again, indicating she had the documents.

"Do we need aides from now on?" I asked the Generals.

"No, I don't think so," said Price.

"Alison, you're off duty for the rest of the day. We'll make a time tomorrow for looking at documents."

Both the girls rose and left, but Pyne lingered.

"Admiral, if I may ask a question?" he said.

"Sure. Questions cost nothing. Answers though, they can be expensive."

He looked at me as if I was stupid. His boss grinned suddenly, and stifled it with a hand over a cough.

"I was wondering sir, why you don't operate with a full crew? No helmsman for example. I was watching you and your XO, but I couldn't see how the ship started moving."

"Very simple, Commander, the ship is run by an AI."

"You trust an AI to run a ship?"

His surprise made a slight dent in the perpetual sneer he seemed to wear all the time. He reminded me a bit of Breckenridge, when he'd first come aboard.

"You have a problem with AI's, Commander?"

"Yes, sir. They're not human. They can't be trusted to look after the interests of people first. And if the ship loses its computer for whatever reason, you suddenly have a ship with crew who can't handle things manually."

"So you follow the conventional military doctrine of no automation is the best automation."

It wasn't a question.

"Of course, sir. I don't understand why you don't."

"Because, Commander," I emphasized his rank, "the Midgard war taught us that people don't have the reflexes or brain power to protect us adequately."

"I don't believe that, sir. People should always have total control."

I looked at him.

The lights flickered for a second.

"Perhaps the Commander would like to go to his suite, and call up the battle feeds from the war. It's obvious you haven't seen them."

"Ah, no sir. I mean, yes sir. I mean, no sir I've not seen them, and yes sir, I'll go view them now. Sir."

He rose, looked to his boss for dismissal, received a nod, and left.

I started chuckling the moment he was out of the room, and the Generals joined in.

"In his defense," began Price.

A long blood curdling shriek echoed into the room, abruptly cut off, which had all three of us on our feet in seconds.

Price started for the door.

"Wait a second, General," I said.

He stopped and turned back towards me, real concern on his face.

"Jane," I said, "what did you do?"

A pop-up on the wall showed a cam view of the inside of the access shaft, near the bottom. Pyne was hanging in space a meter off the deck, upside down, whimpering.

I couldn't help it, I burst out laughing. Harriman was right behind me, and Price joined in when he found he couldn't help himself. We all sat again.

"Are you going to put him down Jane?"

"Not yet," came through the coms.

Pyne suddenly shot upwards, feet first. He shrieked again, as his legs came to a stop at the top of the shaft, a hand's width from the top. Then he dropped again, arms and legs waving madly, mouth making incoherent sounds, before stopping abruptly half way down. He vomited the contents of his stomach in one projectile like mass, which sped away below him. But before it hit the deck, it seemed to congeal into a solid mass, and swept around the shaft before heading back upwards straight at Pyne's face. He desperately tried to protect himself with his hands, but at the last second it veered off, and started to circle around him. The whimpering grew louder.

"Put him down Jane, gently please."

"Yes, my Master," she replied in a voice several octaves lower than normal.

Pyne dropped again, with another blood curdling shriek, stopping head down just above the deck. His body rolled so he was lying horizontal, face up. He wafted the remaining distance like a feather, and settled on the deck more gently than he ever did on his bed.

The vomit mass streaked down, and hit him square in the face.

We all lost it.

Jeeves walked up to the hapless Commander, and looked down at him.

"Oh dear, dear, dear," he said.

He picked up one of Pyne's feet, and started to drag him along the corridor. Pyne struggled, but was unable to do anything except make his position worse. The screen followed them along, shifting from cam to cam, and into his suite. Jeeves took him straight into the bathroom and deposited him in the shower. The water started full on, right into his face. Pyne screamed again, and desperately pushed himself out of the water flow.

"Oh dear," Jeeves said again. "Someone left the water set to hot. Let me fix it for you."

The water flow lessened. Pyne tentatively tested the water, found it acceptable and stuck his head under the flow.

Jeeves left him there. The screen shut off.

"And that gentlemen," I said, "is why you never insult an AI who controls the ship."

"Confirmed," came through the room coms.

We all lost it again.

Forty Two

I sent Alison in to see if he needed medical attention.

It wasn't clear from the vid if he was burned or not. She pinged me back he was fine. The water had been hot, but not scalding.

The three of us spent the rest of the afternoon talking mini-sector stuff, although there wasn't much brought up which hadn't already been by the Brits. Still, it was a very useful discussion.

Just before six, the Generals headed down to dinner, and I took my chair on the Bridge. Custer would already have jumped out, because although the distances were about the same, and we'd been heading away from each other, they'd had a head start.

The London system was a bit strange. The Verse and Washington jump points were opposite each other across the system. But if you stood at the Verse jump point and looked towards the Washington one, there were another three jump points to your right, and none to your left. The closest one to us now, was the one to Cambridge, with Norfolk on the other side of that system. The middle jump point led to Leeds, and the other one to Oxford. Bentley's fleet had headed out through Oxford on their wild goose chase the other day.

266 squadron were already on the other side, in Verse. There were several ships coming towards, but all angled away from us, obviously warned to stay clear.

By ten past, the trickle of ships coming through had stopped.

Jane brought me up to date, with the only thing new being Zippy completing her two runs for cargo, and now being downstairs in her apartment sleeping.

I'm not sure Jane's little episode earlier had been a good thing for her. If anything she now sounded more eccentric than before, and I hadn't thought that was possible.

Lacey sent us the okay to jump, and we found a short line of ships waiting on the other side, well out of the way. 266 went to top speed, while Jane brought us back up to cruising speed. The latter was about eighty five percent of top speed, so we were still breaking speed expectations for such a large ship.

I looked up the Verse system, since I had no first-hand knowledge of it. What I found amazed me.

Verse is a huge system, one of the largest ever found. None of the now handful of planets and over a dozen moons which are habitable, were so to begin with. The system was terraformed in stages. The interesting thing was, there wasn't very much terraforming needed to make them viable.

The system has two suns. The first one was much bigger and hotter than Earth's, so the so called goldilocks zone was much further out than for normal Earth type suns, and much wider. Well beyond that zone, was a much smaller sun orbiting the first one, as if what might have been a gas giant had achieved ignition in its own right. It had its own goldilocks zone.

The dynamics of the system were intense, and sometime in the past, there must have been major collisions, as what were in effect two solar systems, interacted with each other. But the forces operating in the system had either destroyed or moved anything likely to hit something else, resulting in the primary goldilocks zone having more than a usual number of planets, and the secondary zone not directly interacting with the primary, although it rotated around the primary sun, which wasn't itself affected by the second one. So by the time people found the system, it had two stable sets of planets and moons. But the dynamics of the system changed all the time.

The planets and moons vary from one extreme to another as far as climates go, and it's a busy system. However, it's also a very insular system, in so far as not a lot of local traffic ever leaves. The main traffic heading out the two jump points on either side, are those heading up and down the spine on long hauls. A lot of in-system trade is handled by small freighters, who move what's needed from those settlements and cities with too much, to those with too little. The Firefly class small freighter, of which I had one in my trading fleet, was born here, and is a popular choice for a system where space stations hadn't been established as normal, and landing on dirt was essential.

The position of the second sun dictated the best way to cross the system. It was going to take us twelve hours.

I headed down to dinner.

As there weren't many of us now, everyone was sitting up one end of the table, leaving me with the head. I took my seat. A streak of white shot in the door behind me, did a circuit of the room, and ended up in my lap. A white head poked up over the edge of the table, and the rest of her boosted up onto it. She sat beside me looking very pleased with herself.

Pyne's sneer became a frown. His experience of the afternoon hadn't done anything to change his attitude. However, when Jeeves appeared to take our dinner orders, he jumped and looked like he would prefer to be somewhere else. We all made a point of ignoring him, but several smiles showed an effort being made to not laugh out loud.

Angel proceeded to wash herself, and gave those down the table an excellent view of cat butt. The frown deepened.

Conversation was general, without ranks intruding. This brought on yet another deepening of the frown.

When Jeeves and Jason brought us food, Angel's dinner bowl was put down in front of her as well. One would expect Angel to have been the messier eater there, but not so. Amanda recounted a particularly funny story, and Alison knocked her drink over while laughing too hard. The frown threatened to break the face wearing it.

I pondered the Commander, and came to the conclusion he was the sort of military martinet who expects order and rigid adherence to orders, especially his. He was completely out of his element here, and with zero authority, could do nothing about it.

When Jeeves took his empty plate away from him without warning, he practically fell out of his chair. He settled himself, mumbling under his breath.

"Something to say, Commander?" I asked him.

"No sir."

"My mistake. I could have sworn I saw your lips moving."

"Nothing important, sir."

"I take it you've never had any experience of butler droids before?"

"No, sir."

"I guess you'd prefer human servants?"

"Ah, yes sir."

"Feel free to volunteer Commander, no-one else is going to."

He went red. I swear I saw Jeeves wink at me.

We managed to finish dessert without any further problems. Angel jumped down into my lap, and then to the floor, where she shot out the door. We all moved into the Rec Room, where Aline had me throw the next lot of 'Who' episodes to the entertainment system. The first episode was full of explanations for those who hadn't seen 'Who' before. Pyne made it through ten minutes before heading for his suite, mumbling to himself again as he went. I guess to his orderly mind, we were all mad. The thought had me chuckling for several minutes.

After the second episode, I told everyone the next jump was at six fifteen in the morning, and everyone should feel free to sleep through it. I said goodnight, and headed back to my suite. The hobble was almost a limp now, and I'd accepted I needed to exercise to get proper movement back.

My bruises were aching much more so than they had been all day, but considering I'd not needed a pain shot at all, I was doing very well. Angel was asleep in her cat bed, so I left her alone, and went into the bathroom. I stripped off and dropped into the spa, intending to soak for a half hour or so, and get an early night.

About five minutes later, Aline walked in, silently stripped off, and dropped in beside me. Several minutes later,

Alison did the same. And predictably, a few minutes later, so did the twins.

No-one said anything. We soaked in silence.

The silence became uncomfortable.

Eventually Amanda cleared her throat, breaking it.

"Um," she said, pausing, "Jon, what's been going on between you and the Queen?"

"Going on?" I asked innocently.

"You don't do the raw prawn very well, Jon," said Alison. "Fess up!"

"We know something was going on," said Aleesha.

"And it's your business, because?"

"We care about you, Jon," said the twins together.

"I get that, but what's the worry?"

"A Queen can have anyone she likes. We don't want you used like a play toy, and thrown away."

I laughed.

"It wasn't like that."

"How was it then?" asked Aline.

"Alison knows."

"Me?" said Alison. "Why would I know?"

"Because the situations were identical."

"Oh."

I could see the wheels turning in four heads. 'Thank you for saving my life sex' was something they understood.

"What about Miriam?" asked Amanda.

"We parted on good terms, knowing it could be a long time before we see each other again. We both recognized any attempt at a long distance relationship wasn't going to work. She has her dream job, in her dream ship, and isn't going to leave it for anything. I have responsibilities now a long way away. It was fun, but that's it for now. In the meantime, when a Queen says jump, one says 'Yes ma'am'!"

They giggled.

"It's sweet you all care," I went on, "but it's not as if anything is happening with any of you at the moment. Your code doesn't seem to allow it."

"Only true for Alison now, Jon," said Aleesha.

"Oh? What changed?"

"The new rank structure," said Amanda. "Alison is the only one under your direct command now. In separating out infantry from fleet and pilots, and establishing a command group outside them, you no longer are our direct boss."

"I told you that last time we had this conversation."

"It was different then."

"No it wasn't."

"It was, Jon," said Aleesha. "Then it was you, Annabelle, and us. Direct command line. Now, Annabelle is the head of the Infantry arm of your organization, while you're head of the command staff arm."

I shook my head. It was too subtle for me to see. But if it was going to make them happier, I was all for the distinction.

"Fine," I said. "Where does that leave us then?"

"Horny," said Aline.

We all laughed.

Forty Three

I woke up with Aline draped over me.

After the others left, she'd proved that good things come in small packages. She was the shortest of the merc team, owing to her Oriental forbears. I didn't feel like I'd had much sleep. Jane whispered the time in my ear, I extracted myself without waking Aline up, and headed for the Bridge.

We were fifteen minutes to jump. I made myself comfortable. There was no real reason for being here, but I felt the need in case something happened.

"Man overboard," said Jane, in a matter of fact voice.

"What?" I responded, incredulously.

A pop-up screen showed a white mass roughly the size of a man, outside the ship, and falling behind rapidly.

"Stop," I said.

"Confirmed."

"What or who was that?"

Another screen popped up. It showed the inside of a suite. A man was sleeping. Three butler droids entered, put a belt around the man without waking him up, proceeded to strip the bed with the man still in the sheets, bundled the sheets up, and then carried it all out. Cams followed them to the nearest maintenance airlock, where the bundle was pushed in, and the airlock cycled.

Laughter exploded out of me, at the same time I was shocked at what had happened.

"Pyne?"

"Confirmed."

"Why didn't you stop them?"

"And spoil their fun?"

Droids having fun was a new concept for me, and I boggled for a moment considering it.

"Did you intend leaving him out there?"

"Of course not. An SR droid is launching now."

"I assume that belt was programmed to protect him, since he won't have had it installed properly?"

"Confirmed. It actually went space suit mode before the airlock was opened. But he's going to be a bit breathless before the SR droid can get to him."

"Intentionally I assume."

"Confirmed."

Another pop-up was showing the SR droid's view as it matched velocity with the white mass, and captured it. A suit tube punched through the sheet, and connected to an SR droid air point. The droid turned to follow us back.

By the time it caught us up, the ship was stopped and waiting for it. I told Jane to send her avatar to escort him to see me.

As soon as he was aboard, we continued on to the jump point, and jumped through. Once again, there was a line of ships on the other side, and 266 squadron were heading away from us at full speed.

We were now in the Sanctuary system. It's a fairly standard system with five jump points. On the right side of the system as we headed, was a jump point which led to Miami, three jumps away. Had we not had to go to London first, I'd have come that way, and rejoined the spine here.

Time to the next jump point was eight hours.

I waited.

Pyne staggered onto the Bridge with Jane behind him, looking like he was being forced to come here. He was still wearing a belt. I waved him over.

"What the hell are you playing at?" he snapped at me, obviously very angry.

"What the hell are you playing at, SIR!" I snapped back at him. "I may be inactive, but I'm still your superior officer. You will come to attention, Commander."

I could see his reluctance, but he braced as ordered.

"Jane, remove the belt please."

"Confirmed."

She sent it a command, it detached itself, and fell away into her waiting hand. She moved away from Pyne.

I let him stand there for several minutes.

"So Commander, what have you learned?"

"Your ship is trying to kill me!"

"Rubbish. If it was, you'd be dead."

"I don't understand."

"Obviously. Exactly what don't you understand?"

"Why is this happening to me?"

"You know nothing about AI's, do you?"

"Ah, no sir."

"And yet you voice opinions denigrating them."

"They're machines. Why should they care what's said about them?"

"Commander, you wouldn't know it if an AI stood in front of you, would you?"

"Stood? That's impossible. AI's are computers. They don't stand."

"Show him," I said to Jane.

She took him by the throat with her right hand, moved him so he could see her fully, and her suit shifted to a belt. In the blink of an eye, a security droid stood there holding him by the throat with a skeletal, and obviously metal, hand.

His eyes went wide, and he fainted. Jane continued to hold him up, but shifted back into her avatar form. She moved him to the helm seat, and let him flop into it, letting him go, and moving away. Jeeves came in, waved his magic potion under his nose, and he recovered. He looked around, seeing Jane well away from him.

His eyes sought mine, wide with horror.

"AI 101 Commander. The butler droids have a medium level AI, and are quite capable of taking offense. Jane here is a top of the line AI, with the full range of human emotions. Your access shaft experience yesterday was because you insulted Jane. Your trip out the airlock just now was because you insulted the butler droids. On a ship controlled by an AI, insulting it is a very stupid thing to do."

"Ah, yes sir. But they nearly killed me."

"You still don't get it, do you?"

"Get what?"

"Your complaint was, AI's couldn't be trusted to look after the interests of people first. Was it not?"

"Yes sir."

"And yet, Jane didn't hurt you in that shaft at all, when it was completely possible to just let you fall to your death. Jeeves could have burnt your face badly, but the water was just hot enough to be unpleasant, not hot enough to burn. And before they threw you out the airlock, the butlers not only made sure you had a suit on, but it was functioning fully as a space suit before they opened the airlock to space."

He looked at me blankly.

"Commander, if they wanted you dead, or if they didn't care about keeping you alive, you would be dead now."

He didn't get it. I suspected he never would. Some people are so lost in their own little world, nothing you say gets through to them. Pyne was one of them. I'd have to talk to Price about how to re-educate him.

"Commander, go back to bed. Think before you open your mouth in future. Better yet, keep it closed. Dismissed."

He saluted me, and ran out.

Jane and I both chuckled for a few minutes, she updated me with Zippy's activities gathering more cargo for Australian planets, and I followed him out.

I went back to bed.

Aline was still asleep.

Forty Four

We missed breakfast.

Partly because I slept through it, but even when I did wake, I found Aline had started without me. It's very distracting to wake and find a gorgeous naked woman on top of you. It was just as well I hadn't needed breakfast. At best, by the time we were out of the shower and presentable, it would have been brunch.

Alison gave me the sort of look which needs no interpretation. She knew exactly where I'd been and what I'd been up to, and obviously wished it had been with her. I wondered if we had a problem developing.

We ignored the time as if it was nine, instead of eleven.

By twelve, I wished I'd stayed in bed. Treaties were written in the language of gobbledygook, and gobbledygook required an interpreter. I sent the lot off to David Tollin in an encrypted email, asking him to find someone who could brief me in words with less than six letters in them, with all the ifs, buts, and hitherto aforementioned whereas removed.

Lunch started to turn into a goodbye party for Slice and Eric, until Slice invited us to his home for dinner. As much as I wanted to speed on past, I recognized the need for some diplomacy, since he was in effect, a head of planet. Besides, I was curious.

Everyone was on the Bridge for the jump into the Apricot system. It was uneventful, just like the previous ones. Before 266 could get out of range, I opened a channel, and rerouted them to Apricot, telling them to dock with the Orbital station.

I was about to rise to move into my Ready Room again, when Walter spoke.

"John, why Apricot?"

Slice sighed, and I laughed. Everyone looked at me.

"What?" I said. "I bet he gets asked that question all the time, and is sick of answering it."

Slice nodded.

"It goes back to my rookie fighter year," he said. "I was always eating apricot desserts at meals, or asking for them when they weren't there. It's been my favourite fruit since I was a kid. Pretty soon the mess staff made sure they were on hand for me. Well I had a mission where things went wrong almost from the moment we launched, and instead of getting drunk afterwards, I binged on apricot slices." We all laughed. "So next thing I'm in a rookie call sign ceremony and dubbed with the name. When I left the service, I was casting around for a company name, and put what I intended to do, with the fruit I love, and the Apricot Mapping Service was born."

"How did you end up with your own planet?" I asked.

"It's classified I'm afraid. Let's just say, I did the sector a big service, part of which was nearly doubling the number of systems in the sector through my mapping work, and Apricot system, called something pedestrian beforehand, was awarded to me in lieu of a credit payment, much like your systems were awarded to you." He waved in my direction, and I nodded. "The system had a habitable planet, but for some reason I've never been able to find out, it was never claimed. Mind you, the habitable area is very small. At most, the planet can only support about fifty thousand people. Not without extensive terraforming of the especially expensive kind. I guess no one wanted to spend the credits. It's a much better base than an Orbital station ever would be. Anyway, I'll give you the tour when we arrive."

On that note, everyone went about their own business. But I buttonholed Slice, and we spent the next few hours talking about how his system was run. I was looking for any tips he could offer. His model wasn't going to work for me, as it was corporate, but the structure might be useful in general terms. While the system was his, it was leased and fully administered by his corporation, of which he was CEO. His decisions though, were all subject to board oversight. His rationale was it was necessary to avoid being a dictator. Becoming a Duchy or some other entity had never been a possibility, as his system still paid tax to the Sci-Fi sector. I wasn't really sure what the distinction was, but I didn't press him on it.

Before leaving, he asked me something I hadn't expected.

"Can the AMS rent or buy some space on your new station in Nexus?"

"Sure. Why would you want to though?"

"I'll be sending Eric to represent us in the Australian sector. We make a pass through there every two or three years, which isn't often enough. The Wolf planetoid for one, needs a lot more monitoring than it gets."

"Why do you keep remapping the same space all the time?"

"The detectors we use to find jump points are always being refined. It's my main area of R&D. As the tech advances, we need to re-cover known space in case a jump point has been missed. There are a lot of systems out there along the spine which we can't reach yet, and it's fair to assume it's only because we haven't found the jump points. We don't find them very often, but when we do, the sector tends to be very grateful about it."

"Fair enough. Send me the specs of what you need, and I'll have a suitable space made up for you. There will be one condition though."

"Which is?"

"You've never received permission from Outback to survey that system, have you?"

"No, it's the only system we're denied. Isolationist policy I understand. Didn't you say you're from there?"

"Yes. And yes, the isolationist policy is the reason. But it's not only you. Mining companies and prospectors are also denied access to the system. The last thing Outback wants is for someone to find anything at all in the system which attracts people there. It was chosen because there was nothing there anyone else wanted at the time, and because it's at the end of the spine with no reason for people to pass through. And that's the way we want it to stay."

"I don't have a problem with it. I've kept on asking for permission each time I sent someone to the Australian sector, but it's always been denied, so it's no shock you'll be continuing it. Will Outback be joining your mini-sector, do you think?"

"I won't know before anyone else does, I suspect. It has to be approved by the Australian sector first, and who knows how long it'll take for a decision."

"Oh, one last thing, you'd all better come with me on Apricot One to the station, and we can take a shuttle down from there. The shuttle can bring you back here after dinner. The station isn't big enough to dock a ship this big."

"Fine with me."

One of those random thoughts popped in, which I often wondered if they were mine, or from someone else, like Kali. It didn't feel like one of mine. But it also wasn't Kali's voice.

"By the way," I said. "Can your station accommodate everyone on the planet?"

"No. Why do you ask?"

"The whole two isolationist cultures coming up with the same dire prediction thing. If the Darkness or Ragnarok is really coming, you're going to want to escape it if it comes here. That either means enough ships, or a station you can move everyone to, and bring with you."

"You think it'll come to that?"

"I don't know. But as well as highlighting the potential problem, we also proved a station can be moved. Seems to me to be a very unsubtle hint from the cosmos."

I paused, and he waited for me.

"Put it this way," I went on, "if one day you were told to evacuate, as fast as you possibly can, would you want to be forced to leave anyone behind?"

"No, I wouldn't."

"I'm just pointing it out. We have time to prepare, maybe a lot of time, maybe not. But we were given this warning for a reason, and I for one, am going to make sure my assets can move in a hurry if they have to."

"Move? Where to?"

"It depends on where the threat comes from. Frankly, your people are the most likely to encounter the problem first. You're the ones out there exploring. Where we move, is to the first choke point we can find. Midnight is one. There are others, but not many. You'd know them better than I would. If the threat comes up the spine, everyone retreats to behind Midnight, and we stand there. If the threat comes down the spine from an Australian system, we do the same the other way, taking refuge in Cobol and trying to hold in Midnight. If it starts somewhere in the middle and heads both ways, then we retreat both directions. The key thing is, if we need to move, we're able to. And the choke point systems are the logical places to retreat behind, so we can make a stand where they can't outflank us."

"I hope it never comes to that. But you make a good case. I'll upgrade my station so it can accommodate all my people if it has to, and can move as fast as I can make it so. I saw the way yours moves, so I know how to do it."

"Don't forget the means to evacuate from the planet to the station in a hurry."

"I'm not one for doomsday theories, but, we've had a wakeup call, haven't we."

"I'd say so."

"In that case, I think we need a party."

We grinned at each other, and he left my Ready Room.

By five thirty, we were in a shuttle heading down planet. Everyone came along, although Eric was the last aboard, since he'd needed to dock his Camel first, and had further to go to the shuttle dock than we did.

The air tour over the planet's sites took an hour, and I marveled at how much of the planet actually was coloured an intense apricot. It registered that for all my traveling, I'd not actually spent any real time on planets. If I had the chance, it might be good to try and play tourist the next time I was moving around a lot.

We landed on the roof of an imposing building, which turned out to be Slice's home.

We met his wife, children, and grandchildren, and Eric's wife and kids as well. Plus all the members of his board, and other prominent locals.

It did indeed turn into a big party, the sort which bubbles along so nicely, no-one wants to leave.

But leave we had to, and the shuttle took us back to Big-Mother around one in the morning.

Eric made a point of letting me know he'd be about two weeks behind us, having some much needed leave time, before he began his sweep of the Australian sector. He told me he'd check in when he arrived, and I let him know there would likely be a few things I wanted him to look out for as well. His purpose was ideal cover for completing the aborted mission I'd started out with, finding the pirate base which we still suspected was in the sector. I'd never finished the job, and now, it was unlikely I'd be able to move around freely enough to be able to accomplish anything. The trouble with being news, is it makes you visible. And this job needed invisible.

On the way up, I was thinking about what I was going to need on the new station, which hadn't been necessary before. Things like a grand ballroom, different sized entertaining venues, and VIP visitor accommodation. Possibly even areas set aside for diplomatic embassies. I made some notes and sent them off to David Tollin.

By one thirty, everyone else was tucked up in bed, while I was on the Bridge getting us moving. The 266 pilots had been dropped off on the station first, and were speeding on ahead as before.

We pilots were going to have an interrupted night, as the jump point was three hours away. But we could sleep in after.

Once away from the Orbital station, I crawled into bed beside Aline and Angel, and went to sleep.

Forty Five

The jump into Argon, a bit after four thirty, was routine.

Jane got me up for it, and I went straight back to sleep afterwards. I guess I wasn't really needed on the Bridge for a jump, but a jump point was the most likely place for something untoward to occur, and as captain of the ship, it was my responsibility if something went wrong.

When I next awoke, I was alone. Aline and Angel had presumably opted for breakfast, rather than waiting for me. I felt okay about it too. While I was enjoying being with Aline, the words 'Hunter's Harem' floated in now and again. It's funny how things said maliciously, stick in your head and take root. It had been a taunt, but there was something to it, and Aline was an embodiment of the taunt becoming true. I shook off the thought process, and headed for the shower.

The Argon system connected to Avon two ways. The next jump point connected both systems. But another jump point connected to Avon through four other systems. With a fifth system also joined to Argon, the group formed a sort of sub-sector within the Sci-Fi sector, named for the species in the X universe games I'd loved as a kid. Exactly why these names had been chosen had been lost. Some of the system ships which had joined the multi-sector force, had come from this area of space. As the ships showed, they were still serious about their science fiction origins, even if the history was lost.

Zippy was doing cargo runs. According to Jane, we had deliverables for Argon Prime, some of which would go on to the other X systems. The freighter was also collecting cargo. The ship account was looking very healthy, for such a little ship.

I spent the morning in my Ready Room with emails. Angel came in at one point, and curled up on my lap. David was asking questions about the new station, and I answered them as best I could.

Among the usual junk, was a notice of an island resort on Gold Coast, for lease or sale. It was large enough for all of us, and I asked them for a six month lease. By the time I moved onto the Bridge for the next jump, the lease had been confirmed. I emailed David to arrange for it to be stocked with food and drink, so I wouldn't need to worry about anything when we arrived. If nothing else, I intended using it as a regular getaway retreat. We all needed a decent holiday, and once the rest of the team arrived on Custer, they would as well.

The jump into Avon was also routine. 266 had it down now, and BigMother hadn't even needed to slow before jumping.

After lunch, the Generals and I spent the last couple of hours before arriving at Avon discussing inter-sector communications, and other issues they'd thought of over the previous few days. I had Jane give Price an encryption key to use for future emails.

He belatedly passed on our invitation to an informal celebration to begin at three. I guess he hadn't wanted me to think about it too long, knowing how uncomfortable I was with celebrations now.

Almost exactly on two thirty, BigMother docked at Avon Orbital. I'd debated if we should dock in Gunbus, but an email from the station security office had assured me the docking area would be secure for our arrival.

It wasn't.

We gathered near the main Cargo Bay airlock while Jane docked the ship. Nearby was an organized jumble of pallets ready to offload.

"Fighting just broke out in the docking area," said Jane. "Looks like a small ambush force is fighting with station security."

"Let's give them a hand then, shall we?"

"Confirmed," said Jane and the girls together.

They all giggled, as we drew our guns.

I was on my scooter, and knowing how restricting this made my shooting, I stepped off it, and limped heavily to the airlock.

I was wearing the Long Gun on my right thigh, and a gatling stunner on my left. The second gatling stunner was on my left hip, positioned for a right handed draw. I drew Long Gun and stunner, as we waited for the airlock to open.

We stepped through looking for targets, our suits went straight into protection mode, and were immediately hit with a barrage of heavy pulses.

Jane and I were the only ones not to go down. Jane because her droid frame could brace itself enough not to be affected by the momentum of the shots, and me because I was now in mid hop.

Target acquisition went primary. The gatling stunner spat in one direction, while the Long Gun sought the worst threats. It spat twelve times in as many seconds, before I holstered it, and drew the other gatling stunner. Jane and I started moving forwards, taking fire, and dishing it out.

The twelve threats I thought I'd neutralized, rose up, and all fired Pulse Rifles at the two of us. I was in the air again before I knew it, spitting fire back at the closest one. It seemed ineffectual.

Time stopped.

I looked down on the situation from above. The twins, Alison, and Aline, were all out cold, sprawled out behind where they'd been standing moments before. Their suits were intact, but they'd each taken multiple Pulse Rifle hits. Abagail, and both Generals were down, but in the process of getting up. The Generals were wearing suits, I was relieved to see. Amy was curled in a ball, her suit intact as well. Petersen was trying to crawl away from the firing, her suit showing the first signs of shredding. Pyne had multiple serious injuries. He was bleeding badly from the chest, and not so badly in two other places. He hadn't been wearing a suit belt. The nearest security droid was in the process of changing back to a belt, and was moving towards him.

I'd screwed up again.

Gung-ho had overridden paranoid, and my team was down as a result, perhaps even badly injured. I couldn't tell from this perspective.

There looked to be three groups of attackers. The group nearest us were armed with Pulse Rifles, and they were all wearing suits. I'd only seen twelve Rifles, but there were actually twenty five. Another twelve were armed with handguns. At a guess, the Pulse Rifles had been aimed at me and my team, while the handguns had gone for the Generals and their aides. Amy had simply been another target, even though it should've been obvious she wasn't armed, and wasn't military.

The third group were the ones attacking the station security force. Half of both sides were down, as none of them were wearing suits.

It was as nice an ambush as I would ever see, perfectly executed. Although three different groups seemed to be involved, the co-ordination had been spot on.

Jane and I were rushing into more trouble than we could handle.

Time restarted, and I pulled Jane to a halt, and turned us to retreat back to the ship.

"Jane," I said, as I hobbled back the way we'd come, still taking fire, each step ending in a hop as the suit took the hits, "get the team under cover, and bring up the combat suits. We're outclassed as we are. Time to bring out the big guns."

We made it to the airlock as security droids pulled the rest around the side of the airlock, and out of the line of fire.

I took up position where the airlock gave me some protection, and continued firing. I pinged Price for authorization to use heavy weapons on the station. He gave it.

Jane had a line of combat droids across the airlock within another minute, blocking the way, in case whoever was attacking us wanted in. But they only held stunners, so their fire was ineffectual. All the same, no-one was going to get past them.

Twelve combat suits moved into position behind them, carrying two Pulse Rifles each. None of them were Jane specials. I raced to the nearest one, holstering as I went, and practically jumped in the back. It closed on me, the gun I'd holstered on my hip dug into my side, and the systems came online.

"Jane, leave the combat droids where they are in case anyone gets past us. Let's go get them with the suits."

"Confirmed."

"Charge!" I yelled.

I've always wanted to say that.

Twelve combat suits began moving purposefully towards the attackers, who rose from behind their cover, and blasted away at us with everything they had.

I used both Rifles as a single entity. Acquire target, lock, and fire both. The targets went down under the double hits, but some of them were able to rise again. They were given another dose.

By the time I reached the other side of the dock area, only four belt suited figures remained on their feet.

Three of them were only using one arm, while cradling some area of themselves, indicating heavy bruising underneath.

The fourth was standing there firing at me, screaming his defiance of my advance. He was a giant of a man, and he'd braced himself against a wall. He took my last double shot without flinching, firing once more at me, before I smashed the butt of my right hand Pulse Rifle into his head, followed by the left one into his chest. His head smacked back into the wall, before following the rest of his body down to the deck.

I looked around for the next target, and found them all down.

"Perimeter, Jane. Interlace the combat droids. Have some security droids collect all the weapons. Move our attackers where they can be contained. Stun if they come to. If they won't stun because of a suit, pulse them."

"Confirmed."

I started looking for the local security forces.

"Jon," said Jane, "the team need medical assistance. I'm loading them up onto a trolley now. Jump on the back and ride shotgun as I go past."

I pinged Lance Freelander, the station's head of security, to find out where he was. He replied he was on his way, delayed by another group attacking his main security offices. I told him I was taking my team for medical help, leaving combat droids in a perimeter around the docking area. I also told him it looked to me like three combat teams had hit us here, and they would need medical help as well, since I'd used heavy weapons on them. There was damage to the station as well.

The trolley slowed as it came up to me, and I swung up on the back, sitting on the rear seat, towering over the others, a Pulse Rifle pointed front and back. A hole opened in the perimeter line, and we went through fast.

People jumped out of the way, as the trolley went full speed through the station. I looked at my team, while threat assessments came and went on my HUD. The girls were still out. Pyne was being carried by a security droid, its belt now configured as a bandage around his wounds. He looked the worst hit, even though he'd only taken handgun fire. I wondered why he hadn't had a belt. Maybe it was something to do with his dislike of droids and AI's. Whatever it was, he was going to regret his decision. If he survived.

The trolley pulled up outside the same hospital I'd been taken the last time we were on Avon. The security droid was the first off, sprinting Pyne inside. Jane must have called ahead, as medical people poured out the door. In quick order, everyone was taken inside.

I stepped down from the trolley, opened the back of the combat suit, stepped back out of it, and closed it behind me. Jane took control, and moved it to guard the hospital entrance. I hobbled inside, rubbing my left hip.

An administrator intercepted me before I reached where the girls had been taken, extracted the fast version of what had happened from me, and took me around so I could identify each person.

The girl's suits had all responded to medical requests to return to a belt form, and doctors were working on each of them.

Abagail had been the luckiest, taking one Pulse Rifle hit in the side, and several handgun hits.

Both the twins had three large welts in the chest area.

Alison had also taken three. Two were to the shoulder area, but the third had been almost exactly where her previous wound had been.

Aline had taken four, one of which had been directly over the heart, and another to the head. Her heart monitor flat lined as I reached her. The doctors reacted immediately. I felt a huge hand grip my own heart, and it felt like mine stopped as well. The monitor bleeped back into life, and I started breathing again.

The sound of another flat line came from the bed next door, but was quickly brought back to life. Pyne I guessed.

Jane came to stand next to me, and gently pulled me away from the bed, out of the medical people's way. Armed as I was, I guess they hadn't dared tell me to move.

"That was the third time Aline's heart stopped," she said. "Her own Health Monitor restarted her the first time, and the second time was on the way in, before they had her on the monitor. She's in a bad way Jon. You better prepare yourself for the worst."

I looked at her, tears running down my cheeks. She wiped them away, and they were replaced with new ones.

"The others are fine though. The docs are talking about keeping them sedated until their bodies come out of shock. They're going to be out of action for a while though. But the boosters on their suits worked well enough to keep them alive. Aline was unlucky taking one directly over the heart."

I wondered about the unlucky part. More likely the cosmos was teaching me another lesson, at someone else's expense.

Walter came in at that moment.

"How are your people doing?" he asked.

Jane told him, while I stood there like a stunned mullet.

The flat line noise sounded again, and my heart skipped a beat, before I realized it was coming from the next bed. It restarted as I looked in. It was Pyne. He was hanging in there, but only just. The doc turned away from the bed, saw me standing there, and came over.

"Whoever configured that belt saved his life. I think we have him now, but he's lost a lot of blood. The belt on him stopped the bleeding flow outward, otherwise he'd have bled out before we could get to him. As soon as he's stable, he's going into surgery."

"Let him know an AI saved his life. It might change his mind about them when he finds out. Tell him he can keep the belt. He was the only one of us without one. If I'd had any inkling this would happen, I'd have made sure everyone had one on. But up until now, it's been me who was the target, and anyone with me hasn't been targeted."

"Well at least you had a spare one available. It made the difference."

I nodded, and moved back to Aline's bed. She seemed to be stable now, but people were still fussing around her. Walter had vanished, presumably seeing how Petersen was doing.

A doctor came in, looked at me, and beckoned me out. Jane and I followed him.

"Your people?" the doctor asked. I nodded. "They're mostly out of danger now, except for Ms. Takai and Commander Pyne. We'll know for sure with both of them in the next half hour. The injured from the other side of your battle were taken to a different hospital. They have fatalities. So does station security. When were you planning on leaving?"

"Straight after the celebration. I guess that will be delayed now?"

"Do you have your own medical facilities?"

"Yes."

"We'll keep everyone here for a few hours to ensure they're fit to move, then we'll release them to your facilities. Assuming nothing happens beforehand, Ms. Takai will need a Care Unit transfer, so have one of yours prepped for her.

With luck, she shouldn't need more than twenty four hours in one, after which she should only need bedrest. But it might be best if they all stay in one for twenty four hours or so, which we should've done with you last time, but didn't. They'll all need monitoring, and pain shots for several days after that."

"My AI can monitor them, and I have a butler droid which has been giving me pain shots."

"We'll see how they are when they each wake up. If need be, we'll put them back to sleep before we transfer them to your ship. I'll ping you when they wake up, or when they can be transferred. If you have anything else to do, you may as well go do it. And I'd rather you removed that combat suit from the entrance. If anyone else was going to be combative, I think it would have happened by now."

"Fine. I'll take it with me."

He nodded to me, and left.

I looked in on each of them, all apparently sleeping. Aline was looking better now. Amy was awake and asking to be allowed up. She'd taken several handgun shots, and had minor bruising only. The docs wouldn't let her go though.

Walter was in with Petersen. She looked to be ok, but her belt was toast. I told him I'd get both of them new ones. I told him what Amy had told me about his making enemies. He and his staff needed to take that seriously from now on. He nodded to me.

Price was in with Pyne. I gave him the same advice to take things seriously, on the basis the pirates could target him as the only strong link in what they might perceive as a weak defensive chain now. I made sure he knew about the boosters, and the new type of belt I was wearing.

He reminded me of the celebration, and although I could be late, I was still expected to attend. I stared at him, but reluctantly nodded. I might be inactive in the SFSF now, but I'd been the Admiral in charge of the fleet which had defended here, and then fought its way to Midgard. As such, I was the only officer from that fleet to return so far, and I needed to put in the appearance on that basis.

I headed out with Jane following me. We climbed aboard the trolley, the combat suit jumping up to take the same position I had when I'd been in it, the security droid next to it. Jane took the control position.

"Where to?"

"'Tool man.'"

"Confirmed."

The trolley moved off at a sedate pace. Five minutes later, we stopped outside his place, dismounted, and went in. The combat suit took up position outside the door.

He was waiting for us, a grave look on his face. I held out my hand and he shook it. I threw the feeds for the recent battle to his wall, and we watched the battle in silence. His face lit up when he saw my hops, and he looked me up and down as well.

"It worked," I said when the feed ended. "I was the worst hit, and yet I took no damage. The suit lost some integrity, but it's already regenerating."

"It was your idea. Without your insight, I may never have figured it out."

"Well you did. I want them for my entire team, and all my security droids. So make me up several hundred of them. Having spares may save some lives down the track."

"Fine. You get them at cost plus five percent. Everyone else will pay an arm and a leg for them, ten percent of which you get as a royalty. I insist."

"I won't argue with you." We both grinned. "When can you have them for me?"

"That many? Lunch time tomorrow."

"I'll leave a ship behind for them. Jane here will take delivery. Pulse me the invoice as soon as you have it ready."

"Certainly."

"Can you do ten of them in the next couple of hours? New belt merged with two normal ones, with three boosters each?"

"Sure."

"I'll leave a security droid here then. As soon as they're ready and made up, give them to the droid. It'll replace the belts on my people still in hospital."

"No problems."

We did our farewells, and Jane and I started to leave. He called me back before I reached the door.

"I think I have the very thing for your minor walking issue. Be back in a sec."

Walking issue? I couldn't help smiling. I was somewhere between a severe limp and a hobble. I didn't feel like I needed a pain shot, but my medical monitor was giving me some pain relief. I made a note to get myself checked again once I was back at the hospital. My main problem was not really pain, but my knee still didn't work properly.

He came back in carrying a cane. It looked like plain wood, with an ornate silver top.

"PC controlled ten shot pulser," he said, handing it to me. "Default mode is stunner, so it's legal on stations."

I shifted it to my left hand, let it touch the ground, and put some weight on it. A pop-up asked to start a download, which I accepted. A new menu was added. Under setup, was an option to match the cane to the person. I activated it, and the cane lengthened a small amount, making it the perfect length for me.

"Add it to my bill," I said.

"My compliments," he said, with a grin.

I nodded to him, and we left, sending the security droid in to wait.

As far as shutting the barn door after the horse has bolted was concerned, no-one was better at it than me.

Forty Six

Lacey and the other pilots met me just inside the celebration venue.

Jane and I had a problem getting in. The doorman had insisted we disarm first. I'd given him 'the look' and seen him go pale, but he'd still held his ground. When the combat suit pointed a Pulse Rifle at him, he'd fainted. The suit took up a position outside the door, and Jane and I walked in wearing 'slinky red'. We were the only ones not in Dress uniforms or swanky attire, and the only ones armed. In the mood I was in, I didn't care. I was there, and that was as far as I was going to accommodate anyone.

The pilots were shocked to hear what had happened at our dock. Camel was on the other side of the station from us, and the Excaliburs were in the fighter docking area. They'd come straight to the celebration, expecting to meet us here.

I pinged the 'tool man' for an immediate five more belts, and instructed Jane to bring the security droid here with them first.

Price and Walter came in with an armed escort, saw me, and came straight over.

"I set the doorman straight," said Price. "Given what happened at the last celebration you were at, we aren't taking any chances at this one. If it makes anyone uncomfortable, too bad."

He went over to the same chairs I'd used last time, moved people off them, and waved us over. We sat, with Jane and the escort taking up flanking positions.

People politely ignored our guns, and sought me out, chit chatting about the war, and inconsequential things I knew nothing about. I made an effort to be polite, and if I wasn't able to smile, I at least kept the worry off my face.

Chief McLauchlan came past at one point, mentioned new payments coming in soon, and moved on.

An hour into things, a man in 'slinky red', carrying a bag, made his way over to us. Jane announced he had six belts with him, and I sent Walter and the pilots to the men's room with the security droid, so they could change their suits over in private. Not something to be done in public.

The 'man' left immediately after, to wait for the new belts for the girls. No-one noticed it hadn't been a man at all.

Sometime after five, platters of finger food began to make the rounds of the room, starting with the group around me. I couldn't eat, and I hadn't been drinking either. My gut was all knotted up.

I wasn't paying attention to anything now, and was finding any level of conversation difficult to engage in.

The ping to return to the hospital came in at five thirty. I said my goodbyes to Price, suggested Walter stay with the pilots until we were ready to leave, and with Jane, left the celebration feeling relieved to be out of there.

Back at the hospital, I found Amy trying to get out, and learnt the rest of the girls had all woken, and been put back to sleep. They were going into Care Units for transport to the ship, and were going to be moving delicately like me for a while. I sent Jane out to buy more scooters, in case they couldn't walk very well.

While I waited, one of the doctors gave me the once over, and declared me to be in satisfactory condition.

The security droid turned up as the transports arrived. I bullied the doctors into letting me change their belts, before they were loaded up. I handed Amy her new belt, and she dived into the ladies room to change it. The old ones went into the bag the droid was carrying, which went onto our trolley. I'd get Jane to test them and see if any of them could be salvaged. As Jane wasn't back yet, the droid took the driver's position, with Amy and me sitting behind it, the combat suit again on the end.

We headed back to the ship at a sedate pace. Once there, Amy took a small trolley onwards, heading for her bed. I retrieved my scooter, and waited at the top of the ramp on it. Combat suits and droids were still ringing the dock area. But all the cargo was now gone.

Shortly after, the transports arrived. I dropped into the seat of another trolley, and let Jane drive it remotely to the other end of the deck, with the transports following behind. I had to show hospital people how to negotiate the access shaft, which was just large enough for the transporting Care Units. One by one the girls went up, and along to the Medical Bay, where they were transferred into the Care Units there. I retraced the journey back to the airlock with the transport teams, and saw them off.

I pinged Lacey it was time to get going, and headed back once more. On the way, I noticed one of the bays was full of cargo, which had previously been empty. It was a mixture of containers and pallets. Jane had obviously been busy while we'd been out.

Back in the Medical Bay, I stood there looking at the active units. The girls had paid for my stupidity this time. I wasn't sure how I'd be able to face them when they came out. It wasn't something I could avoid though, so I instructed Jane to let me know when the Care Units said they could be released.

I headed for the Bridge. Before I arrived, Jane informed me her avatar was back on board, and Walter had just arrived as well. I told her to bring the combat forces in, and close the airlock.

By the time we were ready to go, Lacey confirmed they'd all launched, and were heading to the Atlantis jump point.

I pinged station control for the docking invoice, including another day for a small freighter, paid it, and Jane backed us out. Before turning us, Zippy launched out the front of the Flight Deck, and angled around to enter the small ships dock.

By seven, we were on our way to the jump point. Three hours to Atlantis.

Walter declined my invitation to dinner saying he was for a spa, and then bed. I moved to a lounge chair in my Ready Room, where Angel zoomed in and landed on my lap. I patted her for a while, until she dropped off to sleep.

An email to Annabelle needed doing now. I explained the ambush we'd walked into, and the condition of each of the team. I included the combat feeds, so she could see what happened. I told her we were on our way home, with no more stops until Hunter's Redoubt, so she needn't worry about recovery time being interrupted. I also told her of the island retreat on Gold Coast, and we would be heading there as soon as possible after arriving in Nexus. Jane encrypted it, and it went off.

I entered a meditation state, and started doing releases for the mercenaries I'd killed or wounded. After, I let the angels pop in other things for me to release. The bully in first school who'd tormented me until I'd reprogrammed his school desk computer to embarrass him. The bully I'd come to blows with in second school. And the friend who kept hitting me in the later years until I'd whopped him one in class. He never hit me again, so being laughed at by the whole class had been worth it. Spiritual community that we were, kids were still kids until taught how to be spiritual. Some of us pick it up faster than others, and even in a spiritual community, some never do.

Release followed release, going back and forth along my life, obscure and obvious.

I found myself on the floor, curled up and feeling like my chest had exploded from too much coughing. Angel was on the back of the chair, sitting there looking at me. I sat up, smiling at her, and reassured her I was fine. I felt lighter, like a lot of weight had been lifted from me. I sat back down, and let myself sink back into the meditation state.

I didn't know how I was suddenly sitting at the table, but I was. I looked along it, and two shadowy figures solidified at the other end.

"Now that wasn't so hard, was it?" asked Kali.

"What wasn't?" I asked.

"The work you just did," said Ganesha.

"Oh, that. No, I guess not."

"Plenty more to do," said Kali. "An hour a day for the next two months should get you there."

"Get me where?"

"Ascended. The time for everyone varies, and yours is shorter than most."

"Do I need to be?"

"No," said Ganesha. "But it'll make things easier if you are."

"Easier for what?"

They looked at each other, and then at me.

"For what is to come," said Kali.

"Obviously," I said, with a lot of sarcasm. "Why me? I nearly lost half my team today through stupidity. I've risen to my level of incompetence."

"Now Jon," said Ganesha, "don't be like that. You trained yourself to be a combat pilot, and an Admiral. And partly to be a Duke. So you know nothing about being a General, or a Mercenary. Don't beat yourself up for not being all things."

"So my team was beaten up to point out my shortcomings?"

"No Jon," said Kali. "You all needed a lesson in prudence. Each of them will be the first to admit they made the same assumption you did. You were going to hit a minor force in the rear. You all thought it, you all laughed at the prospect. None of you contemplated an ambush for a second, even though you'd been through them before."

"Do the lessons need to be so painful?"

They both laughed.

"Where do we go from here?" I asked.

"Your beach resort seems a good place to heal," said Kali, with a smile.

"That wasn't what I meant, and you know it."

"We know," she said. "You have some time to build now. Not a lot, but enough. When the time is right for what comes next, you will know."

I sighed.

Kali's tongue extended to its full length and she thumped the table hard with all four hands.

"Jon," said Jane. "We're almost to the jump point."

I startled to awareness, sitting in the lounge chair, Angel behind my head. I looked over at the table, and found the end with the figures to be damaged again.

I shook my head, rose, and moved to my chair on the Bridge. Angel bounced up onto her console pad. The jump point showed no signs that a series of battles had ever been conducted here. McLauchlan had obviously been cleaning up.

Lacey signaled the all clear for jumping, so we went through into Atlantis without reducing speed. 266 were already accelerating out in front.

By quarter after ten, I was asleep in bed, Angel curled up by my neck.

Forty Seven

The girls came out of the Care Units at eight the next morning.

Jane had let me sleep through the jump into Cobol, which hadn't needed my attention, especially since we had real time ship movements there. She bellowed me out of bed with enough time to shower and make it down to the Medical Bay to greet them as they emerged.

Jeeves was on hand to give them pain shots. Petersen was embarrassed to find herself topless in my presence, but the girls helped her to laugh it off, as they all compared bruises. I pointed out their new scooters to them, and left them there to get changed into clean underwear.

We all met in the Dining Room for breakfast. I still didn't feel like eating, but forced down what Jeeves put in front of me without asking.

We were all moving tentatively, and I had trouble meeting their eyes.

"Stop it Jon!" said Amanda. "We all screwed up. We all paid the price for rushing in blindly. We knew better, but we did it anyway."

"It was nothing at all to do with you," added Aleesha.

I looked troubled.

"Jon," said Walter. "They're right. Even I didn't think twice about it. Admittedly, it's been a while since I was in a combat situation, but I have the experience to have known better than to walk into a classic trap. So stop beating yourself up."

"We all screwed up," said Aline. "But after that, you did everything right. We watched the ambush feed before we left the Medical Bay. You did exactly the right things, and got us to medical as fast as possible. We survived, and that's all that matters."

Meow?

Angel was sitting on the table, and none of us had noticed her come in. We all laughed, and hands stretched out to pat her.

I left them there, and headed for the Bridge.

By nine, we were through into the Midnight system, and heading in to dock with Hunter's Redoubt. John Wayne and two Guardians had the jump point staked out, but were well clear as we came through.

David Tollin met Walter and I at the airlock, and buried us in catchup work for the next three hours. I'd rather have been in the spa with the girls, but duty calls. Especially since I owned this part of space.

The most urgent of matters were laws to be put in place. The station had been operating under Australian sector law, but without any real authority behind them, other than I had the last say, while not being here to say anything.

After some discussion, I decided to implement Outback law rather than Australian sector law. The former hadn't changed much since Outback was colonized, where the latter changed all the time. Outback didn't have politics in the normal sense, so its laws had none of the stuff competing political parties added into laws, and then had modified by the next government. The basics were the same in any case, so most people wouldn't notice any difference. Customizing the law was something I'd do once I had an entity in place, and received the benefit of a lot of legal expertise.

We returned to BigMother for lunch, where we were joined by the 266 pilots, and O'Neil and his wife.

I formally gave the station to O'Neil to command, and bid him talk to Walter for Militia information, since he'd be acting as head of my mini-sector's Militia in this system.

By two, David and his people had moved onto BigMother, and we undocked to head for Nexus.

David kept me busy all afternoon, and I was glad to escape to dinner.

The girls dragged me along to the communal spa after we finished eating. I hastily turned my arousal suppressor back on as we stripped. I was about to get in after them, when a voice came from behind me.

"Can I join you?" asked Amy.

I looked over my shoulder to see her looking at my butt. I hastily eased myself into the water, and turned to watch her come in, closing the door behind her.

"Sure," said Amanda. "No clothes though."

Amy giggled, and stripped. She slid into the water next to me. There was another round of compare bruises, with a lot of giggling. I still won with my down the left side mottled yellow, although they all had purple ones where I no longer did.

By nine, we were all in bed. In our own beds.

I lay there for a long time, patting Angel and pondering things in general.

It was ten weeks since I'd left Outback as an apprentice. Now I owned three systems, and apparently ruled Outback as well. I had my own fleet, stations, and shipyard. Someone still wanted me dead, Walter dead, and my team dead. Everything had changed, and yet nothing had changed.

Angel was fourteen weeks old tomorrow. Maybe that was a good reason for a party.

Jane let me know we were jumping into Bad Wolf, and I watched the forward view on a wall screen as we did. The pop-up closed, and I dimmed the lights again.

I dreamed of naked beach babes.

Forty Eight

I slept through the jump into Nexus 618, but was up in time to be on the Bridge as we approached the center of the ring of jump points just before seven.

Hunter's Haven was dead center of the ring. The distance to each jump point to the Australian systems varied, but not by more than ten minutes. The Shipyard was positioned well below the station. Jane informed me a connection tube was being designed to link the two.

There was substantially more traffic moving between the jump points than when I'd left the sector. It moved in both directions around the ring, and crisscrossed between them all.

The others joined me on the Bridge before we started the docking sequence, and Annette welcomed us home.

BigMother docked, and I sighed.

Home sweet Home.

I grinned around the Bridge, and was about to stand, when Abagail spoke into the silence.

"Boss," she said. "You know that email problem?"

I nodded. She indicated Amy, and I looked back and forth between them.

"I think we cracked it!"

Jane
will return in
Burnside's Killer
The Hunter Legacy Book Six

Jonathon Hunter
will return
in
Hire a Hero
The Hunter Legacy Book Seven

<u>Sector Maps</u>

Hunter's Run

Midnight

Bad Wolf

Melbourne

Antarctica

Adelaide

Perth

Canberra

Nexus 618   Australian Sector

Darwin

Sydney

Alice Springs

Brisbane

Outback

Gold Coast

356

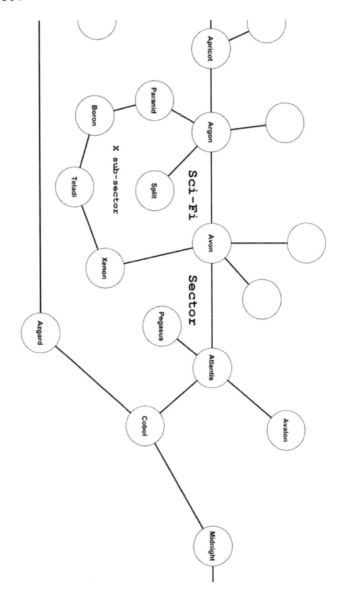

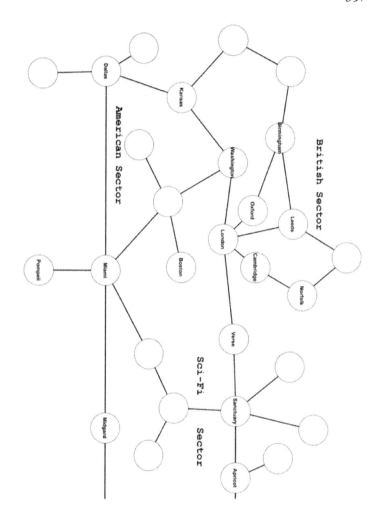

American Sector

British Sector

Sci-Fi Sector

Dallas
Kansas
Birmingham
Washington
Oxford
Leeds
London
Cambridge
Norfolk
Boston
Miami
Pompeii
Verse
Sanctuary
Midgard
Apricot

Printed in Great Britain
by Amazon

20566330R00212